SYLVIA TOWNSE

(1893-1978) was born in Harrow, th send Warner, housemaster and Head of the Modern Side of Harrow. As a student of music she became interested in research in the music of the fifteenth and sixteenth centuries, and spent ten years of her life as one of the four editors of the ten-volume compilation *Tudor Church Music*. In 1925 she published her first book of verse, *The Espalier*. With the publication of the novels *Lolly Willowes* in 1926, *Mr Fortune's Maggot* and *The True Heart* in the two following years, she achieved immediate recognition. The short stories she contributed to the *New Yorker* for over forty years established her reputation on both sides of the Atlantic.

In 1929 Sylvia Townsend Warner visited New York as guest critic for the *Herald Tribune*. In the 1930s she was a member of the Executive Committee of the Association of Writers for Intellectual Liberty and was a representative for the Congress of Madrid in 1937, thus witnessing the Spanish Civil War at first hand.

In all, Sylvia Townsend Warner published seven novels, four volumes of poetry, a volume of essays, and eight volumes of short stories. Her biography of T.H. White, published in 1967, was acclaimed in the *Guardian* as one of the two most outstanding biographies to have appeared since the war.

A writer of formidable imaginative power, each of Sylvia Townsend Warner's novels is a new departure, ranging from the revolutionary Paris of 1848 in *Summer Will Show* (1936), a 14th-century Abbey in *The Corner That Held Them* (1948), to the South Seas Island of *Mr Fortune's Maggot*, and 18th-century southern Spain in *After the Death of Don Juan*.

Sylvia Townsend Warner lived most of her adult life with her close companion Valentine Ackland, in Dorset, then in Norfolk and later in Dorset once again, where she died on 1 May 1978, at the age of eighty-four.

Virago also publishes *The True Heart, Mr Fortune's Maggot, Summer Will Show* and *The Corner That Held Them*.

VIRAGO
MODERN
CLASSIC
NUMBER
327

After the Death of Don Juan

SYLVIA TOWNSEND WARNER

With a New Introduction by

WENDY MULFORD

Published by Virago Press Limited 1989
20-23 Mandela Street, Camden Town, London NW1 0HQ

First published by Chatto & Windus 1938

A CIP Catalogue record for this book is available from the British Library

Printed in Great Britain by Cox and Wyman Ltd., Reading, Berks.

Introduction

At the conclusion of *After the Death of Don Juan*, this brief exchange occurs between Ramon and Diego, two peasants who play leading parts in the bungled siege of the castle of Don Saturno, lord of Tenorio Viejo:

> 'What are you looking at, Ramon? What do you see?'
>
> 'So large a country', said the dying man. 'And there in the middle of it, like a heart, is Madrid. But our Tenorio Viejo is not marked. I have often looked for it. It is not there, though. It is too small, I suppose. We have lived in a very small place, Diego.'
>
> 'We have lived in Spain.'

There are two real subjects to *After the Death of Don Juan*. One is Spain itself, its cruelty, grandeur, desolation, the dignity and beauty of its people, the stark extremes of poverty and wealth, the remote backwardness of the countryside, the age-old traditions, the hospitality and culture. The other, central, text concerns the exploitation and oppression of the Spanish peasantry by the combined forces of Church and nobility. These forces are the same, whether it is the time of Carlos III ('in the seventh decade of the eighteenth century'), in which the novel is set, or the time of the struggling Spanish republic, in the fourth decade of the twentieth century, whose fate passionately concerned Sylvia Townsend Warner at the time she was writing.

She called the novel (in a letter to her friend Nancy Cunard in August 1945) 'a parable if you like the word, or an allegory . . . of the political chemistry of the Spanish war, with the Don Juan — more of Molière than of Mozart — developing as the Fascist of the piece.'* But it is at the same time a very entertaining and beautifully written narrative, rich in the atmosphere and evocation of slow Spanish rhythms, of the dust, the stillness of midday, the harshness of the landscape, the sheer vastness of Spain's mountain ranges and its plains, the isolation of its villages. Spain itself, in its beauty and its deprivation, the country with which she held a continuing love affair, is at once subject and setting of this book.

All Sylvia Townsend Warner's novels are rich in evocation of place — one might compare the treatment of revolutionary Paris in *Summer Will Show* — and paradoxically, in their unique registration of a time and a place, capture a remarkable quality of timelessness. Here is the Spain of the familiar and endearing, 'beef boiled with broth and a slice of the tripe, pigs and chickpeas, thyme and grapes and garlic, law-suits and wool-combing, the wineskin and old women'.

After the Death of Don Juan is set in the small village of Tenorio Viejo, in a remote part of southern Spain, in the eighteenth century. In it Sylvia Townsend Warner portrays the conditions under which Fascism grew and flourished. The novel is woven like an old tapestry, with richly intricate cross-stitching, out of the traditional elements of the legend of the notorious libertine Don Juan. The story begins in Seville, 'after the death of Don Juan'. The early scenes introduce us to a cast of Sevillean grandees, at whose expense Sylvia Townsend Warner employs some of her most acid wit. The most pious, wealthy and obstinate young woman, Doña Ana, has fallen for her would-be seducer. Juan, however, after accidentally killing her father in a duel, lamentably appears to have died, in horrible circumstances

*Sylvia Townsend Warner, *Letters* (Chatto & Windus, London, 1982), 51.

— at least, according to his servant, Leporello. Ana is furious — ostensibly because Juan has escaped earthly revenge, in reality for more pressing personal reasons.

The motif that binds the elements of the original plot together and grafts it upon the material of the lives of the peasants in Tenorio Viejo is Doña Ana's lust for Juan and her fanatical pursuit of him — dead or alive. She insists that her household travel to Don Saturno's estate, to inform Juan's father of his son's untimely death. For seven days they journey — with three coaches, seven mounted attendants, a baggage wagon, many prayers and much stopping of mouths with handkerchiefs — over the 'wide estates of Andalucia', through 'encampments which housed the labourers and their families', where the 'stench was appalling', and finally over mountain ranges to Tenorio Viejo, where 'the olive-trees in their cultivated earth looked like the spots on a leopard's skin, the vineyards were few and poor. There were no meadows. All round were the mountains.'

By this device of Ana's journey to the provinces, attended by discomforts and dismay similar to those of Dr Johnson in the Highlands, Sylvia Townsend Warner sets her scene for the clash between the opposing interests of nobility and peasants. There is a rich vein of humour in the opposition between town and country, and in the discomfiture of the Sevillean grandees and their retinue in their cheerless and godless surroundings — for Don Saturno, like his son, has little time for the teachings of the Church. The tale modulates between the farcical events in the castle and the precisely observed bleak realities of the peasants' lives.

The grandees, Doña Ana's wimp of a husband, her duenna and chaplain, all find themselves miserably trapped: for the visit that was to deliver a message has lingered on like the legend itself, as Ana pursues her hope that, after all, Don Juan is not dead. A young woman of few thoughts, Doña Ana's fixed determination is to remain at the castle, despite the increasing discomfiture of the rest of the house-party. When she and Juan finally do re-encounter each other, towards the end of the book, there are no pretences. When she says that she knew they would meet again, Juan replies that that is no reason to be idle and he cites his latest conquest, whose behaviour he compares favourably with Ana's:

> 'I wooed her and I had her. So she was not obliged to run after me, mewing and spitting and caterwauling.'
>
> . . . 'You devil,' she said. 'You filthy devil!'
>
> 'No more a devil than you . . . No more filthy. It's how we are made, you know, people like you and me.'

Until Juan makes his reappearance, fleeing from the mockery of Seville and a disfiguring attack of nettlerash, Leporello's thrilling account of the legendary death-scene, though subjected to severe scrutiny by the villagers, has nevertheless satisfied most of them, and the grandees— with the exceptions of Ana and of Don Saturno. For the rest of the audience, the tale of Juan's challenge to the statue of the Commendander, the banquet and the grand finale of the devils dragging the infidel Juan down to hell, are convincing.

To Don Saturno's educated and sceptical mind it is a frankly incredible tale: he would be delighted not to have to support his son's debts any longer, but finds little in this story of metaphysical intervention to give him much hope that Juan is dead. The peasants, too, hope to discover that this particular burden upon them has been removed — they have hopes that with Juan's death they may be able to persuade Don Saturno, a well-meaning reformer and a democrat at heart, to implement the scheme for irrigation of their land, 'for barley and rye, and the vine and the olive', long shelved by their lord because of taxes, mortgages and Juan's debts. Only Ramon realises that they have 'more on [their] backs' than Juan — 'One death is a very small thing, neighbours, to set right so much that is wrong.'

Nevertheless, the hopes of Juan's death cause the peasants to organise a deputation to the castle to petition Don Saturno for the irrigation scheme — a negotiation which is going well (Don Saturno greatly prefers his peasants to his visitors) until interrupted by the reappearance of Juan.

Juan makes his entrance to the consternation of the devout Sevilleans, the dismay of Don Saturno and the secret rapture of Ana. Although temporarily reduced in circumstances, for this Juan is no hero — he has run out of funds and is tired of his uncertain life as a nefarious toy boy — Don Juan is no less deadly at Tenorio Viejo than he was in Seville. The drain on the estate caused by his previous lifestyle is only too apparent in the village's poverty, the crumbling school and church; and the peasants' attempt to improve their situation, together with Juan's ready exploitation of it, precipitates a murderous outcome for both peasantry and castle.

Here the tone of the novel makes a decided shift: from its opening as wry comedy of manners in the Sevillean scenes, to the near-farce in some of the set-pieces in the castle, where 'simpering' and urbane aristocrats and rural nobility confront each other with mutual incomprehension and loathing, and the various lackeys and toadies on either side play out their appropriate parts, the novel gradually strips bare all illusion of manners. In the climax the peasants are unequivocally at the centre of the stage, fighting, hand-to-hand, as so often occurred in the Civil War, for their lives.

In this novel, by contrast with her previous novel of the 1930s, *Summer Will Show*, action is not dependent upon character. In

Don Juan, as in her last two novels, *The Corner That Held Them* and *The Flint Anchor*, Sylvia Townsend Warner went beyond character and individual relationships as the motive force: her method, as indeed with other Marxist writers of this period, was to make society itself, rather than the individual, the subject. In a time when the very existence of society is denied, it is all the more remarkable that a whole new generation of readers are discovering and enjoying her work, particularly since she favoured remote societies for her subject. (A fourteenth-century abbey and a nineteenth-century East Anglian family in the case of the latter two novels.)

Although Sylvia Townsend Warner reserves her interest and sympathy for the peasants in *After the Death of Don Juan*, they are treated as a group, rendered individual only by the characteristics of their skills as debaters, olive-pruners, by their piety or their avarice. For example, one of the most individual portraits, a character who adds little to the action of the novel, is Celestina, the miller's daughter, who secretly saves all the money her father gives her for masses to be said for his silkworms: the gold is to provide her dowry, so she may escape into the calm cleanliness of a convent. (Covents cost money.) Her phlegmatic passion for a life in a nunnery echoes many of the themes of *The Corner That Held Them*, for religious bodies were not so much spiritual institutions as refuges in an uncertain and dangerous time, and many who went there did so rather from disgust with the conditions in this world than desire for the next.

Warner's peasants are not sanctified, or seen as embryo social-realist heroes, for all her admiration for the USSR at that time. All are held up to her level, humorous and scrutinising gaze. But this detachment is permeated by an immediacy, a vivid life in the writing that more than compensates for the lack of individuation. It is the result of her tried and tested method in historical novels, in which she would start with a fish-kettle, as she put it, or a skein of silk, a candle or a ball of twine, and re-create from the detail the rich intricacy of the period and the place. *The Corner That Held Them* is well known for this quality, but it is one that the other novels, and particularly *After the Death of Don Juan*, share too. She was always an imaginative materialist.

In scenes such as the one in which Leporello lies hidden to overhear the talk of the women as they wash their clothes in the river, Sylvia Townsend Warner catches the tart flavour of Spanish speech which so delighted her. Discussing the sacristan's daughter-in-law, who has all the gentry's washing, and still gets no fatter, one woman says:

> 'It's my belief she's got a worm. Not an ordinary worm, but what they call a queen-worm . . . An ordinary worm lives in the guts and eats the food you send it. But a queen-worm is more delicate than that. It will eat only the marrow of the backbone. Up it goes, suck, suck! . . . when it tastes the brain it begins to dance on its tail for pleasure, and you die in a convulsion. That's what ails Teresa Mauleon, mark my words.'

And, discussing the affairs of the castle, the tanner's wife offers the information that Doña Ana's husband is no better than he should be, and has been caught, *in flagrante*, with her chaplain ('a fine man . . . a lovely man, tender as veal, smooth as a sausage').

> 'I can't understand it at all,' said the young woman who had listened so attentively to the queen-worm. 'Surely, it is a great sin?'
>
> 'A sin, yes, it is a sin. But the gentleman is an officer in the army, officers in the army are all good Catholics.'
>
> 'What do you mean, Maria Perez?'
>
> 'Eh, what I say. The gentlemen in the army are good

Catholics so they love the priests. It has always been so, it always will be so.'

'Well, it isn't like that with the common soldiers, anyhow.'

'No. They have to drudge along with womankind. Black beans and long families for them.'

Some of the most successful effects in the novel come from the clash and contrast of individual and group scenes on the stage of the small village, and within its church and castle walls; there is an inn scene, where the peasants question Leporello about the fate of Don Juan, while other group or 'chorus' scenes are set in the pruning of the olive grove (the village's main livelihood), at the mill, and in the schoolhouse. The method is not unlike that in Eisenstein's films: a close-up of key characters — Don Saturno, the sacristan, the peasant Ramon — in which their thoughts are presented; shots of groups of characters, taking refuge from the storm; then the full cast — Ana denouncing the imposter Juan to the whole village, the siege, the arrival of the troops, the massacre. Within this dramatic, even operatic structure, Sylvia Townsend Warner highlights the gradual opposition of the two sets of interests: in the last resort, no one can stand aside. Objectively, each character, even the sceptical and reforming Don Saturno, is bound into one interest or the other — in the Don's case, literally, as Juan ties him to a chair to prevent him warning the peasants of their betrayal.

Up to this point, the two sets of interests are deftly interwoven. For example, soon after her arrival in the village, Ana, whose piety is beyond suspicion ('such ladies are the glory of Catholic Spain'), goes into the church for a night's vigil, ostensibly to pray for her father's soul, in reality to pray for Juan: to hale him from hell, in the view of her reluctant duenna, Doña Pilar. The villagers grouped below the church watch with unruffled curiosity:

With the turn of the street the church was visible again, close at hand and dominant. A flight of steps led up to the platform before the porch. It was as though the people who stood there were acting on a stage, and as though it were a play the people of the village stood watching from below. Lord! how tall these strangers were: even the lady was taller than Don Saturno, and as for her husband — an emperor could not have a finer figure, nor an angel a more beautiful complexion. Such broad shoulders, such a waist, such legs! Their priest too was a very fine figure of a man.

Meanwhile, the sacristan, a character through whom Sylvia Townsend Warner exposes the nature of Fascism's appeal, guards the door to the church. Through the night he sits, his cloak wrapped around him, his back to the door, tasting the sweetness of power:

The sentries trudged their rounds, the stars wheeled overhead, and he, Gil Mauleon, sat on guard. Rigid and ornate the church enclosed her [Doña Ana] like a cage. Rigid and ornate her stiff bodice, her massive skirts . . . Like crowning witnesses the images stared down on her with their attentive eyes. But they did not see her better than he did, who sat with his back to the locked door and held the key.

If the Juan legend and the obstinate lust of Doña Ana for the lover who spurned her provide the pretext and framework for the tale, and the setting of Spain and the hopes and sufferings of the peasants provide the immediate concern, Sylvia Townsend Warner was also interested in putting forward certain key ideas in the novel. One of these is to be found in the character of the man who comes nearest to being her hero, Ramon Perez.

In the copy of *After the Death of Don Juan* which she gave to the poet Valentine Ackland, her lifelong companion, Sylvia Townsend Warner wrote 'P.248'. The passage in question reads as follows:

> He was a man of certain steadfast ideas — not uncommon in that, and the ideas were nothing out of the ordinary. What made him peculiar was the steadfastness by which he lived out his creed.

These ideas of Ramon's have to do with justice — a key theme for Sylvia Townsend Warner throughout her life, for nothing enraged her so much as injustice, and, it is fair to say, her views on this played no small part in her joining the Communist Party; with standing by one's neighbour, and with the attempt to improve the world where one can. In other words, Ramon Perez sees further than his fellow villagers, he sees the necessity for combining together, not simply lying down under their wrongs. '*No hay remedio*', there is no remedy, the phlegmatic Spanish response, is not for him a sufficient philosophy.

The other character who is the representative of change is the engagingly eccentric Don Saturno himself. However, his intellectual passions — for astronomy, Aristophanes, his library, his maps — together with his inability to resist his son's demands, or to administer his estate efficiently, render him ineffectual as an agent for any real reform. In the denouement of the novel it is made clear that such a man, however good his intentions, will in the end become the ally of the Fascist powers.

The fatalism of the peasants underlies the flat, even tone of much of the writing; although the novel points the possibilities of change through organisation, through education and through escape from the superstitions of the Church, which exert such a powerful, and class-biased control. (Sylvia Townsend Warner was always an implacable atheist and opponent of the Church.) Even in the last scene, in the final hopeless battle against the troops, one of the peasants, Diego, discovers himself through fighting:

> From the moment when he had jumped down from the wall he had entered into a new life, a life of unassailable happiness, . . . He felt secure in the love of his brothers . . . Secure in love, secure in hate. His hate was released and ran loose, beautiful in the sunlight, rejoicing like some wild animal loosed from a cage . . .'

Under the lax guidance of their Don — atheist and half-hearted reformer — the peasants are less than scrupulous about their religious devotions. And the Sevillean visitors are appalled to discover that Don Saturno has instituted a school, not to teach the peasants useful crafts, but to teach them to read and write — 'One should never deny to any section of mankind the means of feeling itself more miserable . . . discontent, a noble discontent, must be the end of education' — a passage one cannot help appreciating in the Britain of 1989. Unfortunately, because of the Don's failure to fund and take an interest in it, the school remains ineffectual, attended by only a few children.

In the early stages of the Spanish Civil War, in October 1936, Sylvia Townsend Warner went to Barcelona, with Valentine Ackland, to work for an ambulance unit. On her return, she wrote to a friend:

> I don't think I have ever met so many congenial people in the whole of my life, liking overleapt any little bounds of language . . . A people naturally intellectual, and with a long standard of culture, have thrown off the taskmasters who enforced ignorance on them.

At the time of writing *After the Death of Don Juan*, she was also writing a number of reports about the situation in Spain which were published in places like *Left Review*, and as many pieces as possible in widely read journals like *The New Statesman* and *Time and Tide*. As she was to say later, in an interview in 1975:

> . . . it was getting rather hard to get in any propaganda because the English authorities and respectables were clamping down on freelance journalists who had anything to say in favour of the Republic. I had a great deal to say . . .'*

Sylvia Townsend Warner never had any time for the 'respectables'; she was a natural anarchist. In the same interview she described Don Juan as 'definitely a political novel . . . a political fable . . . I think it's an extremely good story because I took the Mozart subject as my framework but continued it into the Spain of this day and age.'

By 1938 the International Brigaders were returning from the Spanish Civil War and in the last drawn-out months of the struggle against Franco, the Italians and the Germans, all the supporters of the Republic could do was to organise evacuation wherever possible of Republicans, and send food-parcels to those who stayed. Sylvia Townsend Warner and Valentine Ackland were active in doing both, as they had been tireless in support of the Republic for the previous two and a half years.

Sylvia Townsend Warner's second and last trip to Spain was for the second congress of the International Writers' Association for the Defence of Culture in 1937. In a piece called 'What the Soldier Said', published in *Time and Tide*, she celebrated the Spanish characteristics and values that so impressed her. It is a fine piece of journalism, but the place to discover Spain in the writings of Sylvia Townsend Warner, enduring Spain, the Spain of ordinary people, is in this extraordinary, unclassifiable novel, ripe with the generosity and humour of a most civilised people.

Readers coming to *After the Death of Don Juan* half a century

**P.N. Review*, 1981.

later may be little concerned with the parallels between the events in Tenorio Viejo, and the development of events leading up to the Civil War in Spain. The novel can be read without any appreciation of this background. It is high-spirited, beautifully written and ultimately moving, a passionate and partisan re-creation of a place and a people with whom Sylvia Townsend Warner felt a deep empathy. But its satire and its realism are barbed with her rage and pity at the forces that in the 1930s were tearing Spain apart, while Britain and most of Europe stood aside and watched the triumphant Fascist rehearsal.

When Franco won, she vowed she would not return till 'the brute' was dead. She kept her vow. Unfortunately the dictator lived too long for her to be able to revisit the country with which she had fallen in love on that first visit in October 1936, the country she described as 'a most ungainly country to love, but . . . extraordinarily beautiful'.

As for the novel, it was published in late 1938. Left-wing reviewers praised her historical imagination, her perspicacity, her style; the major literary reviews ignored it. She herself considered it to be her most personal book after *The Corner That Held Them*, as well as an extremely good story. She thought that it got 'swamped' because it was published so late, and in a small edition. But the tide of politics was turning. By 1939 people had other things on their minds than Spain and historical novels written from a Marxist point of view. As she said when asked if her political commitments affected the reception of her work, 'It affected it very badly . . . I never had reviews from the sort of reviewers that *sell* books.'

Five of her novels have already been reissued in paperback at reasonable prices people can afford to pay, most of them after long years out of print, most of them by Virago. It would have given her especial pleasure that *After the Death of Don Juan* is now the sixth.

Wendy Mulford, Cambridge, 1989

The death—or rather, the disappearance—of Don Juan de Tenorio took place at Seville in the seventh decade of the eighteenth century. It happened under curious circumstances. Don Juan, a renowned libertine, was paying court to Doña Ana de San Bolso y Mexia, a young lady who was already promised in marriage elsewhere. (She was motherless, an only child and a considerable heiress.) Her father, a retired Army man, had expressed his unequivocal disapproval of Don Juan, Doña Ana too averred most steadfastly that his advances were odious to her. Nevertheless, it happened that Doña Ana was alone in the garden-court of her father's house one evening, and that Don Juan encountered her there. He began to make love to her, so forcibly that she protested. The Commander heard voices, and came out. Seeing his daughter in Don Juan's arms, he drew his sword. They fought, and the Commander was mortally wounded.

It was expected that Don Ottavio, Doña Ana's betrothed, would avenge the Commander's death; or at any rate attempt to: Don Juan was a practised swordsman. Doña Ana, however, declared that vengeance must be the business of heaven. Meanwhile there was a very grand funeral, and a superb monumental figure of the Commander, carved by one of the best artists of the day, was set up over his tomb.

So much is certain; for what followed we have to depend on the report of Don Juan's valet, Leporello. According to him, Don Juan, in a fit of bravado, visited the Commander's tomb, and invited the dead man to supper. The statue bowed its head in assent. On the appointed evening Don Juan hired a private room at a fashionable eating-house. The table was laid and a band hired. The band, though, was in an adjoining room, and only Don Juan and Leporello were present when the Commander in the likeness of his statue—or the statue animated by the Commander, have it as you will—entered. With a few stern ejaculations he told Don Juan that the hour had come when he must either repent or render up his soul to hell. Don Juan refused to repent. The room grew dark, the floor opened, devils appeared, and Don Juan was dragged down into the pit. The Commander, meanwhile, had retired.

This was immediately followed by the entrance of Doña Ana, Don Ottavio, Doña Elvira (a lady who had left her convent for love of Don Juan), a respectable member of the lower classes called Masetto, and his wife, who was also one of Don Juan's victims. They had come in search of Don Juan, in order to carry out a concerted reproach. They found Leporello, who with every appearance of terror, told them of what had just taken place.

Doña Ana had constantly affirmed that heaven would

avenge her father's death. But this demonstration of heavenly efficiency was too much for her. For several days she remained in her bedroom, refusing food and refusing consolation, alternately weeping and fainting. During these anxious days Don Ottavio remained in the ante-room, thinking that at any moment he might be called in to receive her dying words, and sometimes addressing respectful condolences through the keyhole. On the third evening, worn out with watching, he became drowsy, and was indeed asleep when a hand touched his shoulder. His dream translated this touch to the stony hand of the Commander, summoning him to follow Don Juan into hell and challenge him there. He woke; and saw Doña Ana, deadly pale, beside him.

'Ana!' he cried, 'Doña Ana! Is there anything I can do for you, anything I can fetch? I live to serve you.'

Ana said,

'Where is Elvira? Has she gone yet?'

Ottavio shook his head. Doña Elvira, a guest in the house, had also taken to her bed.

Ana frowned.

'And where is Leporello?' she continued.

'I really have no idea. During these last few days I have thought only of you.'

'He must be found at once, and taken into your service.'

She spoke with such decision it was as though heaven spoke through her; and it occurred to Don Ottavio that she might be raving. He knew that one should not argue with the demented, nevertheless he began to demur a little. When there were so many deserving domestics for hire, he suggested, would it not look a little odd to engage the valet of such a libertine master?

'Do not cross me, Don Ottavio. After such afflictions' —Tears sprang to her eyes. In a choking voice she continued—

'after all I have gone through, my father's death, myself an orphan, everything . . . then, when I was beginning to grow, not consoled, but accustomed to my wretchedness, the death of this villain bringing it all back to me. . . . Do not argue with me now about this one poor shred of comfort.'

'Comfort, Doña Ana? But am I not sworn to be your comfort?'

'Yes, yes! Of course you are a comfort, or will be. Though I cannot think of marriage at present. But don't you understand, Ottavio? We cannot lose Leporello. He was the last person who saw my dear father.'

Don Ottavio kissed her cold hand, murmuring,

'What sensibility! Heavens, what sensibility!'

Doña Ana dried her eyes, and sat down.

'While I am equal to it, there are two things I must discuss with you.'

Her demeanour was so curiously resolute and determined that again it seemed to him that she must be astray from her senses. But he assured her that he had no purpose in life except to be of use to her; she had only to speak, and he would obey.

She sat silent, staring in front of her, and he waited for her to speak. She turned her head, and looked at him almost as though she had forgotten he was there; and her eyes dwelt on him with a scrutiny at once so blank, so exhaustive, and so desolate that he began to implore her not to overtax herself, to wait until the next day. But she interrupted him, saying, with something of her old grace,

'My grief makes me forget the ways of the world. Would you please ring the bell for Doña Pilar? And we had better have something to eat.'

Yawning and blinking the duena set up her embroidery frame in a corner of the room, and a footman brought refreshments on a tray.

'Heaven has made it clear to me that I have two duties to perform, one as a member of society, and the other as a daughter of the Church. First, I must visit the parents of this wretched man, and tell them of his fate.'

'What!' exclaimed Ottavio. 'Had such a wretch relations?'

'A father and an aunt. They live in the provinces. It will be a very fatiguing journey. But I must make it.'

'But, Doña Ana, consider your health. A journey into those frightful provinces (quite apart from the expense, which would be considerable) might be the death of you. And then, think of the strain of being the bearer of such news. The idea is noble (all your ideas are noble) but the execution of it might be fatal. I am sure Doña Pilar will agree with me.'

He paused; but there was no answer.

'At least, put it off till you are more equal to it. Let the poor things remain in ignorance a little longer. Why hurry on their sufferings?'

'My second obligation is to order masses to be said for the repose of his soul.'

'One cannot fulfil too liberally one's obligation to the dead,' said he, 'but masses for the soul of your dear father are already being said at every altar in Seville.'

'The soul of Don Juan,' said Doña Ana.

Don Ottavio looked at her in astonishment. She leaned back in her chair, her eyes were closed, her features set. 'I'm afraid she's raving,' he whispered to the duena.

Doña Pilar came forward, and began to feel Doña Ana's forehead.

'Leave me alone, please. I am not raving. My wish is a pious and reasonable one, I cannot see why I should be thwarted in everything.'

'But, Doña Ana, with all deference. . . . If Leporello's story is true—and why should we doubt it?—Don Juan went straight to perdition. It would be throwing away money, I mean it would be flying in the face of Providence, to have masses said for the repose of his soul.'

'Don Ottavio, would you attempt to stand between me and my conscience?'

'Not for an instant. But just now your conscience is overheated.'

'Overheated?'

'Overwrought. You have lost your command of theology. No wonder, after the strain of all you have been through. But I must assure you, dearest Doña Ana, that to pray for the soul of a man whom heaven has visibly sent to hell is neither an act of reason nor of piety.'

Doña Ana's foot tapped the ground. Her features sharpened into a resemblance to the late Commander.

'Have I lived,' she asked, 'to be called impious? And by a layman?'

From behind her embroidery frame Doña Pilar signalled anxiously to Don Ottavio. But he felt he must assert himself.

'Let us say no more about impiety. As you say, it is not a subject to be canvassed by obedient children of Holy Mother Church. Let your man of religion decide. But let me speak as a man of the world. Your finances, my dearest, are seriously compromised. Your father's funeral cost a great deal of money——'

'Do you grudge it, then?'

'Not for an instant. But it cost a lot. Then there was the statue over his tomb. It was considerably larger than life-size——'

'Would you have had it smaller?'

'Not by an inch. But it was considerably larger than life-size and carved from a solid block of Carrara marble by no less an artist than—his name escapes me for the moment, but I remember his fee. Then there was the mourning,'—Don Ottavio began to count on his fingers—

'the masses, the endowment of an orphanage for young girls of endangered virtue, the annuities to your seven dear aunts, the diamond necklace to our Lady of Atocha, and a certain number of outstanding debts. Besides the legal expenses.'

Doña Ana's foot tapped no longer. Don Ottavio pursued his advantage.

'You have a soul above money, I know. But let me remind you of the future. I have already the honour and rapture of being your betrothed. If heaven should bless us with children, sons like your valiant father, daughters like yourself, we should wish to bring them up in a way befitting their station. Might we not then regret money spent on these ill-advised'

—'Ahem!' coughed Doña Pilar—

'on this ill-advised journey? It is impossible to travel without expense.'

Ana sipped a little wine.

'I might give up the journey. But I must insist on the masses'

—Don Ottavio threw down a biscuit with a gesture of despair—

'for I feel they are the only reparation in my power. If it had not been for Don Juan's infatuation for me (he assured me, and I believe he spoke the truth for once, that he had never felt such love combined with respect for any other woman), if it had not been for that fatal evening, and my poor father coming into the garden just then—if it had not been for all this, he might never have fetched on himself the wrath of heaven, he might yet be alive and able to repent.

'I can't let him go!' she exclaimed; and burst into tears.

'No one in Seville,' said Don Ottavio, 'doubted the ardour of Don Juan's feelings for you. Everyone recognised that if you had consented to receive his addresses, you would have become the only woman in his life. But you didn't consent. That being so, I don't think it would do at all if it became known that you were now having masses said for the repose of his soul.'

'Why should they know?' Her voice was sullen and choked with sobs, her face was hidden behind a handkerchief.

Gazing attentively at every inflection of the handkerchief Don Ottavio continued,

'How should they not know? Seville is such a chattering place, your beauty and your virtue have aroused so much envy. You have your reputation to think of, Doña Ana, the jewel of your good name. Think how ill-natured people might talk if it came out that you were paying for masses. Suppose Doña Elvira, for instance—'

The handkerchief quivered.

'If your conscience demands these masses for the repose, however questionable, of Don Juan's soul, I would not for a moment combat your wish. Your wish is my law. I have constantly said so. But wouldn't it be better if they were ordered by someone else, by his relations? The effect, you know, would be just the same.'

'Then at least I must break the news to them.'

Once more he reminded her of the fatigues of the journey, the delicacy of her constitution, and once again he asked her to consider the malice of such characters as Doña Elvira. But he spoke to no purpose, and rather acidly she reminded him that her wish was his law. Journey or masses, masses or journey . . . and now it seemed to him that it might have been more prudent to agree to the masses, and hope that the authorities would refuse them as impious. But his brain was whirling for lack of sleep, calculations of expense and expediency flew about his mind like wisps of hay on a whirlwind. At last with resignation he heard himself agreeing to the journey; and immediately after he heard himself saying that if she were bent on the journey, he must, at least, be allowed to accompany her.

'As your husband, Doña Ana. Your father wished it, it is my dearest desire. Our betrothal has been clouded with such melancholy accidents, why should we prolong it?'

Her delicacy will demand at least a month or two, he thought; and by then she may have given up the idea of the journey. He heard her agreeing that the marriage was her father's wish, he heard her say that she relied on his devotion, that she would be guided by him. He waited for her delicacy to demand its month or two; but there was no such word, only a silence which became more and more awkward.

He roused himself, he plugged the silence with expressions of rapture and gratitude. It seemed to him that the preceding pause had been most painfully obvious, that it was all going very lamely, that she might at any moment, and with good cause, accuse him of coldness and inadequacy. But she did not seem to notice anything amiss.

Day was already showing in the sky. Ottavio went home to his bachelor apartment, and ordered his valet to shave him.

Leaning back with closed eyes, lulled by the delicate hiss of stubble and steel, breathing in the mingled scents of fine soap and a linen dressing-cape fresh from the laundress, Ottavio relinquished himself to a childlike sense of repose and safety.

He was an orphan and impecunious; and he had been through a lot lately, more than was good for him. If he were not careful his health would break down. Even at this moment he had indigestion, and of late he had scarcely been able to call his heart his own, it was always leaping and banging like some animal out of control.

The razor hesitated for an instant.

'Is that a wrinkle?' he asked.

'No, sir. A pimple.'

Ottavio sighed. His face was his fortune. His face, his principles, and his elegant legs.

Was it the face and the legs, or was it the principles

which had commended him to the Commander? The Commander had said it was the principles, yet with his cold lizard's hand he had patted the face, saying 'What a complexion! As fine as my Ana's.' Ana, too, had said it was the principles. And so, out of that chance meeting in the avenue, when his elegant legs had hurried him forward to pick up the old gentleman's cane, his fortune had come, a marriage had been arranged. How peaceful, how poetical those days had been!—music, and billiards, and mutual inclination, the Commander's stories, so interesting and extending so far into the past, the Commander's magnanimity on the question of marriage settlements, all the serenity of an ideal betrothal. Dear and worthy old gentleman! With the utmost sincerity Ottavio regretted the catastrophe which had robbed him of such a father-in-law.

The shave was completed. But he did not want to move, to break this spell of being tended, of being a child again.

'Wash my hands, Antonio. Trim my nails, and polish them.'

For then in a moment the fine weather broke, everything changed; and Ana was in hysterics and saying that she would go into a nunnery. 'But your father's wishes, Ana. I will wait, I will wait as long as you please; but I beg you to respect your father's wishes!' And he had spoken of the Commander glancing down on them from heaven. When next he saw her she was in a different mood, rigidly exalted, bearing herself like a figure in a tragedy. She received him in silence, in silence she heard his enquiries, his condolences, his respectful vows. Standing before her, trying to make conversation, he had felt like a bird twittering under the menace of a thundercloud. And then she had leapt to her feet, and from the innumerable folds of her mourning her hand had flashed out the Commander's sword. 'Avenge him!' she exclaimed, 'Avenge him! Vengeance on his murderer! Then I will marry you, Ottavio. But not till then.' It was terrible, terrible, to see how far sorrow had driven her from her usual delicacy. No fishwife could have stated a bargain more frankly.

It seemed as though Ana could only be his upon terms. Heaven had taken the matter of vengeance into its own hands. Don Juan had been carried alive into the pit, on that point there could be no more negotiating. But Ana was still to win. Now there must be this tiresome, this painful journey as the price for her hand. Yes, and she had mentioned something else too, some other stipulation. What was it? Leporello! A strange wish; and yet in a way justifiable. For undeniably Leporello was the only link between this world of the living and the life-after-death appearance of the Commander, he was, as she had said, the last person to see her father.

A divine will orders everything for the best, and no doubt inscrutable heaven had some good reason for ordaining that the only surviving repository of the Commander's sentiments should be this rapscallionly valet. Possibly a scheme for Leporello's salvation. Desperate cases need desperate remedies. But I cannot take him as a valet, thought Ottavio. That would be too ignominious, too painful. Even Ana cannot ask that. They went about a great deal, I had best make him my courier. Again the thought of the journey rose up before him, a sierra of a prospect.

'Antonio, while you are about it you can wash my feet.'

The wedding was as quiet as a wedding can be, as soon as the vows had been pronounced they stepped into a travelling chariot and set out on their mission of breaking the news to Don Saturno.

Though Don Ottavio had tried to keep the excursion free from any immoderate expense or immoderate display, the cortege as it wound through the streets of Seville could not fail to excite considerable attention. There were three coaches; seven mounted attendants; and a baggage wagon. All the vehicles were draped in black and drawn by black mules. The hammercloths were of black velvet, crape bows obscured the scutcheons, and the servants wore black liveries. Men bared their heads, women knelt and crossed themselves as the coaches went by. Crippled beggars crutched themselves along beside the principal coach imploring alms in the name of the saints and the holy souls in purgatory. Ana turned pale, her gloved hand threw out an alms, she sighed heavily and trembled. Ottavio tried to console her; her father's sojourn in purgatory, he assured her, could not be a long one, very likely it was already over. But she remained staring fixedly in front of her.

In the countryside the defile of mourning vehicles would have aroused as much attention as in the streets of Seville, no doubt, only there happened to be no one to attend to it. It was mid-day. Scattered over the wide estates of Andalucia small groups of peasants laboured, they looked no larger than hens scratching a poultry-yard, they paid no attention to what went by on the high road. Sometimes they passed the encampments which housed the labourers and their families. Only a few old women, blind or infirm, sat drowsing through the noon-day. Dogs, pigs, and infants sprawled in the road, sometimes from a hut would come the knocking of a distaff or the wailing cries of a woman in labour. The stench was appalling, and the coachman had great difficulty in whipping the dogs, pigs, and children out of their path. But only by the smell and the expostulations of the drivers could Ana and Ottavio, secluded behind their curtains, have told that they were passing through an inhabited world.

'No songs, no dances, no sounds of happy industry! How different from Italy!'

'Or England,' replied Ottavio. And peeping through a chink of the curtains he found himself staring straight into a festering eye-socket, round which a number of bluebottles buzzed in a languid, unenterprising way.

'I am afraid this will be a very boring journey,' he remarked, 'do you mind, would you object, if I were to divert myself a little by playing the flageolet?'

'Play by all means,' she replied.

The journey, Leporello had assured them, would take three days at the most, and involved only one mountain range. Nor need they anticipate any great discommodity whilst crossing these mountains. He knew the roads from his boyhood; for the more difficult stages of their journey he would sit beside the coachman and direct him. All would pass off with a minimum of hazard, and any inconveniences they might suffer would soon be forgotten in the pleasure they would feel on reaching the valley, and the estate of Don Saturno. There indeed was a rural paradise. Purling streams, linen bleaching on the green meadows like a flock of swans, majestic groves of fine timber, three mills, no less, a fine modern church and presbytery, erected by Don Saturno's great-great-grandfather, neat cottages, sheep fat as maggots, smooth pigs, splendid poultry, oliveyards, vineyards, silk-worms, shepherdesses, a population devoted to virtue, industry and music, all clustering round the ancient family castle, and all devoted to the family. Ah, said he, when their honours reached Tenorio Viejo they would recognise it as a village of the Golden Age. And what joy their arrival would create! With pipe and tabor the villagers would flock to welcome such visitors, Don Saturno and Doña Isabel....

'How melancholy it is,' interrupted Don Ottavio, 'to think that we must overwhelm these virtuous landowners and their virtuous tenantry with news so inexpressibly shocking.'

'You have taken the very words out of my mouth. Jesus! How crushed they will be, how they will lament! What a blow for them all, what a warning! What a story for winter nights, when the wind blows in the mountain.'

Meanwhile, he was journeying ahead of the party in order to arrange fitting accommodation at the inns. He had taken very happily to his appointment as courier, and looked considerably more respectable in his new livery.

They had journeyed for five days, they had crossed two mountain ranges and jolted across dried river-beds without number, and still another mountain range reared itself between them and the valley of Tenorio Viejo. Doña Pilar, sitting with her back to the horses, was suffering so intensely from a sick headache that she had not even the energy to tell her beads, nor to rate the maid-servants when they tumbled out of the second coach to attend their mistress at the inns. With a blank gaze, with pale lips mouthing an incessant heart-burn, too sick even for fear, she looked out over precipices, at sheets of snow, at clouds of dust, at dead mules and wayside crosses.

For after the first day Doña Ana had directed that the windows should be unscreened; and though the scenery was dreary and unpicturesque in the extreme she watched it trail by, staring out of the window with a kind of stony attention. Only when they passed a church or a shrine did she seem to awake. Then the procession would be halted, and Ana would get out and fall on her knees to pray. Naturally the news of a strange lady praying would reach the parish priest. 'A bereavement?' he would suggest to Don Ottavio.

'We travel with bad news,' Don Ottavio would reply. For indeed it would seem both profane and ridiculous to mention that this was a honeymoon journey, and already he looked back on that night at the inn when Ana, displaying an unexpected animation, had yielded her virginity, as something which had happened a very long time ago, and perhaps not at all.

'Wonderful devotion,' the priest would say. 'Ah, sir, such ladies are the glory of Catholic Spain.' And when at last Doña Ana rose from her knees he would go forward, to speak of consolation, of sorrow being the common lot, and to mention, perhaps, the poverty of a rustic parish, the regrettable condition of God's house. And so they would go on again, and Don Ottavio would make another entry in his travelling account-book and, that finished, return to his flageolet. It was being a very expensive journey, almost as expensive as the masses would have been. Still, Ana wished it. And he was getting on wonderfully with his flageolet.

Leporello explained that in his original estimate of the time required for their journey he had not allowed for the factor of religion. Travelling with his godless master had taught him a worldly estimation of speed. The faster on the road, the slower to heaven. How infinitely preferable was a journey like this, interspersed with beautiful hours of devotion. However, this seventh day—they had not, of course, travelled on Friday—should see them at Tenorio Viejo. There, in front of them, rose the mountain range; the pass went through just there, under the crag that looked like a rotten tooth. He regretted that he had omitted to reckon the two previous ranges. But in a country like Spain it was easy to overlook a sierra or two. Besides, they were already surmounted. A mountain before one rises to the skies, a mountain behind one sinks to the plain. Only the inexperienced cat keeps count of her kittens.

He sprang up beside the coachman, saying, 'Have no fear!'

The road was abominable, a succession of boulders and pot-holes. At intervals mountain torrents swept across it, swift and savage as wild beasts. Overhead the wind was banging against the crags, as they mounted gusts of cold air began to blow in through the crevices in the window fittings, stinging them with a gritty dust. The air had a heartless, a terrifying purity, it wounded the nostrils. Looking out between the dust-storms they saw a landscape strewn with blocks of stone, a cowering vegetation, the reddish fangs of the roots of trees torn up by tempests. Below them on the twisting road the other coaches and the baggage wagon laboured upward, dwarfed and ludicrous. A shrill din came from the coach containing the chambermaids; they were singing a litany. The riders were shouting advice and warning, one to another, the coachmen were swearing and lashing their beasts, above the tumult rose the voice of Leporello, crying out, 'Soul of God, to the left! Look out now, this is the place where the man fell. Here is the ticklish corner, be careful here. If we dislodge that stone, then we are lost. Mother of God, how it goes bounding! Look out, you below! Beast! Did I not say to the left, would you ruin us all, driving as though we were in the Alameda?'

At last the summit of the pass was reached, and a pause was made to allow the mules to recover their courage. Before them stretched a rocky plateau, all sight of the world below was lost, and the wind ripped off the fleeces of the thistles. Leporello jumped down from the box and came to the window.

'Well, here we are, safe and sound, thanks be to the Virgin. And now we can sight the end of our troubles. Do you see that row of cairns there, stretching across our path? That is the boundary, beyond those cairns begins the Tenorio estate. And thenceforward we shall travel on one of the finest roads in the province, with nothing to trouble us, and delight before us. A fine road, an easy descent—we shall be there in no time.'

They went forward, they passed the boundary, presently they began to go downhill. The road seemed no better than before, the descent as full of sharp turns and unguarded precipices as the ascent had been. But Leporello shouted out that there was nothing to fear, that it was an excellent road, that he knew it as well as a child knows the way to the nipple; and alternately encouraged the coachman or taunted him with cowardice. Driven on by shouts and blows of the whip the mules quickened their pace, the weight of the great chariot behind them forced them into a wild jerky trot. The chariot swayed, the stones came rattling after it. Suddenly there burst out a noise of angry shouting from the advance-guard. With the driver hauling on their bits the mules came scuffling to a standstill on the very heels of the riders.

They had reined up before a group of raw-boned men who, gesticulating with cudgels and carabines, barred the way. Don Ottavio jumped out, drawing his sword. The other riders came galloping up, the train of coaches halted. An ambuscade!

Bristling out on the retinue appeared swords and pistols. The coachmen drew forth their great blunderbusses. There was a hubbub of voices, threats and curses, the uncouth windy voices of the men who barred the road.

'Let us pass! Get out of the way, or we will ride you down!'

'Try it, then. It will be the worse for you!'

Don Ottavio's chivalry was aroused. 'Silence, all of you,' he shouted. 'Any man who moves or speaks, I'll run him through the body!'

Turning to the man who seemed to be the ringleader he said,

'We wish to pass.'

'You can't,' said the man. All along the line there was a concurring growl.

'We wish to pass, I say. Out of our road!'

'Can't pass,' repeated the spokesman.

'A more wretched troop of half-licked bandits I have never set eyes on. Off with you to your holes! Troop!'

'We aren't bandits,' said the man, 'we're swineherds. But for all that you can't pass.'

'*Swineherds!*'

For a moment this outrage almost overcame him. He glared at the rank of men. They glared back.

'Perhaps you will have the grace to inform me why we cannot pass?'

'A sow is farrowing in the road.'

He turned, and walked back to the chariot. Doña Ana was looking out of the window, her mouth open, her eyes darkened with fear.

He got in, seated himself beside her, smoothed back a lock that the wind had ruffled.

'Peasants. Just peasants. But never in my life, Ana, have I dreamed of such peasants. Such impudence is revolting.'

She sat beside him trembling.

'But there is nothing to fear. It seems that there is some obstacle further along the road. A moment's delay.'

'Oh, hush!' Though she spoke in the faintest whisper he had never before heard such feeling in her voice.

'I assure you, there is nothing to fear. Their manners are disgustingly uncouth, but they intend us no harm.'

She looked at him with haunted eyes.

'Ottavio, I implore you, do not try to make light of it.

This is not a thing we can make light of. When I looked out of the window, when I saw their faces and their bearing, I recognised *him*! Yes, for all their rags and their servitude, I saw on their brows the same profligate boldness which shone like a dreadful lightning in his glances. He is here, Ottavio. His wickedness is here like a taint, and these men are burning with the same devilish pride as he.'

She put her hand over her eyes as though to wipe away the vision.

'How can I bear it?' she murmured. 'Why must I go on?'

'If you wish it, we will turn back. Heaven forbid that you should go further on an errand which costs you so much.'

She crossed herself solemnly.

'I must go on.'

Presently one of the swineherds came to the coach door and told them that the way was clear. On his arm was a basket, and in the basket squirmed a litter of new-born pigs. Already the red bristles stood up on their skins. Don Ottavio gave him money, and he snatched it greedily. Doña Pilar, in a kindly shaken voice, drew Doña Ana's attention to the piglings.

'But they are ugly little creatures, when all is said.'

The valley, and the village of Tenorio Viejo, appeared below them. It was not in the least as Leporello had described it, it was pretty much as Ottavio had expected it to be. The castle stood on a small hill, the original square stone keep rambling off into lower levels of russet-tiled barns and storehouses. On a further hillock stood a church. It had been built with more pretensions to architecture than the castle, but less solidly, and its cupola had slipped awry, like an old woman's head-dress. Between the church and the castle straggled the village, an array of lime-washed hovels. The olive-trees in their cultivated earth looked like the spots on a leopard's skin, the vineyards were few and poor. There were no meadows. All round were the mountains. Some cultivation had struggled up them, forcing its way between the shaggy oak-woods. On the higher slopes the colour of the earth, fading from the valley leopard-colour to an ashen whiteness, showed that cultivation need strive no further.

Just before entering the village they passed the mill. But the river-bed was already almost dry, the mill-wheel turned at a snail's pace, dragging its bantling wild flowers with it, returning them again. In a few weeks' time it would turn no more, and till the autumn rains they would bloom as impudently as on land.

The cortege which had created so much attention in Seville created attention here too. But no one knelt, and no one begged. They stared with a bleak, blank curiosity and, for the most part, in silence. Only the children, pleased with the spectacle, expressed their pleasure by turning handsprings and somersaults beside the slow-moving black-draped coaches.

'Heavens!' thought Don Ottavio, 'suppose they all

remind her of Don Juan? I am sure they are swarthy enough, and impudent enough.' And Doña Pilar, peering first at the villagers and then at her mistress, was obviously nursing the same speculation. But Ana stared straight in front of her, rigid as a wax-white Virgin that passes, jostled, and saluted, and secluded, above the heads of the crowd in the procession of the Holy Images.

The chariot halted, the footmen opened the door and let down the steps. All along the rank of coaches figures in the deepest mourning were emerging and furtively brushing the dust of travel off their sables. Before them was the castle, a plain and shabby building, its only grandiloquent feature a flight of stone steps leading to a gaunt doorway. An open space, where some old hunting-dogs sat scratching or wandered stiffly around growling at the visitors, separated the castle from the village street. Along one side of it ran a wall enclosing a stable courtyard, on the other was a long barn, with a pigeon house at one end of it. Everything was large, old-fashioned, and dilapidated.

It had been arranged that Leporello, for fault of a better, should be their announcer. Leporello did not appear. His name was called hither and thither; at last Doña Ana's coachman in a voice of sour satisfaction remarked that Leporello had jumped off the box when the swineherds arrested them, had vanished in the bushes at the roadside and was, presumably, on the run. Or perhaps he recognised his friends and had joined them, he added. The situation was extremely awkward, and made no easier by the crowd which was now collecting, people strolling up in twos and threes with an air of exasperating nonchalance. Doña Ana, however, showed no hesitation or embarrassment. She summoned her personal retinue to attend her: Don Isidro her chaplain, Doña Pilar, her two waiting-women; and giving her hand to Don Ottavio she mounted the steps. By now a tolerably respectable major-domo had joined the group of gaping or giggling servants collected round the door; and the chaplain informing him of the names and rank of the visitors, added, by his tone of voice, his own witness that they had come on a melancholy errand.

With slow gait and bowed heads they entered the castle. Only Doña Pilar, allowing her eyes a momentary ramble, had seen that a funeral hatchment was displayed above the great doorway. So the news had reached Tenorio Viejo already, Doña Ana was too late. The many delays on the journey, no doubt. But all things are as heaven wills them, and she would not mention the hatchment.

Within they found the usual dusky servants' hall, whence a double stairway led to the gentry first floor. Opening the door into a long gallery the major-domo repeated the chaplain's announcement.

The room was fitted as a library. Between the bookshelves were columns bearing busts of classical worthies, some family portraits hung on the walls. At first it seemed as if the emperors and philosophers, so dominant in their marble rotundity, and the shadowy ancestors whose thin faces sloped to peaked beards, whose almost transparent hands clasped swords or skulls or patents of nobility, were the only inhabitants of the room.

Then an old man came forward. He was short of stature and very spare in build, walking with a gait at once stiff and tripping, the fragile, nimble gait of a bird. He was dressed in black. Rising from a profound courtesy, Ana said,

'I have come at the bidding of heaven.'

'Madam, I can well believe it. From your appearance I should conclude that you had come directly thence.'

'It is with inexpressible regret that I tell you I am here on a most melancholy occasion.'

'Melancholy, indeed,' said he, 'but that you condescend to be here is in itself a measure of consolation.'

Ana shook her head.

'Alas! We cannot speak of consolation. Resignation alone is all that heaven allows us.'

Don Isidro rolled his eyes, primmed his lips, and folded his hands on his bosom. Ottavio also shook his head.

'How sorry I am,' said Don Saturno, 'that I am obliged to add disappointment to your grief. But the funeral took place last week.'

'*The funeral?*'

'Had I realised that you proposed to honour us by

attending it, of course we would have postponed it. But most unfortunately I did not know of your intention.'

'The funeral?' repeated Ana, 'how could there be a funeral?'

'But without difficulty, my dear madam. A funeral requires only the one most simple, most universal condition. However intricate, however long-prepared the ceremonies, a mere death is enough to animate a funeral. The spade, the hammer and the chisel begin to move, the mason and the grave-digger, the candle-maker and the organist, the milliner and the tailor, the priest and the acolyte, the cook, the coachman, the courier, the notary and the notary's clerk busy themselves, the whole mechanism, like some fine piece of clockwork, begins to revolve. One cog-wheel attaches another, delicate impulses of industry circulate through the whole community. And personally I never attend a funeral without reflecting (and finding it a very comfortable reflection, too) what a large number of excellent persons are gaining their bread by it.'

'A philosopher,' muttered the chaplain to Doña Pilar, 'or worse.'

Ana repeated,

'The funeral!'

It seemed to Ottavio that he must amplify his wife's comment.

'We had not altogether supposed that such a ceremony —the distressing nature of the circumstances seemed likely to forbid—in fact——'

'But the body!' ejaculated Ana.

'My dear sister,' said Don Saturno, 'was a woman of very simple tastes. The custom of embalming, though it carries the sanction of classical usage, and doubtless embodies many admirable and interesting notions, such as the natural physical tenderness which bids us preserve a frame, once dear and valued, from the ignominy of corruption, and those first quaint conceptions of a life persisting beyond the grave, did not commend itself to her. If you would care to see it, I can show you the passage in her will in which she writes: *I wish to be buried like a woman of Spain and not pickled like a woman of Egypt.* Accordingly, we buried her. But I cannot say how much I regret that the ceremony took place before your arrival. I feel that I should apologise for a discourtesy.'

There was a total silence. Doña Pilar began to wish that she had mentioned the hatchment after all.

'But I beg that you will honour me by remaining here to take part in the week's mind requiem. And now may I offer you a little refreshment?'

His hand rested on a silver bell. Ana leaped to her feet.

'No, no! Stop!'

Her cry completely drowned the first tinkle of the bell. Don Saturno turned and glanced at her enquiringly. It was the first time that Ottavio had seen his face in profile; and in the midst of his flurry and embarrassment he noticed with satisfaction that Don Saturno's long thin nose turned up at the tip, which gave him a plebeian look.

'We have all misunderstood each other. I did not come here for the funeral of Doña Isabel.'

'These mountain roads!' said Don Saturno, 'how often have I not said that to civilise Spain we must give her a good road-system? But must this accident cut short an acquaintance so obviously indicated by the finger of Fate? I see, I regret to see it, that you are bound to a funeral. Perhaps on your return you will visit me? And at any rate you will take a traveller's bite?'

Again his hand moved towards the bell.

'Don Saturno.'

It might have been the Commander speaking.

'Don Saturno. Prepare yourself for solemn and terrible news. Your son, Don Juan, is no longer on earth.'

'You will forgive me,' he said, 'if I sit down?'

Leaning back in his chair by the writing-table, Don Saturno signalled to Ana to go on.

She went on. Without a tremble of the voice she described the attempted rape, her father's intervention, the scuffle that followed. Avoiding any mention of Elvira or Zerlina she described how Don Juan had visited the tomb of the Commander, bidding the marble man come down and sup with him.

Don Saturno listened with attention. It shocked Ottavio to see how sympathetically, how naturally, as it were, he followed the course of Ana's narrative, fine shades of surprise, critical interest, disapproval or compassion flickering over his countenance. Hearing of Don Juan's taunting visit to the cemetery he shook his head; but he might, so Ottavio thought, have been shaking it over a false note in a sonata.

'The evening came. Supper was prepared, supper for two. At the appointed hour a heavy knocking was heard. Your son, reckless with wine, lost in some dreadful transport of impiety, ordered his valet to open the door. More terrified of the dead than of the living, the man refused. The door opened, my father, in his living likeness but white as alabaster, appeared. He rebuked your son. He bade him take this last chance of heaven's mercy. He spoke in vain. Pointing downwards with a marble finger he consigned Don Juan to perdition. And the jaws of hell opened. With shrieks, with lamentations, with vain appeals, Don Juan struggled in the clutch of demons. The lightning quivered around them, the sentence of heaven spoke in a peal of thunder. And they bore him down to hell.'

Pale as death, with the stately exhaustion of the martyr, she sank into a chair.

After a while Don Saturno said,

'Who told you all this?'

'Leporello.'

'Leporello? Ah! And where is Leporello?'

Ottavio answered for this,

'We think he is on his way here. He was with us until we had crossed the boundary of your estates. Then, for some reason or other, he left our party and set off alone down the mountain-side.'

'And there was no trace of my son's body?'

'How could there be?' enquired Don Isidro reasonably. 'Your son was taken to hell.'

'Frankly,' said Don Saturno, 'I find this story very difficult to make head or tail of.'

Ana sobbed.

'My dear'—he stretched out his hand towards her with a gesture at once caressing and extenuating—'I did not mean to hurt your feelings. I am sure that you yourself believe it. And I am equally sure that motives of the highest christian charity have brought you here to tell me all this. But though I honour your motives I cannot altogether honour this story. As far as it rests on your witness, it is irrefutable, and indeed I am sorry to say it is to a certain extent perfectly recognisable. I know quite well that Juan was a libertine, and often could not distinguish between a virtuous woman and an amiable one. That he killed your father, that too, I must admit as quite in keeping. I need not say how much I regret the occurrence. But I too, in my time, have killed, often for the most trifling motives of passion or honour. And the visit to the cemetery. . . . It is possible. I would rather not think it possible, for it seems to me in the worst of taste, but I admit that it is possible. Is it not a criticism of our social morality that I should be able to swallow with tolerable resignation that my son attempted rape and achieved murder, and yet boggle a little to admit that he committed a breach of good taste? But as for the supper-party and what happened then . . . No, I must in candour say that my reason rejects all that part of the story.'

'Then I must adjure you,' said Ana passionately, 'to cast away your reason. Are there not things stronger than reason? Heaven in a moment can overthrow reason in a man's brain. Can it not also overthrow what we call reason in the order of this world's events?'

'That is a very interesting argument, and I am quite prepared to admit the force of it. But now you address yourself to my reason. Leporello's story addresses itself to my superstitions. That is quite another matter.'

'You cannot ask me to think that my father's spirit is a superstition,' said Ana with energy.

'The souls of the righteous are in the hands of God. And I am positive that your father would not leave such a repose in order to sup at a restaurant. You cannot really wish me,' he added mildly, 'to think that.'

'I must admit that I see what Don Saturno means,' mused Ottavio. 'And it is unfortunate that such a person as Leporello should be the only witness of this terrible event. But heaven often chooses strange instruments.'

'But surely you believe in hell?' enquired Don Isidro.

'The question seems rather, do I believe in Leporello?'

Don Ottavio said,

'Perhaps we had better wait till Leporello comes. We saw him immediately after, you know. I think Doña Ana forgot to mention that. And he was in a dreadful state. And all the furniture in the room was turned upside-down.'

'Did anybody hear sounds of a struggle? There must have been someone within earshot.'

'There were some fiddlers in the next room. They all ran away.'

'H'm.'

Don Saturno's expression was becoming more and more melancholy. Taking heart at this they went on to persuade him of his son's damnation.

'The judgement of heaven. . . . Ah, Don Saturno, how terrible, how lamentable it is! Believe me, our hearts are filled with sympathy, with regret, if such a word is not an impiety. I for one . . . if only we had never met, if only he had not felt this unfortunate passion, if only he had not come into the garden that night! I feel I can never forgive myself. I am the cause of my father's death and your son's perdition.'

'You reproach yourself unduly, Doña Ana. You could not prevent my son from falling in love with you.'

Ottavio hastened to add,

'And it is not as though you were the only woman in his life, Doña Ana. Heaven knows how many——'

'I shudder,' said Ana, reasserting herself, 'when I remember the way he looked at me that night. It was as though a flame had twined about me, as though I must melt in that grasp. I felt even then that some terrible doom was on him, that he was unholy, more demon than man.'

'He had regrettably strong sexual passions, and indulged them far too promiscuously,' said Don Saturno. 'But I cannot admit that there is anything supernatural in being a profligate.'

'Is there nothing supernatural about hell?' enquired Don Isidro.

'A great deal, I should say.'

'Well, then'—the chaplain enlarged his eyes—'you are answered.'

'But you see,' Don Saturno turned again to Doña Ana, 'I do not accept this story about the demons and Juan being taken quick into hell. For the one thing, it rests on the unsupported testimony of a very silly and rascally manservant. For another, I am at all times unwilling to credit stories like this. And for yet another, I have heard it already.'

Heaven help us, thought Doña Pilar, how unfortunate! Checkmated in everything. First that other funeral, and now he says someone has forestalled Doña Ana.

'And so has Leporello. Exactly this legend has been told in the village for three centuries at least. I do not want to stray into genealogical boasting,' he said with a kindling voice. 'But our family is of a reasonable antiquity, though we are only a *casa agraviada* since the Crown of Spain, which we have been glad to serve, sometimes even with honourable mention, has not remembered to ennoble us. However, we have been here for seven hundred years at least, and in such a period of time legends begin to accumulate. This legend of the wicked Don Juan is one of our family traditions, only till now it has always attached itself to the seventh Don Juan not the twelfth. In fact, the story has passed into literature. Molière wrote a play on the theme, an uneven work, but not without merit.'

'Moly-aira,' repeated Don Isidro as though mistrusting

each syllable. The rest of the party looked blankly polite.

'A French writer of comedies. Many of his pieces are charming, you would certainly be delighted with them. He was fond of Spanish themes. It is remarkable how often Spanish names occur in his plays, and his insistence on marital jealousy is thought by some to show Spanish influence. His best comedy, perhaps, is *Le Tartuffe*, or The Hypocrite.'

But the disquisition on Molière was broken off by Doña Pilar, who fell fainting with hunger on the floor.

Ever since he was a little boy Ottavio had prayed nightly that he might fall asleep at once and sleep all the night through; and only on a few negligible occasions had the prayer been unanswered.

The mattress was lumpy, and Ana was restless; but for all that he was asleep in five minutes, his thoughts flowing easily into his dreams. After all, they were not too late for the funeral, and over interminable mountain roads the procession made its way, moving lightly as thistledown, and in every hand was a candle that burned with a steady flame, though a wind was blowing. The church was so far a journey that frequently they sat down and picnicked, but the food was monotonous, always sucking-pigs stuffed with raisins; Don Saturno accounted for the sucking-pigs by saying they always embalmed a great quantity of them in May, when their virginity was at its greatest perfection. But there was no fatigue, nothing to mar the sense of pleasure and grandeur as the procession went onward with its light floating gait. He, Ottavio, was leading it, playing the flageolet with one hand, for the other held a candle; but he found he could play very well with one hand; and executing passages of extraordinary dexterity and compass he explained to Don Saturno that the melody was a very old one composed by Tubal-Cain; but only in his family could it be remembered and performed in its full beauty. Spread over the coffin like a pall was an enormous wig, and in the curls of the wig white pigeons were building nests out of ostrich feathers. The wind blew his hat off, and rising in the air to recapture it he found it more convenient to continue the journey by hovering in the air, and this enabled him to see that one of the hooded coffin-bearers was spitting out melon-seeds, just the sort of mismanagement one would expect. He spat so hard, the melon-seeds positively whistled by—Whee-hee!

He crashed into wakefulness. He was sitting up in bed, reaching for the holy water, and the sweat was standing on his skin. It seemed to him that a cry had woken him, a maniac cry, hoarse with astonishment, and uttered in his very ear.

There was a rent in the bed-hangings, he could see that beyond the curtained alcove a clear blue moonlight filled the room. Somewhere a clock was ticking. He prodded Ana. How heavily she slept!—like a woman of marble.

He prodded her again, it was as though she were sleeping of deliberation, sleeping on purpose to thwart him. When he was trying to go to sleep she fidgeted, now she must needs sleep like the dead.

'Ana! Wake up.'

'What is it?'

Her voice was remote and composed, it might have been the voice of the clock.

'Ana, didn't you hear anything?'

'No.'

'I did. It woke me, Ana. A shriek, here, beside me, in my ear.'

After a while she said,

'What was it like?'

'It was like a shriek. It was a shriek.'

'Perhaps it was a peacock. They often scream on moonlight nights.'

'I don't think it was a peacock, Ana. Ana?'

She had fallen asleep again, lying rigid beside him, breathing like a clockwork. He took hold of her hand. It was burning hot.

Presently the clock whirred for striking. It struck two. A further chime answered it. A dog howled.

Why had he ever consented to come on this wild goose chase, to a house that lay under so many maledictions? At home, in Seville, he had no need to fear ghosts, armoured in his good conscience, neighboured by so many altars, surrounded by so many prayers. But in the depths of the country, and in a house like this . . . Everyone admitted that the provinces were full of evil spirits, unexorcised demons haunting the mountains or crowding like bats into the shelter of old castles. And this house was so godless a one! Don Saturno as much of an infidel as Don Juan, all those books, so recent a death in the house, not a sign of a chaplain. No wonder the place was haunted. That shriek in his ear, so frantic, so astonished, might well be the very voice of Don Juan as the fires of hell took hold of him. In a moment, perhaps, that light gait would cross the floor, a sneering face look in between the bed-curtains. The best thing to do would be to wake Don Isidro. But opening his eyes he saw the rent in the hangings, the icy moonlight beyond; and all he could do was to lie crossing himself below the bedclothes. Each time his hand made its journey his elbow nudged Ana's side. Yet she did not wake. Well, it was for the best. A woman, and so high-strung, she was far more exposed to fears than he. How providential that she had heard nothing, how providential that to-night she happened to be sleeping so soundly. To-morrow, without fail, Don Isidro must privately exorcise this bed: it would never do if Ana should be awakened as he had been awakened.

But it seemed as though the whole morning would go by without an opportunity of eluding Don Saturno, whose garrulous civility encompassed them like a swarm of midges. Vainly did he beckon to Don Isidro, vainly did he and the chaplain approach each other for a few words in private. As though in a country-dance they approached only to be parted again. There was always some book to be examined, some prospect to be admired, some wine to be tasted. Doña Ana, all unwitting of these endeavours for her protection, foiled them again and again, her good manners, at all times exemplary, complying so graciously with her host's demands on them that one might almost suppose that she found the chattering old infidel worth attending to. Nor was it enough to confer. A moment and a pretext must be found for leaving the room. 'I will say that I want to change my stockings, that I have found a ladder in one of them. And you?' 'Rely on me. But it will take me a minute or two for my preparations.'

At last they got away. They entered the bedroom together, and found it full of maid-servants.

It would have been better, of course, to remain. If they had remained, the maid-servants would have gone away. But on an unfortunate mutual impulse they turned and went out again. Behind them the chattering and the scrubbing were resumed, and an unwomanly jest was made.

Don Ottavio coloured with anger and walked hastily down the corridor. The chaplain followed him. For ten minutes they conversed on topics of general interest, then made a second attempt on the bedroom. This time it was empty. Don Isidro pulled his stole from his pocket and slipped it round his neck, produced the whisk, and drew the cork of the holy-water bottle. Ottavio locked the door and fell on his knees. 'The bed first.' Advancing to the alcove the chaplain drew back the hangings.

There was the wooden bed-frame, but the mattress and the pillows were gone.

A difficult doctrinal point arose. They debated it in whispers, Don Isidro with professional confidence being of the opinion that it would be quite sufficient to asperse the bed-frame and the hangings. But to Ottavio it seemed that the shriek had come out of the pillows, for how else could it be so close to his ear?—and as he recalled the shriek, and the long hours that followed it, he became even more convinced that one could not be too thorough, that in a house like this nothing should be left to chance, no loophole afforded to the enemy of souls. And from his knees he reminded the chaplain that Doña Ana was renowned for the lightness of her slumbers, the alertness of her nervous system. 'Then perhaps we should wait? No doubt they have taken out the bedding to beat it in the open air. By this afternoon . . .' 'Dear Father, it has taken us the whole morning to get here. Beside, Doña Ana always rests in the afternoon. We cannot wait.' 'But how shall we get hold of the bedding? Should we send word by a servant? One must be discreet.' The chaplain sighed for the wickedness of the world as he said these words. 'Could *you* go?' 'Could *you* go?' 'Why not send Doña Pilar, then?' 'Yes, she could go. But then she is with Doña Ana, how are we to get her away? It is certainly a difficult question.' In the end they decided to go together, taking a little stroll through the grounds. The noise of thumping would teach them the way to where the bedding was being beaten. And then, quite naturally, a request, a word of command. . . . 'But meanwhile, since we are here, let us deal with the bed. It is wisest to do what we can.'

Scarcely a drop had fallen before bare feet shuffled outside the door, and the latch rattled. In an instant Don Isidro had whipped off the stole, had concealed the whisk and the bottle, and was opening the door to the maidservants with a look of abstracted meditation. As they carried in the bedding he returned, as it were, to this world and his mission there, and gave them his blessing. Don Ottavio meanwhile stood looking out of the window.

And all this, he said to himself, could have been avoided if only Ana had agreed to leave this afternoon. The bed having been made up, and the women gone, he went down on his knees once more.

Not in all Spain could there be another house where conversations were so interminable, where one was kept waiting so long for one's meals. For the twentieth time Doña Pilar drew a strand of grey silk through her needle.

She was embroidering a petticoat against the time when Doña Ana should consent to put off her mourning attire, a sprig design of grey pansies shaded with silver and black, to which she would later add some seed-pearl dew-drops. It was a pity that the old patterns, intricate and branching, the stately couching with gold thread, the embossed plateresque roses and irises, were no longer in vogue.

There was some satisfaction for an embroideress in them, scope and solace for ambition. But these light sprigs were monotonous to perform, and the result, to her eyes, looked insignificant. French taste. Why should Doña Ana, a Spanish lady, wish to appear sprinkled with wild-flowers, like a shepherdess in a comedy? What cause had Don Ottavio to demand daisies on a waistcoat? They would be asking for an embroidery of radishes and little onions before long. French taste. And she looked forward to the day when she could take up her altar-cloth once more, and straining her eyesight over the exasperating little pansies her mind's eye caressed the quilted velvet, the bullion passion-flowers.

The shutters were closed. It was a little after noon. A few flies circled about the marble heads and shoulders of the philosophers. At the further end of the gallery Doña Ana and Don Saturno continued their endless colloquy, he, leaning back in his chair, prating on about irrigation and astronomy, she, as though bewitched, sitting bolt upright, her eyes fixed on him, every line of her body expressing a spell-bound attention. In God's name, why? What were stars or sluices to her? To sit erect, to listen attentively to the aged, is, in a young girl, admirable and befitting; but in a bereaved daughter, a newly married lady, a little more languor would be more becoming. But there she sat, as the cat sits at the mouse-hole, bemused with long attention and attentive still. Was this in order to miss no word of stars and sluices? And why was this daughter of a most Catholic and

Castilian family lending so devout an ear to a disquisition on how the Moors had led rivulets through fields—fields which had afterwards been watered with the best blood of Spain, blood spilled in the driving out of the same Moors? Puzzled and disapproving, Doña Pilar twanged at the sixty-first pansy. French taste, French taste.

Now Don Ottavio re-entered the room.

'We have been discussing this most interesting question of irrigation. To irrigate Tenorio Viejo has been for years one of my dearest projects. Indeed, one may say that in Spain all water is in a sense holy water. Irrigation. . . .'

But it was Doña Ana who listened to his account of how the water-brooks should intersect the valley, with cisterns and reservoirs to catch the winter rains. Moorish ditches, Roman aqueducts, neither seemed to be of any interest to Don Ottavio, who was examining a map, antique and flyblown, that hung on the wall.

The sixty-second pansy. Don Ottavio with a fine forefinger was tracing the road that led over the mountain. Ah, poor young man! It was evident that he, at any rate, had no wish to remain here.

And while Don Saturno prates of water, thought the duena, his son is in hellfire and he himself, no doubt, well on the way thither. And for one moment the thought of the pit was so vivid that it seemed to her that the floorboards were already charred with the passion of the flames so immediately below them. The Commander too, at this instant, how he must be suffering!—

though in a different compartment. How many pansies would be stitched before he was released? Perhaps the whole petticoat. For though a most noble character the Commander had not been without faults. Such fits of temper if he were crossed, such haughtiness and such language. Gout. But gout endured in no christian spirit.

She recalled the terrible day when it was disclosed that he had caught his daughter's measles; when with the blotches already mustering on the countenance so nobly scarred in warfare he had come raging from his dressing-room, the sound of the shivered mirror alarumming the household this way and that, some to attend and others to fly. Immediately after this Doña Ana had been despatched to the nuns to begin her education. And then had come the other painful episode of the Mother Superior's report. Tearing the letter, so beautifully scented, so finely inscribed, into a hundred pieces, he had driven off to the convent to inform them that no daughter of his could be slow of apprehension. Thereafter the reports had spoken only of progress, had stressed the unusually retentive memory, the moral qualities, the soprano voice. Though it was quite true, Doña Ana was undeniably slow-witted.

Don Ottavio continued to study the map, so perseveringly that at last even Don Saturno noticed his preoccupation.

'So you are interested in geography. So am I. I have quite a fair collection of maps, which I shall be delighted to show you. But it is a pity that our cartographers are so often inaccurate, they allow theory or fancy to introduce a symmetry which often does not exist in the original. Place-names, too, so interesting to the antiquarian, are corrupted, delightful examples of rustic metaphor are obliterated on the grounds that they are not seemly. For instance, on that map which you are studying—dear me, how it has faded!——'

'Is this the road we came by?'

'It is, it is. I wish for your sakes it had been a better one. But now we have a road-making King. And I hope shortly to follow the royal example and do something about my own mule-tracks. What an excellent fellow, eh?'

'I don't think a King of Spain should make so many disturbances,' said Don Ottavio guardedly.

'Ah, you mean that Madrid affair about the cloaks and hats? And there I understand your feelings, in fact I share them. One clings to the traditional aspects of Spain. But think of the many improvements, the projects and reforms. I am glad we have a progressive King.'

During this speech Don Isidro entered, sighing regretfully as he realised the subject of Don Saturno's praises. Now he said,

'Leporello is here.'

'Ah!' said Ottavio. He walked to Doña Ana's chair and stood behind it supportingly.

'Yes?' said Don Saturno. 'By the way, why did he not come before?'

'Overcome by his feelings, contrite for his own wickedness, and appalled at the doom of your son,' said the chaplain, reproachfully eyeing the admirer of Carlos III, 'he spent the night in prayer. At the little hillside chapel, he tells me, called The Hermitage of the Angels.'

'Ah yes! Another of these map-makers' ridiculous misnomers such as I spoke of. Actually, it is a Roman cattle-pound, and the herdsmen still make use of it. Leporello ought to know better, every brat in the village knows it is a cattle-pound.'

'You will find him much changed,' said the chaplain.

'No doubt. All that family go to pieces when they are over thirty-five. A very poor stock.'

Don Isidro now looked speakingly at Ana. But she sat with downcast eyes, and said nothing.

Ottavio found this very touching. Yesterday she had taken the lead a little too obviously perhaps, had dominated the conversation unduly—though since the damnation of Don Juan was so much her affair she had every right to the centre of the stage. But now her silence, her diffidence, her downcast eyelashes quivering on her cheeks, gave her new beauties. Had they been alone, he might have patted her. This being out of the question, he gazed at her approvingly, and hoped she would soon look up and become conscious of his approval. But she continued to look at the floor.

All these various lookings led to a rather awkward pause. The chaplain coughed, and said,

'He hopes to speak to you.'

Don Saturno made no answer. Ana said nothing either. More touched than ever, Don Ottavio slid his hand gently upon her shoulder. But he might as well have caressed one of the marble philosophers, she seemed to be deep in thought, or possibly in prayer.

Though it had been a mistake to hint as much to the Commander, all of whose belongings must be perfect, the Mother Superior of the Convent of Our Lady of Good Counsel had been right to describe Ana as slow-witted. She was also justified in praising her for a very retentive memory. With this memory and these slow wits Doña Ana had gone off to bed the previous night, to lie awake recalling every word of the conversation, and every inflection of Don Saturno's voice, and to speculate slowly, clumsily, unrelentingly, what conviction, so opposite to her own, led him to disbelieve in Don Juan's damnation.

She knew that there were some people whose minds, tainted with too much thinking, rejected the teachings of the Church; and Don Saturno, surrounded with his busts and his books, might question the doctrine of hell-fire. Yet he did not say as much, and he spoke of the Commander as being in heaven. To believe in heaven is to believe in hell also. Considering it from every side it appeared to Ana that Don Saturno believed in hell, though with a rather half-hearted belief.

Believing in hell, and admitting that his son was hell-worthy, why should he doubt Leporello's story? No one else had doubted it. True, Don Saturno had described Leporello as rascally. So did everyone else. Elvira, Ottavio, she herself, everyone who knew anything of Leporello knew that he was a rascal, a fit valet for such a master: Don Saturno was only expressing a common opinion. Why then should he nurse this singularity of doubt? Mere wantonness and intellectual pride? No. With all her senses, the five and the others, she realised that there was more to Don Saturno's doubt than that.

Yet, disbelieving Leporello's witness, why had his face so fallen on learning that the other possible witnesses, the fiddlers in the next room, had run away and could testify nothing? And why did he hear with such looks of concern that the room was in disorder? If he did not believe that his son was carried to hell by devils, why should he be perturbed on hearing of an overturned table? Why think seriously of a table, and lightly of devils?

Back and forth her slow wits trudged over the field of her good memory. And suddenly the pattern was clear, and she understood what had been in Don Saturno's mind. Don Saturno thought that Leporello had murdered Juan. Murdered by man, not borne off by devils. Then perhaps not damned. The slow wits made a leap further. There had been no body, there was not a blood-stain anywhere in the room. *Then perhaps not dead!*

Like something far more powerful than she, like some powerful wild bird flying out of her mouth, a shriek of excitement escaped her. And then Ottavio had woken up, pestering her with prods and enquiries. Long after he was quieted she lay beside him thinking that Don Juan might be alive.

Morning came, but could not kill him. Not damned, not even dead. The more she thought of it (and she thought of nothing else) the more convinced she became that Don Juan was alive. A man of such strength, of such aristocratic dominance, how should he be killed by a valet? No body, no stain of blood: only a table knocked over, some broken crystal and crockery, and Leporello's story. No doubt Leporello had knocked over the table himself, to give an air to his false witness.

And yet on this liar's lips hung the only chance of discovering the truth about Juan, why he had disappeared, and whither. Somehow or other that truth must be extracted. How right her father had been, declaring that with these new restrictions on the scope of the Holy Office morality and order would vanish from Spain. But His Majesty, complying much too easily for a monarch with the demands of some trumpery modernists, had given over the judgement of civil offences to civil law-courts. There could be no certain appeal to the austere interrogation of the rack, she must depend upon her own sagacity and resolution. But between her and Leporello stood Don Saturno, who supposing that Leporello was

Don Juan's murderer might well hand him over to justice before she could get at the truth. Execute him, yes, by all means! But only when she had done with him. And so it seemed to her that the first thing she must do was to win the heart of Don Saturno.

'Has Leporello come?' she asked Doña Pilar, while the waiting-maid dressed her hair.

'There is no sign of him.'

Ah, but suppose he never came? Suppose he had vanished, carrying with him the secret of Don Juan's disappearance, its why and wherefore and whither? She thrust away the thought, and descended to the library resolved to please Don Saturno.

If anything could replace Don Juan among the dead, it was Don Saturno's conversation. No, it did more. Such heartless babble, such frivolous speculations and half-witted theories, consigned Don Juan to the realm of those who have never been. How could one credit that this chattering old man, delightedly discoursing, preening like some elderly song-bird, thought himself the father of a murdered son, sat there, all the long forenoon, awaiting the murderer? And revolted by the levity of this conversation about the stars Doña Ana sat slowly wheeling her fan, pressing her foot on the floor lest it should stamp, compelling herself to conceal her passion of curiosity behind a show of being interested. Doña Pilar stitched in her corner. Ottavio and Don Isidro fidgeted in and out. And Don Saturno talked on, and never by word or sign inflected the conversation towards Don Juan.

There were moments when it was agony to control herself; but control herself she did. When the chaplain came in with his news that Leporello had arrived she concealed her excitement, she concealed her anxiety. She even concealed her stupefaction when it appeared that Don Saturno instead of lodging Leporello in a dungeon was offering to conduct her to the dining-room.

She could do everything but eat.

'Doña Ana seldom eats,' explained Ottavio with mournful pride.

'I fear your long journey has fatigued her.'

'Oh, no, no!' replied Ottavio, spying the snare and leaping over it. 'The journey was really not fatiguing at all. And Leporello is a good courier, I must say that for him. The journey back, of course, will be even easier, as we shall know it.'

Her thoughts rumbling in her head like the noise of waggon-wheels, Ana in a moment of lassitude asked herself if that, after all, would not be the best solution: to depart on the morrow, leaving Leporello to his fate, to abandon for ever this barbarous place, this exasperating old trifler, this hopeless hope? It would please Ottavio . . . but now, like a spine of rock appearing at low tide, out of her exhaustion and discouragement reared an implacable resolution to stay for the present in Tenorio Viejo.

'It distresses me when you speak of your return journey. In spite of the rather melancholy background of your visit I am enjoying it a great deal. At my age, and living in this retired fashion, I don't have much opportunity of social intercourse. Perhaps one never properly appreciates society till one has renounced it. If Horace had always lived in Rome . . .'

Don Isidro sighed wistfully. He had been very happy in Rome.

'Meanwhile, you must let me make the most of my chances. Would it be too tedious if I suggested that later in the day I showed you something of my village? The church, of course. And the school.'

'A school?' enquired Ottavio. It was obvious from Don Saturno's tone that someone was expected to say something that sounded interested, and this, at the moment, was the best he could do.

'A school?' said Ana. 'How very interesting. How progressive. Who are the scholars?'

'My people here.'

'And what do they learn? Viticulture? Husbandry?'

'Needlework?' added Doña Pilar.

'No, no! Nothing so specialised as that. Just the ordinary things that we all learn. Reading and writing and so forth.'

'But do you teach your peasants to read and write?'

Don Saturno took another slice of candied melon and settled himself for the pleasures of self-expression.

'Why not, my dear sir, why not? One should never deny to any section of mankind the means of feeling itself more miserable.'

With a hook of the eyebrows he indicated to a footman that the chaplain's glass needed re-filling.

'Ultimately, that is the end of all education. Whether one learns to spell C A T or to forecast the orbit of a new planet, discontent, a noble discontent, must be the end of education. At first, my people were delighted with this strange new experience. Several of them bought books of devotion, spelled out litanies, and imagined themselves half-way to heaven. Then they took to cyphering and casting accounts, and imagined themselves half-way to being bankers. Finding themselves to be still on earth, and no richer than before, they now leave schooling to their children. But in time the arts of reading and writing will force them to realise the wretchedness of their state, and then to resent, and then, perhaps, to amend it.'

'What repulsive sentiments,' murmured the duena to the chaplain.

'He must be mad,' was the reply.

'All progress,' continued Don Saturno blithely, 'must rebound upon the bestower. In times to come, no doubt, my simple village will be a hive of revolutionaries. Meanwhile, they have learned enough book-keeping to swindle the tax-collector.'

Don Ottavio, Doña Pilar, and Don Isidro stared at their plates in disgust and dismay. Only Doña Ana looked at Don Saturno with fascinated horror. For underneath are the everlasting fires; and how could the son of such a father escape damnation? As a spider, light and worthless, dances over the surface of water and scarcely dimples that surface, Don Saturno danced on the face of the pit. A profound impulse to weep swept over her: to weep;

or else to drag her nails over that venerable simpering countenance. Though Don Juan were still alive, such a father would damn him. Though he were still alive?

'You, at least, my Ana, need not accompany us on this dreadful visit to this revolting village.' So said Ottavio. But looking at him coldly above the hemisphere of her black fan she answered,

'Of course I shall come. I wish to see the church.'

The shadow of the poplar-trees striped the road. In an hour it would be sunset. To the miller it always seemed that these shadows, thin and regular, were like the strokes of the angelus bell. He sighed, and looked at his daughter, and frowned a little, compelling himself to speak.

'How are your silkworms, Celestina? How do they look?'

'They don't eat, father.'

'They don't eat?'

He leaned over the window-sill and spat into the stream.

'Everything else eats. The ass eats, the crows eat, the rats eat, the lice and the fleas eat. Down in the graves the worms eat the dead. But these worms won't eat. Are they dying, then?'

'I think some are dying.'

'How many?'

'I don't know. I didn't count.'

'My child, you should have counted. Every time you look at them you should count them: so many healthy, so many sickly, so many dying, so many dead. You should count them and write it down. What is the use of learning to write, otherwise?'

She smiled and made no answer.

'Celestina, go and count the worms that are dying.'

She went out of the room with her heavy lullaby gait. When she came back she said,

'Perhaps nineteen.'

'Perhaps nineteen! Can you not even count, then?'

'Perhaps dying, I mean. There are nineteen.'

'Not twenty, no? Not twenty-five?'

'Nineteen.'

'Such an idiot of a number. How am I to make up my mind? If it had been twenty-five, then I could have made up my mind for certain. Twenty-five, yes, that would be worth it.'

'Some more may sicken. Then you can be sure.'

'Then it may be too late. For I don't expect miracles, Celestina, what do you think. Shall I ask for a mass or no?'

'I shouldn't think so.'

Dionio Gutierrez looked at his daughter just as a few hours before he had looked at the stream which turned, which still just turned his mill-wheel. But all the year through Celestina was a summer stream—languid and sly. And just as that stream, dawdling among the stones, lay on its back staring idly at the heavens so her thick green eyes stared at him. Never since she lay staring in the cradle had she known a day's sickness, never had she wept, contradicted or cajoled. The smallpox which had carried off the rest of his family had not set as much as a toothmark on her. She was as strong as a man, she could write and cypher as well as a clerk. And just as the stream now turned his wheel the household turned on her slow indifferent industry, and just as those weeds rose with the wheel and passed and sank and rose again, so day after day the same mishaps, the same omissions recurred: the wine leaked from the cracked jar, the trivet fell over, the widow Sobrino's cat sneaked into the house at dusk and went to sleep on his bed. Now it was the silkworms. For five days they had been ailing.

He looked at his daughter, and scratched his head, and felt at once a profound melancholy and the reassuring pleasure of scratching.

'It is difficult to decide. If they die, it is a loss. If I pay and they die it is a double loss. I suppose I had better look at them myself?'

'That might be best.'

He went unwillingly. His stomach turned at creeping things, worms and grubs and maggots. The moment he smelled the silkworms and heard their faint seething crepitation his gorge began to rise, and it was only with an effort of the will that he pulled out the tray and looked at them.

Ah, by what creeping squirming devices, with what

wrigglings here and mumblings there, one scraped together a livelihood! One gained, but it only went through one and came out again in an excrement of expenditure. One amassed, and the tax-gatherer came and spun it away.

'Here, take the money, and go. God may as well have it as anyone else.'

But it was sunset before she left the house, and the smell of the water, warmed all day, rose up languid and sour in the dusk, and pervaded the house. It was as though Celestina were still indoors, diffused through every room.

He went to his bedroom and shooed away the cat. It went off insolently, stretching first one leg and then the other. In a little while it will be rubbing itself against my legs, he thought. 'One fine day I'll drown you!' he cried after the animal.

Like a rising water dusk was brimming up the valley. The poplar-trees were two-coloured, grey below, a sallow orange above. The castle on its hillock, the church on its hillock, stood out in a sharp glory of colour and reality. The soft dust of the road was ankle-deep. The cicadas chirped—the noise of a thousand sickles being whetted. Down the road came old Serafina with the goats. Their small feet made a muted pattering in the dust of the road, though it was evening they were still hungry, and grabbed at the dusty wayside weeds. Mixed with their goatish smell was a smell of the mountain.

'Good evening, my aunt.'

'Good evening, child. Well, what is the news, what has happened down here to-day?'

'Nothing to thank God for, I think. It has been a day.'

'No more than that? And what about the grandees at the castle?'

'I have not seen them.'

'No? I can see them now. Look!'

She pointed towards the church. On the platform before the porch figures were standing.

'Don Saturno, our priest, the strange woman and her woman, the man her husband and the chaplain. And our Leporello is down there at the foot of the steps.

'You should go up the mountain if you wish to know what's going on,' she continued; 'I have been watching them for the last hour. And you have not even seen Leporello? Why, he went past your house this morning, not by the road, though, but by the path beside your maize-patch. And Lord, wasn't he footsore.'

'Is that old Miguela's Leporello?'

'Miguela's Leporello, Conchita's Leporello, Rosa's Leporello, Angela's Leporello, Teresa's Leporello. . . . Ah, poor dog, how he used to pant and snap after dowries! But he's as fat as butter now, and wears tight boots like a gentleman.'

She began to bustle among the goats, sorting them out, for some had to go to one yard, others to another.

'I will help you,' said the girl of a sudden. Serafina uttered her flat ill-natured laugh.

'Thank you. But there is no need.'

Celestina walked on a few steps.

'Say a prayer for me,' cried Serafina.

Maria Perez looked out from a shadowy window where she stood suckling a baby.

'She can save herself that trouble, Serafina. To-night there's going to be a proper praying in Tenorio Viejo, such a praying as we don't often have. Even you will get a splash of salvation, I daresay. They say she's going to pray all night.'

'Who? The strange woman?'

'She.'

'Why, what sin has she committed?'

'A most terrible sin, a most unusual sin, such a sin as no woman in this village has ever committed. She has married a husband who is young, rich, handsome, healthy and kind.'

With the turn of the street the church was visible again, close at hand and dominant. A flight of steps led up to the platform before the porch. It was as though the people who stood there were acting on a stage, and as though it were a play the people of the village stood watching from below. Lord! how tall these strangers were: even the lady was taller than Don Saturno, and as for her husband—an emperor could not have a finer figure, nor an angel a more beautiful complexion. Such broad shoulders, such a waist, such legs! Their priest too was a very fine figure of a man.

'Good evening, Celestina. So you have come to see the spectacle?'

Celestina nodded, holding the money in her hand carefully so that it should not be seen or heard. It was the tanner's wife who addressed her, a woman with long ears and a long tongue.

'What a pity you are late. Still, you have seen them. They take the shine out of our lot, don't they?'

'What's happening?'

'She is going to pray all night. They are tidying the church now, to make it fit for the likes of her.'

'Why is she going to pray?'

'Ah! Now she's going in!'

The doors opened. Inside the church was lit up. Outlined against the candle-light the figures on the platform became even more like performers in a play. Courtesying profoundly, her head tilted to one side as though with a weight of sorrow, Ana farewelled the other performers. Within the church the parish priest was visible, fidgeting from foot to foot. Don Ottavio stepped forward and offered his arm. Leaning on it, scarcely moving for her burden of sorrow and dignity, she entered the church. Doña Pilar followed at a civil distance. The doors closed.

After a while they opened again to let out Don Ottavio and the parish priest. The sacristan had come out by a side door, locking it after him. The remaining party, despoiled of its drama, came down the steps, Don Saturno talking briskly and nodding to the onlookers. A plump middle-aged man in a black livery moved nimbly forward, and bowed himself into Don Saturno's notice. Don Saturno gave him a glance and a nod and went on, not interrupting his sentence. Presently the sacristan brought a stool and a lighted lantern and sat down with his back to the west door, and a couple of men-servants wrapped in black cloaks began to walk slowly round the church.

'And will they stay here all night?' someone asked. A man's voice answered, 'So will not I.' It was Ramon Perez who spoke, and he was the first to walk off.

The plump man in the black livery now began to thread his way among the onlookers, talking in a voice at once pompous and servile, and using elegant phrases: 'One would not wish to disturb . . . vigil . . . sacredness of grief . . . my good people. . . .' A feeling of dislike at once spread through the little crowd. Without answering him they turned away and walked off, the men in silence, each one walking by himself and as though unaware that any other persons were walking with him, the women following in groups, making conversation, enquiring artificially about the health of children and domestic concerns. As if by common consent no one mentioned the scene they had just been watching. Maria Perez was still leaning from her window and talking to Serafina as the others came down the street. She was telling Serafina the remedies she had used in vain to cure an attack of shingles, but seeing the others she broke off, and cried out,

'Well, has she begun to pray?'

'Bah!' Ramon walked on.

'Enjoy yourself at the inn,' replied his wife, and slammed-to the shutters in a hurry.

Celestina inserted herself between two of the married women, Teresa Espiga and Teresa Mauleon. She did not wish to be picked up by Serafina. For a while they continued their painstaking conversation about any subject save the scene they had just been watching. Then, feeling the heavy presence of the virgin beside them, they broke off.

'Well, Celestina. How goes it with you?'

'Not well. I am worried about'

—But the coins in her hand reminded her. Though she, for one, had a perfect reason for going to the church, it would not do to mention it—

'my father.'

'Why, what ails him?'

'I do not know. But for five days now he has scarcely eaten.'

Before she reached the mill she stopped, wrapped up the money in a dock-leaf so that it should not clink, and slipped the clammy packet between her breasts. With such a prayer going on, it would be silly to waste money on a mass. Maria had said that even Serafina would get a splash of salvation. If the strange woman's prayer could embrace Serafina it would certainly help the silkworms.

Dionio looked up as she entered, lifting his furrowed brow towards her.

'Well, my girl, there you are. I have been thinking, perhaps I did wrong to send you. I have been to look at them again, and now it seems to me that there is something wrong with the leaves, for they are blighted, and probably with leaves from a healthy tree the insects would recover by themselves. What do you think, Celestina?'

'Very likely. But it is paid for now.'

He made a sad grimace. Then, as though to console himself,

'Well, remember to write it in the book.'

'Yes, father.'

It was ten o'clock, the hour at which the married men began to go to the inn. The young men had their drinks earlier, and after a glass or two went out to talk to the girls at their windows. It was a long narrow room, running back from the street, and below the street-level. Three steps, two shallow and one deep, led into it. In the thickness of the wall by the door there was a privy, to enter the inn one passed through a cloud of flies and a stink. At a first glance the lime-washed walls appeared to be hung with pictures in frames, but at a closer inspection it was seen that the pictures, frames and all, were painted on the wall. The subjects were all still-lifes, and though it was easy to recognise the objects, for they were painted with great accuracy, it would have been difficult to say what the pictures meant. There was a black cross with a green snake twining round it; a skull, with a cluster of grapes held between its teeth; a ham with a toad sitting on it; a woman's slipper filled with coins; a red lily and a mattock tied together by a rosary. They were firmly and sleekly painted with cheap house-paints, and the frames were depicted so accurately that they appeared to stand out from the walls. Even the nail-heads and the supporting strings were represented. These pictures were the work of the inn-keeper's son, a boy who had been intended for the priesthood; but taking part in a rock-blasting he had seen a man blown to bits, and from that day had developed an appalling stammer. Then he had begun to draw and paint, and Don Saturno, seeing some of his work, spoke of a new Murillo; indeed, he had supplied the paints for this series, and talked about sending the lad to study in a town. But nothing had come of it.

The inn-keeper was telling Leporello this, and Leporello was strolling from picture to picture with an air of connoisseurship, shutting sometimes his right eye and sometimes his left.

'And what is he doing now?'

'The paints came to an end,' said the father. 'He was no good for this trade, so now he works with Luis the tanner. One must live,' he added.

'Just so, just so.'

One by one as he neared them in his perambulations the drinkers shrugged up their shoulders and ignored him. Losing his temper he said,

'A fine talent. A pity that it should be lost in such a hole as this.'

But no one rose to that either. So he sat down by his

wine and stared at the cross and serpent opposite. Lord, what a dead-live place, what a pack of risen Lazaruses!

The flies buzzed, another man came in. It was the big rusty-coloured fellow who had held up the cavalcade because of the sow in the road.

'Oho! So you're here now. How did you like your night in the cattle-pound?'

Turning to the other drinkers he told them how he and his mates had hunted the valet over the mountain, caught him, and shut him up in the pound for the night.

'A night under the stars,' said Leporello good-naturedly, and asked the man to drink with him.

'A morning among the briars,' retorted the rusty-coloured man. 'Why did you sneak into the village by those by-ways with a good road before your nose?'

Without raising his eyes from the draughtboard, Ramon Perez said,

'The old Miguela died only this spring.'

Uncertainty as to whether his formidable grandmother was still alive was indeed one reason why Leporello had approached the village by such a hindward route. But looking jocose he told the swineherd that he had been so drunk with dew that he could not find his bearings.

'First she grew blind, then she starved, then she died,' continued Perez.

One death should lead to another easily enough, it was just a question of finding the right word. But from the moment he had set foot in Tenorio Viejo nothing could go right for Leporello, and despite his grand story which had entranced the gentry of Seville he could not find a single listener here. When he reached the castle all the servants knew already that Doña Ana had come to say that Don Juan had been carried off by the devil; and all the afternoon he had waited in vain for Don Saturno to send for him; and at last escaping to the village, hoping against hope that there he might still find an ear to hearken, at first they would talk of nothing but Doña Ana and her prayers, and now they would not talk at all. Meanwhile the swineherd had picked up his cue from Ramon. He finished his wine in a hurry, and left the inn. After a while Leporello also got up, and with a courteous salute to the company, took himself off.

In the mill that death had left so roomy, Celestina had a bedroom to herself, a room properly furnished, with a bed, a walnut-wood chest and an image of the Virgin. There was also a small rickety table, and on this was the unusual bedroom equipment of a pen, a little pot with ink in it, and a leather-bound book.

It was late. Outside the last glimmer of the sunset had faded, the cicadas on the poplar trees sharpened their noise on the hot summer air. But the rushlight still burned, and Celestina in her chemise sat on the bed, slowly transferring the dockleaf packet from hand to hand. The leaves were melted into a pulp now, one could feel the hard coins inside. Heavy and motionless, in the small room she seemed enormous. It was as though the bed must give way under the weight of those thighs, as though the heavy tresses of her unbound hair were momently growing longer, would spread and stretch until they lay all over the room while she sat motionless and absorbed, exhaling her two smells, the sweat smell of her body, the smell of stagnant water that rose up from her hair.

The clock at the castle struck eleven.

Dionio, lying where the cat had lain and thinking drowsily that the cat must bring the widow Sobrino's fleas as well as its own, roused up at that sound and listened attentively, counting the strokes. Eleven. He knew that it would be eleven, he counted from motives of pleasure and piety. Numbers delighted him. Not because some were lucky and some unlucky, not for any associations. He loved them with a pure love, he loved them for themselves. One was as noble as another, had as real and valid an existence. The twelve hours of morning, the twelve hours of afternoon, the twelve months of the year. The seven stars of the Great Bear, the seven days of the week. All millers are dishonest, and in Tenorio Viejo everyone said 'As cheating as Dionio Gutierrez.' But actually he was perfectly honest in all his dealings where money or numbers took a part, not so much that he valued honesty as that he revered numbers. If a thing was seven, he could not say that it was six or eight. Consequently he was a poor man, for everyone guards himself against the dishonesty of a miller by cheating him as dexterously as may be. But he had gladly paid for his daughter to be educated so that she could keep his accounts. The school was free; but one had to pay the schoolmaster. Loving numbers as he did, it was his greatest, his most solemn satisfaction to think how well Celestina kept the accounts. Whether it was money gained or money spent, the sums were written down, written as well as a clerk could write them. No number, not the least, was slighted. There they were in the book, honoured with a fair hand and a faithful remembrance.

Eleven.

Celestina got off the bed. She opened the account book and wrote in it. *A mass for the silkworms. 2 Reals.*

She waited till the ink was dry on the page, closed the book and laid it aside. Then, as though to pray, she went down on her knees by the bed and pulled out from under the mattress another book, a bundle of cheap paper, such as was used at the school. Stooping still more devoutly she prised up a loose board and pulled out a knotted handkerchief that bulged heavily. Untying it, she put in the mass money, and knotted it again and put it back. She carried the paper book to the table, opened it, and added to the column of figures *2 Reals,* staring long and sweetly at the page.

At midnight the two sentries at the church had been changed. The first pair had been drawn from the visitors'

retinue, those who now took their place were from the castle. A good thing, thought Don Gil the sacristan. If the first pair had stayed much longer they would have become an interruption. As it was he had heard them exchanging remarks about ghosts and evil spirits. Townspeople are like that. The pair from the castle also muttered to each other as they passed on their round, but only to grumble because they were being kept from their beds.

He shifted his position a little, rubbing his back luxuriously against the door of the church, warily holding the sides of his cloak together so that no warmth should escape. It was a thick hooded cloak, it covered him like a tent. The lantern at his feet gave out a gentle warmth. He was not in the least sleepy, he was enjoying himself. The sound of those trudging feet, at regular intervals augmented by the echo to a throng and then shorn into singleness again, was soothing and agreeable, it had a liturgical quality. They trudged around the base of the platform on which the church was built; he, Gil Mauleon, sat above them keeping the door. It was as though they were waves, the waves of a tide that would not reach him. Aloof and solitary he sat above them, founded, like the church, upon a rock, and with the key of the church across his knees.

From his station he looked down on the square and the street, the huddled houses with their dark features of door and window. Except for the two sentries, not a foot stirred. Times had changed. In the old days half the people of Tenorio Viejo would have been on their knees round about the church. Beyond the village were the mountains, outlined against the sky where the moon would later appear to keep him company; they lay there high-haunched as cats lie. At his back, familiar, an ally, rose the bulk of the church. There was not an inch of it that he did not know as a man knows his own bedstead. It belonged to him by sight and touch and smell and hearing: the weight of its different ornaments and trappings, the smell of the Easter and Christmas and Trinity vestments, the creak of the pulpit steps and the steps to the loft, the varying answers of the stone flags, the collection of candle-ends in the sacristy cupboard, the missing and the blackened sequins on the robe of Our Lady of Victories, the scratched toe-nails of the Christ of the Pieta, the place where the plaster showed through the yellowed cheeks of the Mother of Sorrows, and the greasy marks that so many kisses had left on the wounded dangling hand: they were all his by long right, and undisputed. He understood the church and the church understood him.

Inside the church was a woman on her knees, locked in there for the night. And heavy on his lap was the weight of the great smooth key.

The sentries trudged their rounds, the stars wheeled overhead, and he, Gil Mauleon, sat on guard. Rigid and ornate the church enclosed her like a cage. Rigid and ornate her stiff bodice, her massive skirts, contained the riches and suavity of her body, and her smooth knees pressed the stone flags. Like crowding witnesses the images stared down on her with their attentive eyes. But they did not see her better than he did, who sat with his back to the locked door and held the key.

'*Ah me, ah me! O King Jupiter, how fearfully long these nights are! Will it never be day? And yet how long it is since I heard the first cockcrow! My servants lie snoring. They would not have done so in the old days.*'

From the ante-room indeed came a most regular snoring. Don Saturno stretched a slippered foot towards the floor. He had been sitting huddled in his arm-chair with his legs under him, his chin propped on his hand, the light of the candelabra shining on his bald head and on the page of the folio which lay across his lap. Just so might a boy have sat, benighted in a library, absorbed in some long-winded romance or ancient bawdy, motionless except for the shuttle-movement of the reading eyes; but age and rheumatism will rust the most obdurate limbs, and as he stretched out his foot towards the floor a twinge of pain ran up his leg. He closed the book with a bang. The night air had become chilly.

Again he repeated the words, in an animated and not very correct Greek. He felt a tenderness for Strepsiades, just such a country squire as one might find in any corner of Spain. Of all the classical authors Aristophanes was the one most akin to the Spanish character; and there, in the bookcase yonder, lay his translation. To popularise the dramas of Aristophanes: long ago it had become clear to him that Spain could have no better teacher, no more wholesome liberator, than Aristophanes; and in a flash he had conceived the life-work of translating him. The life-work, often laid down, but taken up again as often, proved most congenial; and in his thoughts Aristophanes became a Spanish author. Just as Cervantes poked fun at the romancers, so did Aristophanes deride the high-minded Euripides, and on every page there was something familiar and endearing to a Spanish heart: beef boiled with broth and a slice of the tripe, pigs and chick-peas, thyme and grapes and garlic, law-suits and wool-combing, the wineskin and old women. '*Of love, of bread, of music, of sweetmeats, of honour, of cheesecakes, of manly virtue, of dried figs, of ambition, of barley-scones, of military command, of lentil-pottage*' . . . it was the authentic olio. And slyly, too, the lever could be inserted, and without a word of offence to church or throne the power of both might be shaken by this author whose plays included so many deities and no kings. For many years he had offered his translations to the players; but in vain; for either something would be objected to on the grounds of the censorship or the actors would complain that there were no noble characters in the play. Once he had persuaded a travelling company to accept his version of *The Wasps*; but in the rehearsal they made so many alterations, adding a heroine and a love-interest, that the performance had no trace of Aristophanes.

He walked over to the bookcase and pulled down the portfolio, and turned over the sheets of manuscript till he came to *The Clouds*. For a while he read with the pleased look of authorship. Yet he had made a bad choice, for he did not want to be reminded of the subject of bad sons. Whether in Spain or in Attica, he thought, that is how it goes. One begets, one loves, one takes pride in, one gives, one pampers, one is made a fool of, one is bled (God knows how much Juan had cost, and with what difficulty the money had been coaxed from the severe soil); and in the end indulgence defeats the motive of love, and the darling exasperating phoenix of a son dwindles into a habit, and the wound is a dry scar that tickles in rainy weather. And thinking thus it seemed probable to him that Juan was still alive, just as likely to be alive as dead.

No doubt the romance, the fascination, were still there for others. This beautiful and stupid and high-flown young woman, for instance, to her eyes Juan had appeared in all his splendour; she was prepared to believe that a Deity was as much impressed as she, thought as highly of Juan as she did, and sent devils to fetch him. But to Don Saturno duns, without any act of God, seemed as good a reason for the disappearance.

'I don't want to think him dead,' he said to himself in an impulse of midnight candour, 'for then I should have to admit how little such a thought moves me. And at my age one is unwilling to admit to any lack of feeling, it is too close a reminder that after death one feels nothing at all.'

He looked down at his hand, so white and dry, and at the long, well-tended nails. He flicked his finger-nails against the thumb. *Ut, re, mi, fa.* In the silent room it was almost as if he were plucking the strings of a lute.

He turned on from *The Clouds* and came to *The Knights*. Oh, but this was a worse draw! If it was uncomfortable to be reminded of a bad son it was worse to be reminded of a bad son's scoundrelly servant. And after all, it was possible that the valet had killed the master. If there was any weight at all in Doña Ana's story, it tipped the balance on this side.

Don Saturno felt the horrible slow flush of old age mounting behind his ears. Plainly, it was his duty to interrogate Leporello, and probably it was his duty to hand him over to justice. The handing-over was not so bad, in many lights it would be a pleasure. But he shrank with the whole fastidiousness of his nature from the interrogation, for there was something profoundly repulsive in the prospect of a wrestle with the slippery wits of this fellow. He was all for a democracy, and the people were dear to him. But it was a painful extension of democracy to step down from loving the working-class in the mass to hating a valet in particular.

A foible, a weakness. He looked at his long clean fingers, and sighed, and shrugged his shoulders. And with the gesture it seemed to him that he was extremely cold, that it was inordinately late, that the best thing he could do was to go to bed and order his valet to bring him a cup of hot chocolate. For what was the sense of sitting up in order to persuade himself to an interview with Leporello? He might as usefully spend the night in prayer, like that silly beauty down at the church yonder. Well, to-morrow they might go, and that would be a good thing. He was tired to death of making conversation to this pair of elegant waxworks, one of which had a mechanism enabling her to sing as eloquently as a canary, the other incapable of saying more than *Papa* and *Mamma*. Would they were gone, and their courier with them!

He folded up the translations of Aristophanes. Though to-night Aristophanes had played him somewhat false with Phidippides and the Sausage Seller, at any rate those admirable comedies did not contain one high-bred virtuous woman.

'Poor, poor Ana,' murmured her spouse, looking down on the wide well-plumped bed. 'Poor noble creature! My latest thoughts shall be of her.' But actually his latest thought was of the pleasure of having the whole bed to himself; and still luxuriously rolling and gathering the pillows about his ears, and pulling up the coverlet, he had fallen into an immediate and tranquil slumber.

But it seemed that even now, when the wide bed had been blessed, and he had its safe expanse all to himself, Ottavio was doomed to sleep badly. Last night an unsanctified shriek had roused him. Now he woke for apparently no reason at all, unless the lifelike sweetness of a dream had awoken him. It had been an amorous dream; and as he quitted it for waking he remembered that Ana was spending the night in the church, and wished that she were not. How delightful—and indeed how soothing—to have turned from the dream to the reality!

He bit his lip, and stirred himself fretfully about the wide bed. Ana was in the church, her mind absorbed in exalted thoughts. The Ana of his dream had not a trace of exalted thoughts about her, she had been as passionate as the Ana of the first night at the inn, but she had also been considerably pleasanter to lie with. A pity—a considerable pity—that Ana was in church. But there was nothing to be done, he must just fall asleep again.

He thumped the pillow and the bed creaked. The creak had a most unpleasant tone, it was as though a raven had uttered its leathery sarcastic note. Everything in this house was intolerable, and the expense of the journey had been far beyond his calculations. Now he lay here, mocked with a false dream and a creaking bedstead.

Leporello, too, was already getting out of hand, half a day in this deplorable household had ruined his demeanour and the night on the mountain-side had taken a month's wear out of his livery. Mother of God, what a place for vigils! Last night Leporello in the ruined hermitage, to-night Ana. And really, for what purpose? Praying for a damned man.

I shall never go to sleep like this, thought Ottavio. It would be better to turn back to that dream. More cautiously, this time, he pulled at the pillow; but for all that he had moved so warily, the bed creaked again.

The clock chimed out two melancholy notes. Last night he had heard the same hour announced.

He began to think of the holy souls in purgatory who, watching in torments, have the christian obligingness to wake one at any hour one specifies. Then he thought of his father-in-law, whose image at this moment towered moonlit and severe among the cypresses. That marble head had bowed. Those heavy feet had walked, and the hand had been lifted to knock stonily at the door, and from the cold marble lips, wet with the dews of night, had rumbled the severe syllables, falling by one as stones fall down an echoing gully.

But he had been avenged, it was most improbable that he would walk any more.

Somewhere in the depths of the house a door opened and shut.

There was a moment's pause, and then slow feet began to mount the stairs. At this juncture it seemed to Ottavio imperative that he should have the spiritual reinforcement of Don Isidro. He leaped out of bed, he ran from the room. The feet were still mounting the stairs, a glimmer of candlelight moved up through the darkness, and even in his haste he noticed a singular warm perfume. To reach the chamber where Don Isidro lay he had only to go along the gallery, to cross the stair-head, to mount beyond it the little flight of steps which led to Don Isidro's door. But he had forgotten this little flight of steps. And the footsteps and the faint light were all this while steadily approaching, and in his haste he stubbed his toe on the first step, scrambled, lost his balance. Recovering it, he raced up the remaining steps and began to hammer on the chaplain's door.

A voice behind him said gravely, 'Señor!'

Trembling at the summons he turned about, and saw, as it seemed, the grey head of the Commander. With a cry of filial submission he cast himself down and embraced his father-in-law's legs. And in the same instant a liquid scorching as the liquid fires of purgatory fell on his back, and he and Carlos and the candlestick and the remains of the tray of chocolate rolled downstairs together.

The last cheap little candle had guttered itself out and only the sanctuary lamp cast its vague light on the tinselled altar, the smoky gold of the vaulting overhead, the motionless figure at the praying-desk. Since the candles had gone out the church had become much colder. The solid chill of stone, the shuddering chill of fatigue and lack of sleep had got into Doña Pilar's vitals, it was useless to pull her wadded cloak closer about her, and for some time now she had ceased to fidget for a more comfortable attitude, since there were no comfortable attitudes left. Yawn followed yawn, tears of sleeplessness ran down her cheeks, the blood in her ears whirred drearily on and on. She sat heavily and patiently as any peasant woman might sit, with her mouth half-open and her body drooping forward, and the counter-thrust of her stay-busk reverberated by the heart-burn behind it.

Her rosary had slipped off her lap some hours ago but

she was not going to trouble to pick it up. Doña Ana's prayers could get to heaven unassisted. By day she would sit embroidering those despicable little pansies, and not complain. But to spend the night repeating Hail-Marys at the bidding of the same mistress—no, there were limits to her complaisance. Watch she must; but to pray seemed no part of her duty. One's days and nights, one's strength, eyesight, liberty of action: these, in the position of duena, one gives over, and measures every word before it leaves one's lips. Every profession has its honour, and Doña Pilar had been fortifying her professional pride ever since she entered the Commander's household, twoscore years ago. But one's prayers one may call one's own, and she had no mind to buttress Doña Ana's petitions. The libertine could writhe in eternal fires before she stirred a bead between her fingers. For she had no doubt as to the reason for this vigil. Though the poor Commander were to smite on this very door, and burst the lock, and come clanking up to the altar steps, and lay his heavy hand on Doña Ana's shoulder, her prayer would not turn aside for him. It was another ghost that walked to-night. And because a limber reprobate had glanced, and whispered, and dallied in the garden, and twanged an instrument of music, Doña Ana was on her knees, and Doña Pilar must watch with her. As though we were sitting up—she framed the words savagely in her thought—for a serenade.

Shifting herself, she saw with bleared eyes that a dusky grey was trembling through the windows. And there was Doña Ana, motionless as ever, the gothic arch of her white hands rising above her veiled head. There she knelt, the image of devotion, the image of penitence. Ah, no! The image, for all that bowed head and those rigid imploring hands, of headstrong stubbornness. She would hale him out of hell, would she? No, no, my girl, you won't fish him thence, angle you never so patiently. And what a way to pray!—how arrogant, how ostentatious! For not once had she stirred from the praying-desk before the altar, and not once had a word escaped her lips. Mere decorum alone might have prompted the Stations of the Cross or some ordinary civility to the side altars, and whether one salutes the denizens of earth or heaven, it is usual to utter some sort of how-do-you-do. But not so Doña Ana. She must needs pray like one of the blood royal of paradise. All the discomforts and annoyance of the journey, and the tedious misery of this night, and the fatigues and slightings of years past, with every finger-prick of every pansy, accumulated in Doña Pilar, whose old bones and sleepy flesh must dance attendance on this imperious young woman; and now, when a cat began to yowl outside the church her drooping jaw pulled itself up into a grin.

Passionately, slavishly, the cat yowled and yowled, venting its shameless desolate sexual cry. It yowled, it uttered guttural contralto moans. After a while a voice was raised to curse it, and then followed the noise of a stone smashing against a wall. After a moment's silence, patiently, slavishly, the cat began to yowl again.

Doña Pilar coughed once or twice.

'What a shameless animal!' she exclaimed.

Doña Ana continued to pray, and the cat went on yowling.

He had watched the reflection of the eastern sky, the first beam fasten on the mountain-ridge, the inundation of light. But in the chill of the porch sunrise served no purpose, and Don Gil kept his lantern beside his feet, and his hooded cloak wrapped well around him. Out of the dusk emerged the beginning of colour: the dull raisin of the village roofs, the battered blue paint of doors and shutters. The light swept down the hillside, and the earth appeared in its true tints of drought. The dark masses of the oak-woods became a rusty green, and soon after appeared the first severe green of the olives, and the scanty ribbons of the vines on their terraces. The castle on its mound came into the next sickle-stroke, a moment after the summits of the poplar-trees were dipped in gold, and presently the low roofs of the village had received the sun, and the raisin-coloured roofs became etched over with a brilliant criss-cross of shadow where the tiles were broken and awry.

By then, life had begun. The first bands of workers for the vineyards and olive-yards had set out, the clatter of a loom could be heard, a wreath of smoke was going up from the tanner's yard, and the women with their water-jars were trudging to the well, the dust rising after their heels. The two watchers from the castle had given up their sentry-go. They were sitting in the sun eating bread and sausage and flipping pebbles at a piece of dusty grey fur that lay in the road, stirring slightly every now and then as though a wind wagged it.

Don Gil looked towards his own house, and frowned. Still no sign of life. Those idlers would never wake unless he were there to rouse them. And thinking of his daughter-in-law, with her startled short-sighted eyes that looked at every familiar pot and pan as though it were some sudden enemy and her long back bruised with child-bearing, he became impatient with his watch. She would let the children sleep too long; or they would wake, and do themselves some mischief while she lay sleeping and sighing in her sleep. A hateful woman, a vilc mother, a creature without energy or ambition. And yet he had heaped perquisites upon her: the washing of the church linen, and the linen of the priest's house; all the char-work for the priest's housekeeper, Doña Adriana; the cleaning of the school-house; the weeding of the presbytery garden. All these honourable occupations he had, little by little, procured for her, saying, God forgive him: 'Teresa will do it gladly; though she doesn't look well-put-together she's a wonderful worker.' Any other woman, knowing how to put her best foot foremost, would by now be the most powerful woman in the village with such opportunities; but Teresa, dead to any sense of family honour, must be goaded and prodded to it, and went through her days with no more pride than an ass round the threshing-floor.

Devil take the woman! Suppose she chose this morning to oversleep, this very morning when Ricardo was to serve Don Tomas at the first mass? Already she should be awake, combing the boy's head. But there she lay with her mouth open as though sleep had thrashed her. Yes, that was Teresa, thwarting him at every turn. And on this remarkable morning, with the strange woman within there, entrusted to his guardianship like a golden jewel of whose strong-box he held the key, and with all the visitors attending mass, Don Tomas would come—but the server, the grandson of Don Gil, would be lacking. And here he was, tied like a dog to a kennel. Under the cloak he grasped the key in his fist and shook it. At last he called to the watchers, at first softly, then imperatively. One of them turned round and said, grinning, with his mouth full,

'Are you hungry, Don Gil? But you must stay for mass.'

He beckoned with the hand that held the key. Compelling his voice to sound benevolent, he said,

'You would do me a great service if you would step down the street to my house, and knock on the door until you waken my poor daughter-in-law. I know she wanted to wake early, for the boy is to serve mass. It would break her heart if on such a morning she were to sleep too long.'

'Why not go yourself? We shan't split on you.'

'Ah no, my friend.'

The man went off, saying something in an undertone to his fellow, and Don Gil sank back into his cloak, trying to recapture some of the princely suavity of mind which he had felt during the night: for not on every night of the year does one keep watch over such a treasure, and hold the church key so powerfully.

It had been better during the dark, with nothing to distract him from his contemplations, with no one to infringe his dominion. This common daylight and all these usual people going about their errands were unravelling, shred by shred, the magnificent mantle he had worn during the darkness, and already he was beginning to share her with day and with mankind. Alas, it was over, the powerful and sumptuous night! But there was still something to look forward to, for in a little while he would unlock the door, and see her as the long night had re-made her: pale and trembling and tear-stained, with her silken petticoats crumpled, and the black shadows under her swollen eyes.

Not long now. And the man-servant returning had brought word that Teresa was already awake, and the boy being washed. Now the coach from the castle was in sight, almost filling the narrow street as it jolted hither. It drew up by the church steps. And now came Don Tomas, with Ricardo behind him, and a congregation larger than usual. The door of the coach was opened, Don Saturno and the visitors' chaplain got out. As they came up the steps he rose, and fitted the key in the lock, and turned it, and opened the door he had guarded so well all night.

On her ears the accustomed words fell dry and sapless as the dead leaves of autumn. The night was over. The wafer was put on her tongue, and seemed in the same instant to have been laid as a film over her senses. She swallowed it with a deadened greediness, as though her hunger had waited too long. 'It is over, it is over,' she thought, 'I have not managed it, and it is over.' Kneeling with her hands sheltering her face she heard the mass ended, the altar vessels carried away, the noise of people going out, the breathing of those who still waited. And it seemed to her that she had mismanaged everything, that by some unanalysed negligence or stupidity her intention must certainly have miscarried. It was over, and to-day was to-day, and in a few hours they would be leaving Tenorio Viejo. She knelt on, it was as though she were kneeling on a little island of sand which at every moment was being washed away around her. Some more people went out, and through the open door came the sounds of a day already launched.

She rose from her knees, giving one long, hopelessly farewelling look at the altar before which she had knelt all night. Even when she turned, its imprint was on her sight, she saw the two priests, and Don Saturno, and Doña Pilar only as vague figures behind a golden palisade.

Through the open door she saw the brilliant vignette of the world in sunlight, and walked towards it. They followed her. In the porch she gave money to the priest, and walked on down the steps. What was it they were trying to say to her? Ottavio. Something about Ottavio. Yes, quite true, Ottavio was not with them.

'Not with you?' she repeated politely.

What was this? Fallen downstairs? How? Why?

'Why did he fall downstairs?'

'There is no need to be alarmed. Don Ottavio is not in the slightest danger, it is only a minor accident. And when we left to come to you he was sleeping quite comfortably.'

'Yes,' she said. 'Sleeping?'

They stood round her, as though to protect her. Don Saturno laid a fatherly hand on hers.

'I give you my word that it is nothing to cause you the smallest anxiety. It seems that your husband was walking in his sleep. At any rate, he stumbled, and fell down a few stairs. He has sprained his knee, he has a few bruises. But it is nothing more than a week's rest will set right. You must stay with us a little longer, that is all.'

She heard him out attentively. Her face, as the innkeeper afterwards remarked to his customers, was like the face of an angel listening to the word of God.

'It is the will of heaven!' she exclaimed.

She moved away from them towards the coach that was waiting. The sun, the strong heat of day, seemed to her unexpected and transcendent as a burst of music. On the golden air the golden altar glittered, the altar that she had farewelled in such desperation of disbelief. As though she were the only denizen of this newly invented world she walked on towards the coach. Don Saturno stood bowing to hand her into it. As she glanced downwards towards his hand she saw at her feet something lying—a dead cat, or almost dead, for its tongue was stretched out and draggled in the dust. She gathered up her skirts and stepped into the coach.

Would they were gone, and their courier with them! So he had exclaimed, a few hours ago. But now the aspiration must take the more developed subjunctive of, Would they had never come!

How remarkable, thought Don Saturno, is the difference between class and class. Often in the village a hovel caught fire, and burned to the ground; or the wind blew its roof off; or a flood undermined it; or without the help of any element save time it fell to pieces. And within an hour a family, with its children, its livestock, its pots and pans and scraps of rescued bedding, is established at some neighbour's. The one narrow roof covers them, the same smoke stings the eyes of Perez and Lopez, the greasy spoon goes a wider journey, the bread is divided into twelve portions instead of six. The turmoil is indescribable, the discomfort is beyond contemplation, from the two miseries packed into the space of one ascends a complicated incense of stink and uproar; and yet they seem to settle down under it. For however much they may quarrel, squall, and backbite, the common people, at bottom, bear each other a permanent affection.

But not all the empty rooms of the castle, nor the breadth of its kitchen resources, nor the civilities and etiquette of education, could make the incursion of Doña Ana with her retinue of husband and chaplain and duena tolerable to him for long. And now, Mother of God! they might be here for weeks.

'I beg of you,' he had said to Ana, 'to treat this house as your own. Naturally, you will not wish to leave Don Ottavio's bedside.'

She had replied that Don Ottavio was sleeping, and seemed to be doing nicely. 'Your presence,' he continued, 'is the best surgery. Any refreshments can be brought up on trays.'

And with a further strategic movement he had dislodged Don Isidro with the suggestion that Don Ottavio might be in more immediate need of spiritual consolations than one would like to contemplate, since a blow on the head is always a threat to the reason.

And so for a minute or two he had walked about the library with the sense of having swum from a noisy shipwreck to the security of a desert island, and to its discreet silence he repeated his words to Don Isidro, humming them over again with pleasure, as though they were a melody. But there had been a tap at the door. And

Leporello sidled in, fat in his mourning suit, his chops reeking of shaving-soap, his hands dangling in idleness, his air compounded of gloom and smirk.

'Well?'

He was astonished at the tone of his own voice, its ungarnished dislike; and at the same moment had the surprising thought that to have spoken thus was not only discourteous but dangerous.

'Well?'

This time the tone of voice was even harsher, and gave him no surprise at all.

'I don't like to trouble your honour . . . but since they are all upstairs . . .'

Out of his pocket he pulled a little book.

'I didn't like to mention it to them. I shouldn't like anyone outside the family to discuss these matters. But there are a few little bills.'

He laid the book on the desk.

'I'll look into it,' said Don Saturno, and turned to his book-shelves.

'Ah-h!'

A fat greasy sigh—it might have been a fart—broke the silence.

'My poor master!'

Don Saturno turned round. Leporello's dull black gaze was sliding off like a blackbeetle.

'My poor young master, I mean.'

'He was forty,' said the master. 'I do not know if you call that young.'

'He always seemed young to me,' replied the valet. 'And in any case, forty is young to die.'

The blackbeetle paused, halted, returned a little way.

'O sir, what a dreadful end for one of the family! Every night I dream of it. And though it's wonderful to be back in the old place again, it does bring alive the past most cruelly. Ah, what a catastrophe, what a merciless affair!'

With his right hand he gathered up his left, as though it were an utensil, and began to count on his fingers.

'Seven. Eight weeks come Saturday to a day. Sometimes it seems longer, sometimes it seems less. It's a relief to me to be able to unbosom myself to your honour. I would not say a word against my new family, the shirt must be true to the back that wears it—but there isn't the same confidence, the same feudal feeling. No!'

The blackbeetle gaze was now circling Don Saturno's feet.

'No! A gentleman that lives in a town, your honour, can never be the same thing as a gentleman that lives on his estate. They say his mother was an Italian, too. Quebrada de Roxas y Pellico. Pellico is an Italian name, I believe, sir?'

'Tell me,' said Don Saturno—the blackbeetle gaze rushed up him with alacrity—'tell me, since you feel inclined to unbosom yourself, how my son came by his end. Sit down,' he added. 'Take your time, Leporello.'

'By the Virgin, I can scarcely bring myself to speak of it.'

'Go on, Leporello. It will do you good.'

'Living or—the other thing, flesh or stone, I never trusted the Commander,' Leporello began. 'From the moment I set eyes on him something went down my back that said, Beware! Here comes a misfortune. And many a time I begged your honour's son to flee such an orbit. These premonitions are very mysterious things, sir.'

'Very. But go on.'

'If he'd listened to me, ah, I shouldn't be wearing black at this moment. A paltry symbol, compared with the heart. Not good cloth, either. More show than body to it.'

'Pray go on. We had reached your premonition.'

'But he wouldn't listen, he wouldn't give his mind to it. The truth is, those two ladies, Doña Ana and Doña Elvira, were pestering the life out of him. He got to look so pale, poor gentleman! As for the fight, I didn't see much of it, it was all over in a flash. It's my belief he never meant to finish off the old gentleman, but his skill ran away with him. What a swordsman!'

'And then?'

'You might have supposed that after that the two ladies would have quieted down a little. But they were worse than ever, chasing him hither and thither and yon. One of them out of a convent, too. Ravening as two black bitch-hounds they were, out of their senses for him. One would not believe it of Doña Ana, seeing her now. But I blush to say she was the worse of the two.'

'Don't stay to blush, Leporello.'

'All the time my presentiment was growing worse. I

warned him, your honour, I begged and prayed, I did all a poor servant could do. But what can one do against destiny and the gentry? He went to the cemetery, and I went with him. There was the statue, all white marble, tall as a tree, with an inscription in Latin as long as a litany. And all around were the cypresses, shaking their heads, as much as to say, Dare no further. There stood my master, in front of the statue, inviting it to supper, naming the very hour. The sweat burst out of me like blood when I heard such words and said in such a place. Mother of God, I said, what are you provoking now? And before the words were off my lips the statue nodded its marble head with all the marble feathers on it.

'Lord, how I prayed! Lord, how upset I was in the bowels. I went around as trembling and stupefied as a man in a fit of the ague. And there was my poor master, driving me on, with this to be done, and that to be done, the wine to be bought, the fiddlers to be hired, the finest meats and the purest wax-candles. The Commander will relish a good meal, said he, after mumbling cemetery mould. Shall we have in some young ladies, Leporello, or shall it be a sober bachelor party? O sir, said I, falling on my knees, consider your immortal soul, think of your dear father and your dear aunt, think of . . . Excuse me, your honour, but I fancy I hear Don Ottavio's bell.'

'Never mind if you do. There are plenty to answer it. But your story, Leporello, only you can tell.'

'I don't know if I can bring myself to it. I would really prefer not to lacerate your honour's feelings. A poor serving-man like me, how can I find suitable words, how can I adequately impart such an astounding and horrible event? My powers are not equal to such a recital.'

'But you are doing very well. And I only want plain words.'

'In God's name, then! Well, the hour came, and everything was ready, and the fiddlers were playing in the next room, and there he sat, calm as the snow on the mountains, and there was I with the serving-cloth on my arm, and praying inwardly as no man has ever prayed before, saving Jesus in the garden. And at the very appointed hour, footsteps came up the stairs, one-two, one-two! And then a thundering knock. Open the door to my guest, said he. Never, said I. Not though you hale me to it with red-hot pincers, your poor faithful Leporello will never open the door to your destruction. It knocked again, a sound like an earthquake. Come in, said he. And the door opened, and the Commander came in. Such a blast of cold air came in with him, in an instant the room was as cold as a charnel. Don Juan de Tenorio, said he, will you repent? No, said my master. Repent, said the Commander. Again my master said no. Then—O your honour, how can I tell it?—then the Commander raised his arm, his arm of stone, with the stone drapery hanging from it. The candles burned blue, the floor opened, up came flames and devils, and Don Juan was carried off alive into hellfire. Ah, what a terrible shriek he gave! It has rung in my ears ever since.'

'About how many devils?'

'Sir, how could I count them? But they were there in dozens, leaping and prancing all over the room, and my poor master struggling in the midst of them. To think that this was how I had my last sight of him!'

'But no one else saw anything, or heard anything? Not the fiddlers?'

'They all ran away, your honour.'

'Nor the people on the ground floor? One would suppose,' said Don Saturno, 'that if flames and devils ascended to the first floor, someone in the room below would notice them passing.'

'Does your honour doubt me?' said Leporello in a wounded tone.

'I find your story difficult to believe.'

'But I saw it with my own eyes, your honour. Alas, that I should have to say so.'

Don Saturno looked thoughtfully into the eyes which had seen so much.

'You saw it with your own eyes? Distinctly?'

'Surely, sir. With my own eyes. Could one invent such a thing? Of course the room was a trifle dark, the candles went out, the flames gave only a hither and thither sort of light, the clouds of sulphur made my eyes water, the presence of so many devils created a great deal of confusion, I was half-fainting with anguish of mind. But see it I did. Yes, to the best of my belief, your honour's son was carried off by devils, more's the pity. On-whose-soul-Jesu-most-pitiful-Mary-most-powerful-have-mercy. One can't but say a good word for him, hell or no.'

The black eyes seemed bulging with candour. He sat leaning forward, his hands dangling between his thighs. It was as though a fat spaniel sat there, devoted, attentive, meekly quivering, awaiting a bone, a word, a lash.

'That bell seems to go on ringing. Perhaps you had better attend to it.'

The spaniel went off with alacrity, wagging its plump haunches. What other country can breed such natural Homers, thought Don Saturno. A really detestable fellow, though, capable of any baseness and perhaps of any crime. What lay beneath this fable? What should he do next? With a glow of relief he recollected that Leporello was in Don Ottavio's service, was Don Ottavio's responsibility. Meanwhile, a certain responsibility remained with him. Sighing, he opened the account book, and turned its greasy pages. It had been kept as though it were from the royal exchequer, the maravedi its unit of reckoning. Entries carried forward of five thousand, of twenty-five thousand farthings, gave it an air of majestic grandeur. Even with the maravedis reduced to crowns it was a considerable total. Leporello's unpaid wages were a steadily recurring entry.

It seemed to Leporello that he had earned a little relaxation. As Don Saturno had remarked, there were plenty of people to answer bells. Besides, was he not now a courier? Couriers are under no obligation to dawdle about in the servants' quarters. He would take a stroll through the grounds.

Like everything else about the castle of Tenorio Viejo the grounds were wretchedly dilapidated. Their formal alleys and quincunxes had outgrown the shears, within arm's reach the evergreens were roughly clipped but above that level their boughs spread out bushy and unkempt. It was obvious that for many years the garden ladder had been mislaid. The channels, dug for water to flow along them, cooling the walks, were dry and half-filled with rubbish. On the floor of the belvedere a heap of last year's pumpkins had rotted to discoloured shards. Though it was the month of May the plane-trees were already wilting with drought.

A dry sheltered fustiness filled the air. It was as though one were in a church whose woodwork is devoured by dry rot. Beyond the belvedere he found his path barred by some hurdles. They guarded a queer sight. The formal plantations had been grubbed up, in the dusty trenches one could still see the fangs and whiskers of the tree-roots that remained in the earth. The space of ground thus cleared had been sown at some time with grass but now only a few patches of lawn survived among the common herbage of low-growing thistles, skinny clover and couch. Scattered about at irregular intervals were sapling trees, all dead. And on a small artificial mound studded with bits of rock, stood a wicker-work summerhouse, warped askew. It seemed that at some time or other Don Saturno had decided to have an English Garden.

A few thin sheep wandered about, plucking at the clover, or shredding the remains of bark from the dead saplings. The sight of this garden raised Leporello's spirits. He began to whistle and to throw stones at the sheep. The designer of this miscarriage was nothing for a man of intelligence and enterprise to be afraid of.

Thinking over the interview, it seemed to him that he had acquitted himself very creditably. If Don Saturno had not believed all of the story, he had not wholly denounced it either. It was a ticklish business to tell a gentleman his son was damned, any good Catholic would resent such tidings with energy. But Don Saturno being so lukewarm a son of the Church, the resentment was tempered also, no doubt. Anyway, the story was not all. Let him believe it or no, as he pleased; the essential was that he should believe the account-book. Lord, how hard it is for a poor servant to come by his dues! For the rich, quarrelling never so much among themselves, corrupting each others' wives, driving steel into each others' bellies, were as one in cheating the poor. Where could one find a worse paymaster than Don Juan? So he had thought; and changing to the service of Don Ottavio had looked forward to better days. There was a deal more money in the new establishment, but there were many more locks on the money-chest, and his hopes that the new master would pay the debts of the old had been disappointed. Indeed, it seemed that he had changed for the worse. With Don Juan there had at least been sundry little windfalls, a gratuity here and a bribe there. But in the household of Don Ottavio and Doña Ana there was nothing but virtue and equity. So he was reduced, as Don Juan would say, to squeezing the old cow once more. It had taken some courage to come on this expedition, on the hillside, indeed, he had lost all heart, had been ready to give up. Yet here he was, his guardian angel must have willed it so. And the first step had been taken, not too ill, and he had good hopes for the rest of his affair.

Beyond the waste of the English Garden was an inappropriate wrought-iron gateway. He vaulted the hurdles, walked past the sheep and the dead saplings, and tried the gate. As he supposed, it was not locked.

The ground sloped away towards the stream. To his right he could see the village, to the left the dusty road crept on towards the mountain. He heard the sound of thumping and splashing and the voices of women, he must be near the washing-place.

Here might be the relaxation he sought. The presence of women is always refreshing, the act of eavesdropping brings many consolations to a philosophic spirit. He insinuated himself into the thicket of bamboos and rushes which edged the river-bed.

They were kneeling with their backs to him. Through the screen he could contemplate their rumps, shifting and swinging as they leant forward to beat on their washing-boards. Clack-clack went the stones and the washing-bats, and from the linen still unwashed the sun fetched a penetrating odour that he snuffed up with pleasure. Like a Sultan, he lolled here in the shade, observing the rumps and listening to the talk of silly women.

'So they are going to meet this evening, and have it all out.'

'Bah! What difference will that make?'

'A crosser husband to-morrow morning.'

'The difference between to-day and yesterday.'

'A new petticoat for Maria Hernandez.'

'Aye, that's true. Talking of grievances makes a dry throat. Empty your heart and empty the cask. On the day of mourning the innkeeper rejoices.'

The last speaker sat up on her haunches, straightening her back, turning her head from side to side.

'Eh! Here comes Teresa Mauleon, dragging along as usual. Lord, what a basketful she's got!'

'The church washing, the priest's washing, the schoolmaster's washing, Doña Adriana's fine chemises—she'll nibble up all the work in the village before long.'

'But she doesn't look the fatter for it.'

'It's my belief she's got a worm. Not an ordinary worm, but what they call a queen-worm. Such worms are rare, praise God for it, but I've known of one or two others in my time. An ordinary worm lives in the guts, and eats the food you send it. But a queen-worm is more delicate than that. It will eat only the marrow of the backbone. Up it goes, suck, suck! A little further every day, but not much. For it is a thin worm, you see, and the marrow of the spine being very nourishing it needs but one suck a day, it lives like the holy nun Maria of Mexico, who existed upon nothing more than a sanctified wafer each morning. Up it goes, this queen-worm; and with every inch of the marrow sucked away your back grows weaker and weaker, until it reaches right up to the brain. And then when it tastes the brain it begins to dance on its tail for pleasure, and you die in a convulsion. That's what ails Teresa Mauleon, mark my words.'

'The virgin-protect-us! How do you get this worm, Aunt Serafina? Where does it come from?'

'It enters by the fundament, my child. A little creature, no longer than a skip-maggot. And you catch it by squatting to piss in a place where dead Moors lie buried.'

'Good gracious! But how can one tell where dead Moors lie buried?'

'Not in any way, my dear. Only by the queen-worm. Heaven does not condescend to mark out Moors by any other method. Well, Teresa? You are well-laden, I see.'

The newcomer flumped down with a sigh, and began to work immediately, as though the steeping and thumping and turning were but a continuance of something long performing in her mind.

'Your household have been busy this morning. The boy did very handsomely, spoke up well.'

'Ah, but he should not have scratched himself in the Gospel.'

'Poor child, he was hard put to it, no doubt.'

Serafina began to give her opinion of the morning's affair.

'A very nice little ceremony. Our Don Tomas was at his best, one would scarcely have known that he has the asthma. And the strange woman is certainly handsome. But the beauty of the party is her chaplain. What a man, what a man! The very image of Saint Sebastian, grown a few years older and with the arrows taken out.'

'What, do you admire him so much? His mouth hangs open half the time.'

'His toes turn in.'

'He rolls his eyes like a duck in a thunderstorm.'

'Why, Leporello is better than he.'

Serafina laughed.

'The truth is, you are all so faithful to your husbands that you do not know a fine man when you see one. I tell you, the strange woman's chaplain is a lovely man, tender as veal, smooth as a sausage.'

'It seems,' remarked the tanner's wife, 'that he is too handsome for the lady's comfort.'

Serafina clucked her tongue against the roof of her mouth.

'I can't blame her.'

'You needn't,' replied the tanner's wife drily, 'it's her husband who might be blamed.'

'What?'

'Impossible!'

'Impossible! How do you know this?'

'It seems that all yesterday morning the two were bawling for a bed. My cousin Antonita told me. Locked up in the bedroom they were, the blood bounding in their veins, their faces red as fire, the chaplain simpering, the gentleman panting like a tiger. Aye, no wonder she went off to the church to pray.'

'I can't understand it at all,' said the young woman who had listened so attentively to the queen-worm. 'Surely, it is a great sin?'

'A sin, yes, it is a sin. But the gentleman is an officer in the army, officers in the army are all good Catholics.'

'What do you mean, Maria Perez?'

'Eh, what I say. The gentlemen in the army are good Catholics, so they love the priests. It has always been so, it always will be so.'

'Well, it isn't like that with the common soldiers, anyhow.'

'No. They have to drudge along with womankind. Black beans and long families for them.'

Teresa Mauleon twitched her heels. In a constrained voice she said,

'How low the water is getting.'

'True. It has not been so low in May since I can remember.'

'That will irk our Dionio, down at the mill.'

'It will irk him the more since his days of cheating seem to be numbered.'

'Why, is he sick?'

'He has not eaten for more than a week. Shrunken away to nothing, he is.'

'What a close-mouthed place this is! I had not heard a word of it.'

'For all that, it's true.'

'Yes, it is true,' interposed Teresa Mauleon, 'for I heard Celestina say so last night.'

'Celestina? Ah, what a fortune that girl will have—the only child of the miller! What a prize! Odd, that no one seems to be after her.'

'What's the use while he is alive, the close-fisted reckoning beast? But if he's dying, that puts a new colour on it.'

'But what about Conchita Hernandez? She'll have as much.'

'No, not so much.'

'Not so much by half. 'Tisn't her money the boys run after.'

'Did you hear . . .'

The Sultan moved into an easier attitude, burrowing a pocket for his elbow in the soft dusty earth. It was pleasant to lie here in the shade hearing talk about girls.

For his master's taste in women was not his taste; and for years he had scarcely a moment to pick a girl for himself, he was like a man who has so many errands to run that he can never find time to visit the shoe-shop, and pounds along in leavings that don't fit him. God, the malice he had endured from some of those inherited dames, who had solaced their wounded feelings by wounding his! He was not by nature an amorous man, and for too long he had seen much too much of love; but now a sort of timid lust put out its snail's horn, and thinking over the conversation he had overheard he decided to look into these girls of Tenorio Viejo.

Indeed, why should he not marry? It seemed that there were two girls in Tenorio Viejo who had dowries, the miller's daughter and the inn-keeper's. Why not marry and settle? If he could get his money from Don Saturno, and add to it a trifle of dowry, he might leave drudging in service and open a small business in a town. A wife is a great help in commerce; for either she is handsome or she is thrifty. The Hernandez sounded the most invigorating. A sharp girl like that would be more apt to appreciate his urban manners, the fact that she had already tried to kill herself for love suggested an amiable responsiveness. And Celestina should be her rival; for there is both prowess and safety in numbers. The more he mused, the more interested he became; and hearing that a woman had come up from the village with a message for him it seemed already a go-between.

Spruce and suave was the Leporello who stepped into the kitchen courtyard. There was the woman, her petticoats rattling in the arid breeze, a middle-aged woman with a swaggering figure and a taut countenance.

He laid his hand on his bosom, and bowed, graciously. She stood unmoving, her hard strong legs rigid among her flowing petticoats, and rapped out in a harsh voice,

'Are you the one called Leporello?'

He replied that he was her servant.

'And can you read?'

Out of her large hand came a piece of paper.

'For if not, I can say it.'

He put on, a robe for the occasion, his master's manner: that often-seen expression of slightly quizzical interest, the body withdrawing itself, as it were, in a suspension of judgement from the letter in the hand, the eyebrows mounting like two blessed spirits. The eyebrows remained there, stranded, as he read,

Sir,

You will oblige us greatly if you will come to the tavern this evening at ten o'clock. I have the honour to sign for all. Ramon Perez.

Ramon? Ramona? The name remained in the masculine.

'Well, can you read it?'

'Certainly, certainly. It is most elegantly written. But who are these . . .?'

'The men,' she rapped out in her harsh, indifferent voice. 'The tenants.'

It was not what he expected, and this was a most intimidating woman.

'Well, what message do I take back?'

'Oh, I come. Certainly, I come. With pleasure.'

'Can you not write?' she enquired flatly.

A most hateful woman, a mouthful of bitter herbs. It was distressing to learn from those within that this was the mother of the very Conchita Hernandez towards whom his fancy had so hopefully inclined. Maybe it would be better to essay the miller's daughter who had, so he had gathered, no female relations.

Because he felt nervous, he asserted himself by being over an hour late. There were twenty or so men sitting in the long room of the inn, and it was clear that they were waiting for him, and no one made the least comment on his delay in keeping the appointment. Every countenance wore the same look: serious, intent, and non-committal. The furniture had been rearranged, the tables and stools were grouped together, they sat close-packed, like an audience. The man who had been so conspicuously rude to him the night before now greeted him, introducing himself as Ramon Perez, and beckoned to the innkeeper, who came forward with the wine.

'We have met to ask you a question,' Perez began, 'or rather, to ask you for information. We here are all tenants of the estate, and this matter concerns us all equally. This is our request. We wish to hear from you how Don Juan met his end.'

The rusty-coloured swineherd glanced towards the speaker.

'Jesus Morel wishes to speak. Speak, Jesus.'

'If we wished only to gossip we would not ask you. For already the place is ringing with stories, and if gossip were all we wanted then the more rumours the better.

Don Juan was carried off to hell, so the tale runs. To speak for myself, the destination is not interesting to me, nor the sins that he took to hell with him. If I seek for sin, I can read the Lives of the Saints. If Don Juan is in hell, that is his business. Our business is to hear from you how he died. How, where, when, in what manner, and with what witnesses. If I judge rightly, that is what we wish to learn. I say no more.'

And this was the fellow who had thrust him into the pound.

'Speak, Esteban.'

'Jesus Morel is right. What matters to us, though with all reverence to damnation, is ourselves, our own lot on these acres. If Don Juan is dead, let him go to hell, purgatory, or heaven itself, that is not our concern. *But is he dead?*'

A third man was on his feet.

'Yes, that's the question to be answered. Is he dead, is he off our backs at last? Or must we still sweat out the wine he drinks, sow him crowns and guineas when we think we are sowing corn for ourselves, shear our sheep to make satin tails for his harlots instead of coats for our children. He drinks wine, and our land gasps for water. How long have we been promised water, sluices, channels, God knows what?—and still it is put off because his turn must be served and his debts paid! Our houses fall to pieces, but they cannot be mended, because his coat needs retrimming with gold lace. We have land, and we work it, and by rights we should be making every year a little money to put by. But every year we fall more into debt, because he owes money to the jeweller, and to the tailor, and to the coachmaker, and to the pastrycook. Is he off our backs or not? Are we to live or die?'

A fourth man rose.

'Speak, Andres.'

He spoke in a sharp thin voice, high-pitched and fluent, the voice the shepherd hears all night on the windy mountain.

'I don't wish to speak uncongenial words, but for all that I don't agree. Suppose Don Juan is dead? We shan't find much difference in our load, there is more on our backs than the son of Don Saturno. Don't let us fool ourselves. If Tenorio Viejo were to become a paradise, it would still be in Spain. There would be the taxes to pay, wouldn't there? We should still be taxed. And the better crops we raised, and the better we did for ourselves, so much the higher would the taxes be. I am sorry if I am uncongenial, but I speak the truth.'

'It's true enough,' said Dionio Gutierrez, lifting a heavy forehead. In his face, full of weary wrinkles, clear round eyes shone innocently.

'It's true enough, the taxes are heavy and many. There is the tax of the Tenth, and the tax of the Eighth. There is the tax on bread, on flesh-meat, on oil, on wine, on fat, on soap, and on tobacco. There is the tax on salt, and the tax on wool. There is the tax on stamped paper. There are also the dues to be paid to the Church. These are . . .'

He was launched on a further reckoning when the third man broke in with,

'Stamped paper! Stamped paper! That's not a tax that troubles the likes of us, that's a tax for millers and such-like, a rich man's tax. It seems to me that Dionio Gutierrez did not grow so glib at counting taxes on his fingers from reckoning what goes out from the mill, neighbours. 'Tis from what comes in, peradventure. He can count what he makes while we are too busy to count what we pay. I think a miller had better not lift up his voice among peasants. It's an old saying that a miller is as greedy as the King, the Church and the Landlord in one.'

'I have not heard that saying,' said the man presiding, 'nor do I think much of it. We did not meet here to abuse each other before a stranger.'

The angry laughter and the growls died down. There was an uncomfortable silence, broken at last by a man who was clearly only speaking in order to break it.

'It cannot be denied that we have been promised water, and still have not got it. If we tenants had water for our land, we should do better. Water is what the land needs.'

An old man leapt up and said in a furious bellow,

'Marl! Marl! That's what the land needs. Water alone cannot nourish the rock. And what else is the land here but the dust of the rocks. Get your water, and see what you have: a puddle! We have to grow barley and rye, not salads. And for barley and rye, and the vine and the olive, we need marl. Good marl, a bed of good marl!'

On this, everyone struck in, even the miller was allowed to have an interest in this question. Only Ramon Perex said nothing, sitting patient and observant amid the brawl of opinion. When of itself it had died down he turned to Leporello, saying,

'You perceive how serious to us is this question of our land. To say the truth, it is our life. As Jesus here said a while ago, our reason for wishing to hear your account of the death of Don Juan is not idle curiosity, or the wish to listen to a strange story at the inn.'

He began.

Neither by flourishes of eloquence nor flashes of bawdy could he move them from their fixed and silent attention. It was as though their combined attentiveness followed him step by step through the narrative as a pack of wolves follows the traveller through the wood. Never had he had so intent an audience; and never had he told his tale so lamely. His lips grew dry, his tongue swelled, his heart pounded. In a daze of effort he trudged through the splendid familiar narrative, the words to come and the words past jangling in his mind above the words he spoke. Nothing came right. Swords, ladies, cemeteries, blasphemies, ortolans, hellfire, and devils, all the plump words turned to sawdust; no extra garnish, no jokes or appealing sentiments could revive the narrative. He had, in fact, gone stale.

And they listened and listened, tracking him to the end

of the story, to the moment when he must emerge into the bare moonlight of silence. When he had finished the sweat was running off him, and the horn drinking-cup refilled with wine clattered against his teeth as he drank.

He had thought that the wolves would pull him down and tear him, but they swept on. They began to talk among themselves, slowly and warily.

'It must be getting late.'

'Yes, it is certainly late.'

'Very late. One forgets the time in listening to a story.'

'It must be midnight. I think the wind has fallen.'

'It does not usually blow so hard at this time of year.'

'Such winds mean long drought and great storms to follow.'

'Yes, it will be a bad season.'

'The third drought running.'

'What can you expect, when the world is full of such wickedness?'

'Such wickedness as his? He was certainly a great sinner.'

'And better dead.'

'It sounds to be a fine statue, however. All of marble.'

'And able to walk. When I am dead, I doubt if I should want to bestir myself much.'

'Nor I. However, he was in a manner obliged to walk.'

'Some are active in this world, some in the next.'

At length the man presiding gave him a small dismissing nod. He stumbled to his feet, stumbled through a valedictory flourish; and then found he must stand like a schoolboy while Perez and one or two of the older men gave him formal thanks.

He heard the heavy door pulled to after him.

The street was empty. No! A man in a hooded cloak was walking slowly a few paces ahead, cat-walking close to the house-fronts. A dim moon face turned. It was the sacristan.

'Ah! Don Leporello, if my old eyes do not deceive me. What a charming night. So serene.'

'Is it you, Don Gil? I should have supposed you would be in bed at this hour, after keeping vigil all last night.'

'At my age one can do with very little sleep, my son.'

The intonation was perfectly religious.

'As a matter of fact I had to do a little errand for our good Father Tomas—a little reminder to a parishioner. But I suppose some more gallant business has brought you out to-night. Ah, Don Leporello! You must not turn our heads with your town gallantries. We are a simple people in Tenorio Viejo.'

'Nothing of the sort, I assure you. I have been all this while at the inn. Some good fellows wished to hear the story of the death of Don Juan. I was glad to please them.'

'Just so, just so. How I wish I had heard you,' said Don Gil.

They had gathered closer, still silent. Suddenly a

clamour of voices broke out.

'He's dead, neighbours, he's certainly dead. We're rid of him at last.'

'Now for the water!'

'What a story! One can scarcely believe it. But there's no doubt that he's dead, praise to the Virgin!'

'For me, I don't believe a word of it.'

'Nor I.'

'Listen to them! And if he lay dead among us, I suppose you would not believe it. Why, he saw it with his own eyes.'

'With his own eyes. Flames and devils carrying him off. What more do you want?'

'The word of a man who does not look like a liar and speak like a liar. That's what I want.'

'Don't listen to them. He's dead, that's good enough for us, whether the man who speaks it looks like a liar or no. He's dead. Now we can get water for our land.'

'Marl!'

'Water!'

'If he lay dead among us, that would be another matter. But as for this story, it is a story for children, and the man who believes it is a fool.'

'Oh yes. Everyone knows that Jesus thinks one a fool to believe in the teaching of Holy Mother Church. Say hell to Jesus and he will say, Liar. He'll find out one day.'

'There will have to be sluices, little gates, to regulate the flow.'

'And watchmen, neighbours. We must choose out watchmen, or our water will be sneaked from us.'

'Yes, but when will it be brought?'

'Yes, that's a point to consider. When will it be brought?'

'It must be brought at once. Three droughts! Name of God, are we to see our crops fail three years running?'

'Down through the olive-yards to the maize-plants.'

'Cisterns.'

'It will be a puddle without marl, nevertheless.'

'Well then, name of God, we'll have the marl too. Pedrillo shall have his marl.'

'I say again, when will it be brought? It has been promised us often enough.'

'We'll demand it. He can't put us off this time. We'll see that we get it.'

'Ask, and ye shall receive.'

'It depends on the manner of asking. We'll ask, and we'll receive.'

'We'll get it, our water. Have we not suffered long enough? We'll get it. And we'll get other things too. We will be masters now for a change.'

'An old man without an heir. . . . What's that to stand against us? Now that the heir is dead, the land is ours, in a manner of speaking.'

'Manner of speaking? It shall be more than speaking, if I have a word in it. The land is ours by right now. The old spider, we'll break his web! Think how he has oppressed us for all these years, neighbours, think how he has ground us down.'

'Always promise, never perform.'

'Always take, and never grant.'

'Dumped that school on us and made us pay the schoolmaster.'

'And talk! Ameliorate, that's his word.'

'Look at those paintings on the wall here. Didn't he promise to send Angel Hernandez to study in the town. Where's Angel Hernandez now? In the tanyard!'

'For generations they've oppressed us. Did not our forefathers build the castle with their own hands, hew the stone and carry it and set it up with forced labour?'

'Yes, and did they not fetch artisans from the town to build the church under the noses of those here who should have been paid for doing it?'

'What a pack, I say. One after the other, each worse than the last. What a devil's rosary! But it's told now. He's dead, Don Juan is dead!'

They had split into two parties, and the larger party was made up of believers. Pedrillo was murmuring to all and sundry, 'Water and marl, that's good husbandry. I say nothing against that.' Another old man, completely absorbed, was tracing out an imaginary system of irrigation with the wine spillings, leading the dark watercourses through visioned fields. Diego sat rocking himself to and fro, staring with burning eyes, biting his lips. Every now and then one of this party would turn and look over his shoulder at the others, at the unbelieving.

Jesus, and Dionio, and the young man who had patched things up after Diego's attack on the miller, were listening to Andres, who with lean forensic hands and shrill voice was expounding the various reasons for not believing Leporello. Whenever he gave them a loophole for speech they thrust in a word of assent. Only Ramon sat silent, leaning forward, his hands resting on his knees, his elbows stuck out. A heavy-built, ugly man, he looked now like a thoughtful toad; and like a toad he had bright sorrowful eyes. By degrees, because he was the only one who did not speak, those who glanced towards him glanced more often and with a sharpening of anxiety or defiance, till at last Diego threw out the words,

'And what do you say, Ramon Perez? Is he dead, or no?'

Looking round on them, he answered slowly,

'Dead or no, what difference do you think it would make?'

There was a silence of absolute astonishment. Then with one accord they broke into a clamour of furious eloquence, reiterating grievances, hardships, injustice, promises broken, and hopes frustrated. They talked themselves out, and he said,

'One death is a very small thing, neighbours, to set right so much that is wrong.'

A man who had not spoken till now said,

'Well, there can be other deaths, I suppose.'

'There will be!' exclaimed Pedrillo with energy. Surprised, they looked at the old man.

'Yes, there will be other deaths. Don Saturno will go soon, mark my words. He is younger than I, he has lived easy and I have lived hard, he has eaten more flesh-meat than I have eaten bread—and maslin bread at that. But I'll outlive him, I pledge you my word for it.'

The man who had spoken of other deaths looked contemptuously, and Diego winked at Jesus. But most of the others seemed relieved at this turn, and Esteban said,

'With one gone, and the other, then it might be our turn. They say, too, that now we have a King who divides the ownerless land among those who live by it.'

'Don't trust in *him,* Esteban. Don Saturno talks of our King as though he were his brother. Our robber is a splendid fellow, said the thief.'

An argument followed, Andres averring that it was impossible for a king to do anything for his people save eat them, Esteban, proud of his information, speaking of roads constructed and brigands put down. Every time he praised the King the innkeeper, hovering in the background, shook his head vehemently, and crossed himself.

'And so he has trampled out the robbers, has he? And who are those same robbers? Poor men, desperate men, like the rest of us. That's how a king takes the part of a poor man.'

Diego slammed his fist on the table.

'If we are to wait till Don Carlos comes over the mountain a six-foot-long trench and a sprinkle of holy water will be all the land and water we shall need. For God's sake, Ramon, let us get back to the point. You set them off on this ramble. This time, give me a plain answer. Is Don Juan dead or no?'

'I say nothing as to whether he is dead. But I do not believe this story.'

Andres caught at this.

'Believe it? Only a fool would believe it. For one thing, it is a servant's story. For another, it is full of improbabilities and contradictions, such as . . .'

His voice toppled under the weight of the other voices.

'I agree with Ramon,' bellowed Jesus, 'the man's a liar, and the story's a fable. An old fable, too. Our grandfathers sang the ballad of Don Juan de Tenorio. Blood of God! If I could not invent a new story I would be content to sing the old one. The words are better, too, than any of his half-licked phrases.

> Is it a lady or is it a nightingale
> That sings so sweetly, that cries so sadly?
> Lady, though you sang to a harp of angels
> You would not fetch Don Juan from hell.
> No, would not fetch him.
>
> And is it a mattress or is it a pillow
> You spread so softly, you wet with weeping?
> Lady, though you wept like an autumn river
> Your tears would not quench the burning he feels,
> No, would not quench it.
>
> And is it a fire of oak-wood or of olive-wood
> That burns so brightly, that burns so fiercely?

They had listened, beating the measure on the table, humming the burden of the song, carried away by the singing that sprang like a powerful fountain out of the uncouth man. But the spell did not last. They began talking among themselves, the voices grew louder, Andres was expounding once more, again the argument broke out and was much nearer a quarrel now. But they still deferred to Ramon Perez, and Diego said, almost as though to persuade,

'Why not believe the story, Ramon? Others believe it, his own father believes it.'

'Has he told you so, then?' interjected Jesus. Ramon snapped his fingers at the interruption.

'Up there, they all believe it. I don't say they are better judges than we, but maybe they know more of it than we have heard. What we have heard is a servant's story, sure enough; but it may be true, for all that, at any rate the gist of it. Where there's smoke, there's fire.'

A voice behind him asked why all the town gentry should have come to Tenorio Viejo if not to bring tidings of importance.

'Exactly,' continued Diego. 'They are not here for nothing. They came to say Don Juan is dead.'

'But who did they hear it from? From Leporello.'

'They believe it. Why should not we? Man, man, why not believe it? All these years we have been ground down and denied so that this fellow's debts should be paid and this fellow's whims gratified. Have you so lost heart that you can't lift your head to believe he is dead at last, that at last we are rid of him? Have you so lost hope that now, when the good news comes, you can't believe it?'

'It is because I hope that I am cautious. Don Juan has been our curse—though I do not say he is all of our curse. But I do not believe Leporello's story, and I will build no hopes on it.'

A heavy sigh came from Pedrillo.

'Our hopes are desperate, just as we are. As Diego says, whichever way we turn, Don Juan stands between us and our purpose. Promises have come like clouds. And like a wind his insatiability has swept those promises away, the rain has fallen on his ground, never on ours. Each man here would rejoice to see him lying dead.'

Raising his voice above the growls of assent he went on,

'But has our adversity made us mad, as well as miserable? Are we men of bone, or men of paper to be blown this way and that on the breath of a story? Because we hate Don Juan must we believe Leporello?'

With the effort of raising his voice he began to cough. Dionio, looking at him with admiration, said,

'Ramon speaks like a prudent man. Why should we believe this story?'

At the back of the room a voice said tauntingly,

'Why indeed should Dionio Gutierrez believe this story? Why should he long for the death of Don Juan? He has all the water he needs. It turns his mill-wheel and that's all he cares for.'

The voices went up again, voices shouting of water and the death of Don Juan. Belief was triumphant. Diego called to the innkeeper to bring more wine.

'All, all!' he said magnificently, gesturing the wine towards Ramon and his unbelievers.

'To Don Juan in hell!'

'May he burn there!' came the devout response. And in a moment they were singing,

> And is it a fire of oak-wood or of olive-wood
> That burns so brightly, that burns so fiercely?
> Eternal are the fires of hell that burn him,
> And endless the pangs of hell that pierce him,
> Ah, how they pierce him!

The parish priest before Don Tomas had been Don Pablo, a man from the province of Castellon, with the growing of large pumpkins in his blood. It was he who had made the presbytery garden, and it was because of him that Teresa Mauleon was weeding-woman there. Don Tomas was no man for a garden. The smell of flowers or of herbs brought on his asthma. But Don Gil insisted that the garden should be kept up. The castle had a garden; and it would be a slight to religion if the presbytery should lack what the castle possessed.

To-day Don Tomas's asthma was particularly bad. It was a hot still day with a threat of thunder. All the morning he had been lying on a sofa, gasping for breath, wiping the sweat off his face with a handkerchief. Yet now he appeared in the garden, walking hastily. Teresa was weeding among the tomato vines, stirring up the pungent smell. He went through it as a man goes through a line of fire; but as he passed he said in a strangled voice,

'If anyone should look for me, Teresa, I would rather not be disturbed.'

There was a fine hedge of artichokes at the end of the garden and he disappeared behind it.

Down the garden path, two sets of footsteps approached —Don Gil the sacristan and Don Francisco the schoolmaster. Teresa went on weeding.

'We are looking for Don Tomas,' said her father-in-law.

'He is not here. All this morning I have not seen him.' She was careful not to look towards the artichokes.

'Not here!'—Don Gil spoke in a loud clear voice— 'Not here? How very odd! How unfortunate! Is it not unfortunate, Don Francisco?'

Don Francisco agreed.

'I can scarcely believe it.'

'Perhaps Doña Adriana knows where he is. Did you ask her?'

'She is asleep,' said the schoolmaster. 'We could not wake her. It is a pity she eats so much, and sleeps so grossly.'

'Many things are a pity,' continued Don Gil, his voice still pitched unnaturally loud. 'Most of all it is a pity when one cannot find one's parish priest at a moment like this. It is always painful when God's representative cannot be found, how much more so when afflicted spirits are flying to him for advice and consolation.'

The afflicted spirit's voice was now declamatory.

'He certainly ought to hear about it,' said Don Francisco. 'The flock is threatened, and the shepherd is absent. The Evil One is abroad, and no one can find the exorcist. Sad! Deplorable! Our houses may be set on fire over our heads at any moment.'

'What can you expect in a place like this? They are hogs.'

'And that the scandal should come just now, when people from the polite world are with us. When I heard the news my first thought was for Don Tomas. Let us warn him, I said to myself, let us put him on his guard. Feeble he may be, neglectful he may be. But surely he will not wish a thing like this to happen in his parish while that party is at the castle. Not in front of another priest, no. Surely that would awaken some proper pride in him.'

He looked round the garden as though challenging it.

'It is certainly alarming!' said the schoolmaster.

'Alarming? It means riot, it means revolution! Property will be destroyed, women raped, grey hairs torn out with ignominy. And the sacrilege! There will be no end to it.'

'Where do these disgusting ideas come from, that's what I ask?' said the schoolmaster.

'Some say, from education,' replied the sacristan.

'No! That's a mistake, I assure you. You, Don Gil, are the best educated man in Tenorio Viejo. Do not deny it. Your career shows it. You have property,'

—Don Gil opened his hands with a gesture of regretful denial—

'you have reared up a virtuous family, you have sons in the army, daughters in religion. Your grandchildren ornament your roof like young fig-trees, you hold a most responsible position in the village, you are esteemed by everybody, our poor Don Tomas would be nothing without you, you are a prop to Church and State. That is what I call being an educated man. And when has an idea of rebellion crossed your mind?'

'The Virgin forbid!' said the sacristan.

'No, no! Do not blame education, Don Gil! Revolt is a most uneducated idea, only held by the ignorant and vulgar part of mankind. I think I see the mischief elsewhere. There was no talk of revolution in Tenorio Viejo till the strangers entered it. And I may tell you, for your private ear, that Leporello never spent that night on the hillside in prayer. He was swilling and gossiping with Jesus and his lot. Look there, Don Gil, for the fox with the firebrand tied to its tail.'

'Don Francisco, I entreat you, do not say a word against that worthy creature. He may have been wild in his young days, and he certainly has kept shocking company, but I can assure you, he is no firebrand. On the contrary, it was from him that I first heard of this affair.' His voice had fallen, but now he raised it once more. 'Ah, if only I could find poor Don Tomas! Surely this would rouse him, inattentive as he may be.'

'But why not speak to Don Saturno?'

'Bah!'

'After all, it is he who is most threatened.'

'No, Don Francisco, not so. It is the Church that will suffer. And our unfortunate Don Tomas.'

These last words he uttered in a bellowing tone, so loud that it obliterated the sound of a desperate stifled cough.

'But what will happen, what is all this about?' asked Teresa sullenly from among the tomatoes.

'It is a business for men,' replied her father-in-law.

'A business for men? Then it will certainly be bungled.'

They turned with a start. There, behind them, was Doña Adriana, holding a rabbit by the ears. She was a handsome raw-boned old woman, and over her head was a brilliant silk handkerchief, and her apron was trimmed with wild arabesques of scarlet tape. Except on the point of age she seemed wholly unsuitable for a priest's housekeeper.

'Eh?' she said derisively, and swung the rabbit.

'And if this is a business for men, then why are you telling it to Teresa? She has work to do, she had no time to waste on men's business. And if it is a business for men, why are you telling it with the voices of jackasses? You shout so, you woke me up. And what are you doing here, anyway?'

'We are looking for Don Tomas.'

'In that case, I can tell you that he is not here. Good day to you.'

Nursing the rabbit, she watched them go.

'My fat little heart,' she said, 'they are gone, those two swindlers. Now I will kill you and cook you.'

She glanced towards the artichoke hedge, gave it a friendly smile.

'Pull up the weeds, Teresa my child. How pleasant a garden can be! How wise of our Don Gil to insist that we should keep up the garden!'

Her grim face puckered with mirth. She smacked a violent kiss, that almost stunned it, on the top of the rabbit's head and marched back to the house.

There was a rustle, and Don Tomas came sliding across the garden, lean and black as the shadow of the finger on the sundial. Teresa did not look up; but he paused beside her.

'Teresa?'

He began to struggle for breath. The powerful scent of the tomato vines streamed up, she flapped her hands above the plants as though she could dissipate the smell. She listened in a fluster to that laboured breathing, knowing that sooner or later he was going to say something to her. All conversations were more or less a misery to her, and though Don Tomas had never given her a rough word, she was afraid of him: because of his office, because of his sickness, most of all because of his unearthly inattention to the things of this world. A simple question from him or the most perfunctory commonplace was as alarming as though it had come from a tree, or a cloud, or a wheelbarrow.

'Teresa, what do you think about Don Juan? Is he in hell, or is he on earth?'

'Doña Adriana thinks he is in hell.'

'What do they say at the inn?'

'Some one thing, some the other.'

'Teresa, what do you think?'

'I am too ignorant to have an opinion.'

She grubbed her hands in the mould, pursuing a withwind root, obstinately shrunk into herself. But at last she was compelled to look up, to confront his drawn face and its intent and bleary gaze, to answer his delving query. Raising her earthy hand she crossed herself and whispered,

'Hell.'

But still he hung over her, breathless and unsatisfied. He whispered,

'But suppose he had been in hell and has come back again? *To tell us*. Suppose that, Teresa.'

After a while she whispered back,

'It would be a terrible miracle.'

And crossing herself her hand halted on the familiar journey, and stayed trembling above her heart.

He nodded. He seemed to be about to speak, but his long eyetooth caught on his lower lip and locked up the words. He looked away from her, passed his hand over his face, rubbed away the dream. He raised his fingers in the gesture of blessing,

'You are a good woman, Teresa, I am always glad to have a word with you. You have an exceedingly pure soul, and the weeding is very nicely done.'

He gave his little nod, and walked swiftly to the house.

The schoolhouse of Tenorio Viejo was a building called the Moor's House. It was a two-storey building, very old, very solidly built. The ground floor was arcaded, and at one time there must have been stout doors filling the apertures, for one could still see the great iron stanchions through which the bolts had been passed. And a Moor had once lived in it, that was certain, for his ghost walked there still. Since those days the Moor's House had been put to various uses. Once, it had been a jail; and then the stanchions were useful, for iron chains were riveted to them. When the great pestilence had come to the village the dead and the dying had been carried there. It had housed the hired artisans who built the church, and once or twice, when harvests were exceptionally abundant, it had been used as a granary. But all these various uses had been long ago, when Tenorio Viejo was twice the size it was now, and populous enough to support a jail or make a pestilence something illustrious. What was the smallpox or the fever now?—said the old people. A poor scrannel performance, a dozen dead, or a score, if one counted the small children. But the great, the splendid pestilence had slain three score in seven days, the dead and the dying had been laid in the upper room of the Moor's House as close as olives in a vat, and it had needed a strong man to close the door on them.

In those days too the Moor's House stood in the village, instead of standing apart, as now. Year by year, house by house, the eastern part of the village, where the pestilence had raged its worst, had crumbled, till only the

Moor's House, built so solidly, remained. The walls were as good as ever, the roof only had perished. There was no harm in that; if the wind blew and the sleet fell it but incommoded the ghosts: the old Moor, the tyrant, and his meinie of those whom the jail had slain or the pestilence, and the dead babies that bad girls carried there.

Naturally, when Don Saturno decided to have a school the Moor's House came to his mind. The upper room was given a coat of whitewash, the roof was patched, maps of old and new Spain, some hornbooks, and a teacher imported. Don Francisco was cousin to a notary who had done some business for Don Saturno, and highly recommended as an industrious and penniless young man. By hearsay he was perfect, but on arrival he was a disappointment. For he was not particularly young, talked like a book, and turned his toes out. Pay him and send him back, said Doña Isabel; but her brother decided to polish the dull diamond, at any rate till the loan manœuvred by the notary had been paid off.

Don Francisco too found disappointment. He had picked up some liberal ideas, he believed that the spirit of man had only to be enlightened to become virtuous, virtue in due course leading as inevitably to prosperity. He believed, too, that it was not overly difficult to enlighten the spirit of man. 'Personally,' said the cousin, 'I consider Don Saturno a dangerous madman. But you and he will be as thick as thieves. In fact, if you play your cards properly I daresay you will soon be able to drop this schoolmastering business, and live at the castle as his secretary.'

'A teacher's is a sacred calling. Naturally, I would be glad to assist my patron in my spare time; but teaching must come first,' replied the scholar; and during the journey his fancy ran ahead to a Tenorio Viejo thriving under a dispensation of liberal ideas, a contented peasantry, young minds unfolding, etc. He found that Tenorio Viejo was much like any other village in Spain, and that the liberal ideas had got no further than Don Saturno's lips. But he set himself to teaching with a good will, made out a list of equipment overlooked when the maps and the hornbooks were purchased, and prepared himself for the antagonism of the priest. The man of pumpkins was old and sleepy, he led no forays against the newcomer. And Don Francisco started with considerable popularity; for one thing, he was a distinction, and for another, he had given a very impressive diagnosis when called in to prescribe for Pedrillo's cow.

At first the school was well patronised. Not only children but people of all ages were studying the alphabet and asking questions: he saw minds unfolding on all sides. But by the end of the first year Don Francisco was bored to the pitch of heartbreak. Though he could not call an hour of the day his own he was appallingly lonely. The minds unfolding in questions, harassing him with enquiries as to why stars fell and where they went, how many crowns the Queen of Spain had in her jewel-chest, why there was no word spelled XYZ, what happened to the sting in nettles when you boiled them, folded themselves over the answer and went away again. With these constant irruptions from mothers and fathers, with Don Saturno coming in and out to expound some new idea which had just struck him, or to give some question a totally different answer to that which the schoolmaster had just given, the children learned nothing and were completely out of hand. The mob of elders could not be kept in order with the ferule; but one day Don Francisco beat three of the young ringleaders. That evening he was summoned to the castle, to be rebuked for brutality. 'It is mediæval,' said Don Saturno. 'I cannot have children treated like slaves. You would not beat a flower because it was slow to blossom?'

Politeness forbade Don Francisco to say that he could see no likeness between Serafin Mauleon and a flower.

After a few months he was beating freely, but no one said him nay; Don Saturno's interests had flitted to chemistry, he came no more to the Moor's House. It was a sickly autumn, many of the pupils died. Don Francisco's liberal ideas became positively Jacobin. Alone in his leaky house he cursed the institution of landowners and his inattentive tyrant in particular. It was all talk, nothing but talk. The people died, the wind clattered the makeshift roof. He sat alone, thinking of his dead pupils and listening to the wind, while at the castle they were eating and drinking, and Don Saturno was speaking of the equality of man. For all the equality of man, the schoolmaster was not invited to the castle. 'I would scorn to go!' he exclaimed, and the wind answered him with a whoo-hoo that rang through the Moor's House.

A week later he was at the castle, pouring out his misery to the tyrant, his hideous loneliness and boredom and discouragement. Don Saturno was sympathetic, and advised him to take up some new interest, the flute or the study of magnetism. 'But do not go on with it too long, my dear Don Francisco. Let thought be free. It is a great mistake to fetter the mind to any one preoccupation. I never do. And consequently, I am never hipped.' And with ready goodwill he hunted out an old flute.

He was just as affable when the schoolmaster called on him some months later to say that it was a long time since he had received his monthly stipend, and hunted for the money just as good-naturedly as he had hunted for the flute. But the payments became no more regular, and after a while Don Francisco took no scholars unless their parents paid him in kind or in coin. This meant that the poorer children came no more to the Moor's House. Freed from the rabble, his life became more tolerable. Don Francisco settled down.

He had lived thus for ten years, making by degrees a little money, making no friends. What friends could he make? The castle forgot him from one year's end to another and he scorned the village. Lately, though, he had struck up an acquaintance with Don Gil.

By now, if it were not for the fees, Don Francisco might have forgotten that he was the schoolmaster. It was a matter of hazard how many children turned up, whether five voices, or six, or ten, droned together through the reading lesson and the multiplication tables. This morning the attendance consisted of Juan and Pepito Perez, Ricardo Mauleon and his two brothers, Vincente Morel, and the Hernandez twins, Engracia and Fernanda. Having arrived and found no schoolmaster, they were passing the time by playing at lions and christians.

It was a game invented by Fernanda. Lions and christians were chosen by lot, the lions, hiding in the shadowy ground-floor of the Moor's House, rushed out in a pack to tear up christians advancing one by one. This inequity was compensated for by each christian, when thoroughly devoured, being allowed to climb to the top of an old ladder, and pose there in an attitude while the lions ramped about dejectedly below. For all that, it was better fun being a lion.

Or so one would say, seeing Engracia being a lion. But just now she was a christian and had reached her heavenly reward, prolonging the compensation by singing a hymn. Four verses had been intoned with every possible glory of grace-note and roulade, straining her narrow chest she attacked the fifth. It was astonishing that so loud, so passionate, so mature a voice, should come from that wren's body.

The lions began to threaten and expostulate. With a toss of the head the virgin martyr ascended another rung of the ladder and sang on, swaying her hips and snapping her fingers. The earlier martyrs sat at the foot of the ladder, clapping their hands to the measure and fending off the lions with kicks. The hymn ended with a leap to the higher octave, and a prolonged twanging howl.

'In-the-name-of-the-Father-and-the-Son-and-the-Holy Ghost. Lions, you are wicked animals. O lions, you ought to repent. First, O lions, you should be contrite. It is a great sin to chew up christians, it is also bad behaviour and against good manners to tear my petticoat. Furthermore, you have made great fools of yourselves, for here I am in heaven, torn petticoat and all. All this calls for much contrition. Secondly, O lions . . .'

They rushed the ladder. With a shriek the martyr launched herself into the air. With an answering shriek her twin rushed forward to break her fall, and the two rolled together on the earth floor.

Trudging up the sandy path to the Moor's House, scowling at the thistles and the starveling poppies that edged the track, Don Francisco heard those shrieks and cursed aloud. Sin and Death were not a more baleful pair than Fernanda and Engracia. Time and again he had refused to admit them, on the ground that they were too ignorant for any schooling, on the ground that their presence set up a riot, on the ground that girls had no need for education. But four times a year Maria Hernandez silenced him with an exact payment of his fees, and on the evening of the day when he called up enough resolution to turn them out and bar the door on them he was very deftly and accurately stoned and found a dead rat under his pillow.

'Get up,' he said. 'Silence!' and marched up the stone steps which projected from the side of the house like huge snails. The children shuffled after him. Fernanda said,

'Here comes old Carlos from the castle.'

'Silence!' he said again.

'He's waving, he's hurrying,' she continued, standing on the steps. 'Engracia! Give me the kerchief, and I'll wave too.'

'It's lost.'

'No! It would be better if we all went down on our knees, for no doubt he is coming to tell us that the strange gentleman at the castle is dead.'

'Oh yes! Another funeral. At Doña Isabel's funeral we collected the drippings from the consecrated candles, and ate them. Pure wax. They were delicious, especially while they were still warm.'

'I wish we could have a funeral once a week.'

'That's all the rich are good for—a fine funeral.'

'Don Juan had no funeral, though.'

'The cheat!'

'Huh! Maybe he doesn't need one yet.'

'Oh yes. Your father thinks he's still alive. Clever!'

'Now, Engracia, now, all of you! Holy-Virgin-Mother-most-pure-pray-for-us-now-and-in-the-hour-of-our-departing. Is he dead?'

Carlos laughed. On each step was a kneeling child. Those Hernandez girls were like puppet-masters, all the other children were on strings to them.

'No, Señorita Doña Fernanda, no one is dead. But where is Don Francisco? I have a letter for him.'

'. . . a brilliant career at Oviedo,' continued Don Saturno. 'In fact, if he were not kept here by his devotion to our school, his merit would now be recognised by the whole of Spain.'

'But I thought he was a schoolmaster?'

'An educationalist. But that does not prevent him from knowing a great deal about anatomy. The man is an Admirable Crichton, there is no subject he has not mastered. He had not been here a week before he performed a really remarkable cure.'

'What sort of cure. I mean, who was the person? Some peasant?' asked Ottavio.

'No, no! No peasant. A very valuable member of society.'

Don Ottavio was suffering a great deal of uneasiness on account of his leg. It seemed to him that the alarming nature of his symptoms was not appreciated by anyone in the castle, that bones were broken and gangrene setting in, that something more than salve and bandages was needed. Doña Pilar had tried to reassure him by explaining that what was really wrong with his leg was his head. The bruise on his head, she said, had been so violent that it had scattered his animal spirits, causing them to take refuge in his extremities. The pressure of animal spirits in his leg caused the leg to throb; the absence of animal spirits from his head made him a prey to doubts and gloomy forebodings. He should be cupped; or more and livelier leeches placed behind his ears.

Old Carlos and Don Saturno then took a turn. Carlos prescribed a poultice made of figs and dock-leaves mixed with sour milk; but he was very clumsy in applying it, as his hands had been considerably scalded with the hot chocolate. Don Saturno had the poultice removed, and tried magnetism. After stroking Don Ottavio's leg for an hour or so he remembered Pedrillo's cow, and prescribed Don Francisco. The cow, to the best of his recollection, had also suffered from a swelling in the leg.

And Doña Ana sat at her husband's bedside, sat for hours and hours, unstirring and loftily resigned, with her eyes half-closed and her mouth a little open. Somehow she gave the impression of a person recovering breath after a sustained effort. It was as though she had run for a long distance and suddenly left off running. All remarked on her self-control. Don Isidro was especially impressed. He only hoped she would not suffer for it afterwards, for such elevation of mind, he said, achieved in the delicate frame of a woman, must be paid for.

Ottavio, too, could not fail to notice his wife's self-control; and the thought of being parted from such a jewel after so brief a wearing made the notion of gangrene even more distressing. She would, of course, pray for him. He could imagine her as a widow very clearly, as a wife she had been so markedly an orphan that a further step in bereavement seemed only too natural.

'Ana. Will you go into a convent?'

She looked at him with a steady uncomprehending gaze.

'I said, Will you go into a convent?'

She laid a hand, cool as lettuce, on his forehead, told him that it was heated and that he should not talk.

She had not understood him, she did not realise, poor Ana, the dangers of a leg like his. He would say no more, for why should he alarm her, why should he cast a shade over this saintly and well-bred tranquillity which was so delightful in her? And the moment after he said,

'I fear that the injury to my leg is more serious than these people here believe.'

'I am sure it is,' she answered. 'I am convinced that both time and patience will be needed before it is cured. But try not to fidget, Ottavio. Fidgeting can do no good.'

She was at his bedside, as a vase of lilies might be, when Don Francisco was ushered in.

He arrived in a filthy temper. The letter had contained only a pressingly courteous request that he would come to the castle immediately in order to give his valued advice on a matter of importance. 'Why should I be at his beck and call?' he had said to himself. 'I am a gentleman, not a lackey.' And the social agony with which in earlier years he had waited for those invitations that never came rose up, a grotesque apparition. But all the time his hands were fumbling with a clean neckband, and pinching up the curls of his shabby old-fashioned wig. A cloud of dust hung above the track, the dismissed children had scuffed it up with their feet and it hung there still, so quickly had he made himself ready to obey his patron's summons. As he went he rehearsed the cutting things he would say when he got there. It was the eloquence of his thoughts, perhaps, which hurried him along. Hurry he did, whatever the reason, and sweat prickled him and dust stifled him. Little phrases danced about in his thoughts, danced stiffly, on the points of their toes: *this unexpected honour . . . certainly a trifle informal . . . my pedagogic obligations.* Then, in the dusky corridor, he confronted himself in a long mirror: a rather elderly man, stoutish, with bow legs; and a shabby wig awry over a red face grimed with dust; and daubed in the red face two staring black eyes. How long, since he had seen himself at full length?

Trembling with mortification he was turning from the mirror when it showed him the approach of Don Saturno, minute and trim, skating like a spider over the polished floor. In the village, many nicknamed him Old Sorcerer. It was true enough, he could bewitch when he pleased; and as though yielding to some transcendent nausea Don Francisco felt himself yielding to the pleasure of being addressed in cultured speech and with all the cordiality of culture; and forgot the dust and the sweat and the ignominy; and remembered only his eloquence. God help the man, how he prates!—thought Don Saturno, at the same moment offering his snuff-box. In five sentences he had woven the spell, and with the sixth as lightly abolished it.

'. . . not only Socrates, but Aesculapius too.'

That cow!

On an impulse of rage he got up, saying,

'Do I understand that one of the castle horses is sick?'

'Actually, a cavalier, not a horse. But is there so much difference, after all? The animal kingdom includes both. Pray finish your wine. I cannot let you be in such a hurry, even to do a kindness.'

So the horse-doctor sat down once more, and listened to one gentleman's account of another: an account censored and restrained, as though the whole of Tenorio Viejo did not know that Don Ottavio had fallen downstairs in the middle of the night, and why.

His eyes were hot with rage as he entered the bedroom. He entered and cooled them on Doña Ana.

She said little, and what she said was no more than the suitable conventionalities of a wife. Her fan moved to and fro, like the censer swinging before the altar. Once or twice, as Ottavio winced and cried out under the schoolmaster's handling, the fan closed with a whirr, and she turned her head, frowning slightly like someone interrupted in an elaborate calculation. Meanwhile Don Ottavio recounted in detail all the various expedients which had been tried, and his reasons for thinking none of them applicable.

'But I do not suppose,' he said, looking towards his wife, 'that this is anything to cause real alarm?'

'A contused joint,' replied Don Francisco, prodding his finger into the swelling, 'must always be a matter of some days.'

'Some days?' The fan stood still. 'He cannot think of moving for at least a week. And then he must only walk a step or two, from one room to another, perhaps.

'You must forgive me,' she added, 'for speaking so emphatically. But I am positive I am right.'

Bowing, Don Francisco said that Doña Ana was perfectly right. In using the words *some days* he had meant a week at least, probably a period even longer. She inclined her head, as though the words were an offering and she accepted it. After the women of the village she seemed to the schoolmaster not only extraordinarily lovely, but also extraordinarily modest, even timid. He began to expand, to fetch out the crumpled disused graces of his young days. Tenorio Viejo must seem to her very uncouth, very tedious? On the contrary, most interesting; it was her first experience of life beyond a city. Might he ask what city had been graced? Seville? Andalucia, the garden of Spain. Had she by any chance visited Oviedo?

Ottavio fingered his bandages. No doubt it was interesting to hear about Oviedo, but he would rather hear more about his leg. He gave a recalling cough or two, took up the whisk and began to drive away the flies. Then he had a spoonful of quince paste.

'Doña Ana,' he said, a little severely.

She turned from the schoolmaster with such grace that

he forgot to remind himself that these grandees turn up their noses at men of intellect. Beautiful and virtuous, she was intelligent too. He followed her to the bedside, asking himself what he should say about the leg. The thought of Pedrillo's cow dogged him, he heard himself advising viper's fat.

Viper's fat, viper's fat! What an insane suggestion, a vulgar remedy with the most unfortunate associations. Where had his wits been? Now they would tell Don Saturno, and Don Saturno would remember Pedrillo's cow, and the scholar of Oviedo, the polished gentleman clouted in poverty and rusticity but a gentleman still, would be pinned in her memory as the horse-doctor of Tenorio Viejo. He halted in the dusty track. Before him was the Moor's House, that lumber-room where they had housed the criminals and the plague-stricken and the dead. He turned, and looked back at the castle, where Doña Ana sat stirring the devout air before her beauty, where her husband played the fool with her priest, where the Old Sorcerer took men's hopes and brewed them into slow poison: to the castle whither he had been summoned and whence, having served their purpose, he was dismissed. They cared little, those who lived within those walls, of what went on outside. And with a torrent of anger he recalled Don Saturno's airy voice.

'It appears that Don Ottavio sometimes walks in his sleep.'

That was how one recounted these scandals to the

extramural herd. But if they cared little for what went on outside their walls, they did not know much, either. 'I know what may burn you out of your castle one fine night,' he thought, 'and I could tell you, too. But why should I, for you are nothing to me.'

Because of the threat of drought the summer pruning of the olives was being hastened forward. It began on the morrow of the meeting at the inn, and for a week now the men had been working in the olive-yards. They worked together. For though, since the partition of the land, each tenant had his own strip, the old custom held, they worked as they had done when all the olive-yards belonged to the castle. There were good reasons against this conservatism, every one knew them and some people urged them: it was foolhardy, and it was inequitable. The trees that were pruned earliest got a week's advantage in ripening over the others, and if a storm came, trying the boughs weakened by too heavy a burden, the owners of the trees still unpruned might lose the chief of their crop. But for all that the work was done in company. It seemed, at any rate, to go faster so, to be less monotonous, less oppressive to the mind. It takes a strong will and good nerves to work all day alone, hearing only the sigh of the hoary trees, the hiss of the falling twigs.

But after the first hour or so they worked as silently as though they worked alone, overcome by the weight of the heat, bemused by the riddling choice of what to lop and what to leave. At the beginning of a tree one might have a clear enough theory of attack, but after half an hour's work the knife had only uncovered another aspect of cross-purposes, and the tree's form would seem as confused and fluctuating as the journeys of the ants up and down the tree-trunk, crossing and re-crossing, toiling this way and that.

The trees were old. Tenants could not afford to set new stock. The trees were old and had the prolix fertility of old age, branches bushed out everywhere, weak straggling growths obliterated the original pattern of the tree. Pruning them was slow work.

The order of the olive-yards to be pruned was settled among the owners, changing from year to year. There were many considerations to be taken into account, the position of the yards, the prevailing type of tree in each man's ground, their condition, and the condition of the owner. Pedrillo's trees were finished, and Esteban's, and the yard shared by the two Espigas. Now they were at work in Diego's ground. His trees were difficult to handle because at various times he had experimented with grafts, counter-pointing the problem of the original stem with the idiosyncrasies of the interpolated growth. Ramon, pruning a very old tree in which several grafts had been set, called out, 'Now I am getting to work on Diego's breeches.' Though they had headed the differing opinions at the inn there was no antagonism between them as they worked.

Diego's patchwork trees had been chosen for early pruning because they grew in a particularly dry ground. The wood was so parched of sap that at a careless movement a bough might split off. It was impossible to hasten, and the pruning of the upper boughs had to be left to those of slender build, to the 'Cats.' Andres was one of the Cats. His analytical mind, which made him such a terror in argument, also made him the best pruner in Tenorio Viejo, even Diego's grafts could not shake his hold on the problem. And one could tell at a glance where he had taken over the upper-bough pruning, he worked with such style. Brilliant and unerring, he was swift into the bargain. 'If the rest of you could work like Andres,' complained Pedrillo, 'we might save something yet. But there you go, lumbering like oxen.' As his trees were finished, Pedrillo could urge the need to work quickly without seeming to show an uncivil anxiety for his own crop. And for a while his scolding would speed things up. It was quite true. Speed was necessary. If a storm came before the pruning was finished, before the sap, going on its shortened journey, had strengthened the wood that was left, half the olives might drop off. Already undeveloped fruit, wizened by drought, was pattering down. But after a while the pace of the work would fall back again to the same pondering rhythm.

The air was thick with dust. Each man saw his neighbour through a reddish cloud. The sweat of the hand spread to the blade of the pruning-knife, the dust clung on the steel. Ants ran up and down them, biting fretfully, the cicada's strident note clanged against the ears. The smell of the dust obliterated the smell of the olive-wood that had been so sweet in the first hour.

At mid-day they sat down to eat, eating bread, with garlic for flavouring or a handful of fennel-seeds, and quenching their thirst from the pitchers that were filled with a cold broth of water flavoured with oil and garlic. Afterwards they sat in silence. And along the column of the spine, jarred with the weight of the head tilted back to look into the boughs, a tickling ache ran up and down, and behind the brow and the drooping eyelids the brain seemed to be turning heavily, and the blood drummed in the ears.

With the appeasing of hunger they grew paler still, like men in a dream they got up to continue their work. Diego and Ramon were working on adjacent trees. After a while Ramon said,

'Where would you lead the water?'

'In a trench along the upper rows. And I would dig the trench, not straight, but serpentine, so that the current of the water should press against the sides, and make its way into the soil. And those trees that are dying there, I would grub them up, for they are worthless, and plant the sweet-olive instead.'

He slashed with his knife, and a patter of falling fruit answered the movement.

'But why should you talk about water, since you have made up your mind we shan't get it? Ramon, why did you turn against me that night? We have been friends all our lives, we have grown up like brothers, thinking the same thoughts, feeling the same anger. Why did you turn against me?'

'I disagreed with you.'

'No, you rejected me. It was ill done, I say.'

'I disagreed with you. I was right, and you carried the day. It was you they followed. We grew up like brothers, you say. But brothers are not a match, one prevails over another. We are brothers, but we are not equals. You are quick, and I am slow. I am right, but it is you they follow. If I could live for a hundred years, then I might match you. They might listen to me then.'

'And in a hundred years, what would you be saying? *We must go on as we are, for Don Juan may not be dead.*'

There was a chuckle overhead. The boy in the upper boughs was listening to their talk.

'You hear?' said Ramon. 'It is as I say. It is you they follow. But in a hundred years, though Don Juan will be dead, we shall not be rid of him. What Andres said puts it in a nutshell. We have more on our backs than the son of Don Saturno.'

'And for that reason we can do without water? A hundred years, a hundred droughts. Good!'

'I did not say we could do without water, I have never said that. And in a hundred years perhaps there will be water here, though I would not stake on it. But suppose there is water? Then, I say: More than water is needed to wash away the castle.'

'Water *and* marl,' quoted the voice above them.

'For suppose the water is brought, it will still be theirs. They can turn it away if they choose. It will be another weapon in their hands, and we shall have put it there.'

'Why did you not say all this the other night, then?'

'Did you let me? Don Juan is dead, say you; a valet says so, and so we shall have water. Then you ask me if I believe the story and I say, no. I ask you my question, why are you so sure, I say, that the death of this man will bring the water, that the water alone will wash off our miseries? But you do not listen, no one listens. For you have made it seem that everything hangs on the death of this man.'

He frowned with the effort of speaking. Words were not coming easily, exasperated with himself he gave the tree a blow with his fist. The wizened fruit pattered down.

'There!' he exclaimed. 'There fall a dozen Don Juans. But here'—and he smote the tree again—'here is the tree.'

Diego sucked in his lips. He too was frowning. As it was an effort to the one to speak, so it was an effort to the other to listen. The boy overhead called out,

'*Oye!* There is a cloud behind the mountain. I think a storm is coming.'

Through the olive-grove went the word of a storm. From the upper boughs Cats described the look of the cloud, debated whether it would cross the valley or turn to the westward. The pace of the work quickened. Presently Andres hallooed,

'Here come the women, too!'

They came with cloths and nets to gather up the prunings which would be stacked in the sun to dry out for fuel. At once they began their conventional scolding: the pruners had idled, they had not lopped off enough to boil an egg. They brought the day's stories with them. Don Francisco had gone to the castle to cut off the strange gentleman's leg. Pedrillo enquired why so much trouble need be taken. 'My cow died of the schoolmaster without all these cuttings and hewings. The poor animal gave him one glance, and her forelegs gave way under her.'

At the mill Dionio Gutierrez was wasting fast. It would be neck and neck between him and Don Ottavio to the burial-ground. But Sancha had seen him this very forenoon mending a shed, and he drove in the nails as well as any man alive. Yes, he still crawls about, that is his stubbornness; but death is written in his face and he can keep down nothing but herb-tea.

Angel Hernandez had killed a snake in the tanner's yard, and threw the body up on the roof to rot. Afterwards he said to the tanner's wife, 'I've k-k-k-killed . . .' and then stuck fast and could not get out another word; and she, after waiting a minute or two, had answered, 'Well, if you've killed poor Luis, the best amends you can make is to marry me in his stead.' Angel, with no more wit than a worm, had gone off in a hurry, crossing himself against the wickedness of women. Back in the yard, he saw the snake. For being killed before midday there was a day's strength left in it, and it had writhed itself along the tiles and dropped off. 'Alive, alive!' he yelled in astonishment. And the tanner's wife called out, 'All right, Angel. Even if you haven't managed it this time, I'll wait for you.'

Doña Adriana turned round from a tree.

'Ah! In the province of Catalonia we would have paid gold and diamonds to possess such a ninny as Angel Hernandez. For everyone knows that a fool brings luck and promotes good feeling. But here, in Tenorio Viejo, we scarcely value him.

'We're so rich in fools,' she added.

Women did not prune. They were not considered to have enough judgement for it. But Doña Adriana, coming up with the wood-gatherers, had scarcely troubled to throw two or three twigs into her net, but going to a tree had started work on it. She pruned very well, rapidly and conclusively; even Andres, pausing to look at her work, gave it an approving nod. In spite of her queer ways and her aggressive Catalan swagger, the old woman was popular. She was clever and open-handed, though she was the priest's housekeeper and her nickname Doña Iglesia, the village felt that her loyalty was to them, and she fought incessantly with the sacristan, which endeared her to every one. The nickname commemorated the fact that not only was she the cousin of Don Pablo Bau the priest before Don Tomas, but, as she boasted, a true, daughter of the Church, the bastard of a very eminent Dominican preacher.

The cloud had enlarged and now it swallowed the sun. Not a breath of air moved, the dust of the olive-yard, trampled by so many feet, rose up like a blast from a furnace, people coughed and snorted and spat. Thunder grumbled a long way off. If this storm were to break ?—but under the imminent threat no one worked the faster. Fatigue was stronger than any threat; and as the sky darkened and the thunder rumbled more often, the pace of their labour slackened, and this man, and then another, and then a third, shoved the knife into the belt, stepped clear of the trees, and looked up into the sky, measuring the weather with fatalistic appreciation.

A few large drops of rain spattered the dust. They ceased. The air became lighter.

'This time, it will pass,' said Esteban.

'Yes, we shall be at it again to-morrow.'

The darkness of the storm went over, leaving the smoky look of evening behind it. Dusk welled up from the valley, the narrow lacing of the river, skeined over the hollow river-bed, glimmered like an inlay of silver, the poplar-trees were like columns of smoke rising. The cicadas clanged louder than ever, and suddenly their senseless changeless note seemed filled with desperate melancholy. The women began to tie up their nets and hoist them on their backs.

'Well! To-morrow,' said Pedrillo; and they set off, walking heavily, the weight of the exhausted body jolting with every step on the uneven ground. The women with their rustling burdens followed a little behind, murmuring a small-talk among themselves. In the village was the smell of woodsmoke and excrement and oil, comforting after the acrid dust of the olive-yard and the austere evening. Entering his house Ramon Perez almost stumbled over something rounded and motionless, spilled on the earth floor. It was two of the children, sound asleep. He stepped over them carefully, stooped down and caressed the small hot skulls where the hair lay moist and subdued. The girl child opened her eyes and uttered a profound sigh. He heard Maria dumping her net of olive twigs and speaking to the goat. Presently she came in. He pointed to the sleeping children. She nodded, and stepped over them as he had done. She laid some bread on the table, and a knife, and yawning, they began to eat.

'Where are the rest of them?' he said after a while. She moved about the room, staring into its shadowy crannies.

'All here. All asleep.'

He stood up and stretched, and clawed his ribs as a cat claws the bark of a tree.

'Let us sleep.'

She took something out of her bodice, and laid it in his hand.

'What's this, Ramon?'

His hand recognised the texture, he took the flabby vine shoot over to the window and examined it in the last ashes of daylight.

'Ours?'

'Others' too. It's a mildew, isn't it?'

'Yes. It comes on the young shoots with lack of water.'

'Now they will be madder than ever,' she said.

He gathered up one of the sleeping children, she the other. They lay down on their straw pallet. The fleas sallied out, but did not wake them.

Over a fortnight had gone by since the night of Doña Ana's vigil, when Don Gil kept the key of the locked door. The taste of that sweet pleasure was fading from his palate. Why would she not repeat the performance? But though she came to mass, and to the requiem for the soul of Doña Isabel (a stiff-necked old Tartar, Spain was well rid of her) the Doña Ana of the vigil came no more, never again yielded that exquisite perfume of agony which he had snuffed that night. Now she swept past him, stately and serene, as scentless as the duena who followed her holding her ancient bony nose in the air.

He grieved for the lost joy, for the fading recollection of how much he had enjoyed himself.

Beyond anything else, more than money or position or security or crayfish with saffron or a cigar in the summer dusk, Don Gil loved the sense of power. Long ago, a whimpering orphan in a choir-school, he had fallen in love—not with a sense of power, for he was powerless—but with an ideal of power. With a melancholy calf-love he abased himself before the choirmaster, learning by heart every inflection of the oppressor: the veins in the bloodshot eye and the veins on the hand that gripped the rod, the missing buttons on the cassock, the smell of cloves. And one day he saw the choirmaster flinch and turn pale; for Don Ignatio, one of the Canons, had said, 'That boy, what's he called, Gil?—you bully him overmuch.' A new conception of power burst on the child. The tyrant he knew was afraid of a greater tyrant; and the greater tyrant of a greater tyrant yet. A hierarchy of bullying opened before him, fear ran through the social order as blood flows through the man; and behind the social order was God, the source and support of all fear, God like a heart eternally pumping fear into the universe, God in whose image and to whose glory man dresses himself in authority. He saw, and adored, and dedicated himself to becoming powerful.

And in a modest way, he had done pretty well. Though Doña Adriana, the Daughter of the Church, disputed his rule over the presbytery, he had held the past and held the present priest under his thumb. Though his children had grown up rebellious, he had disposed of them in marriage, in religion, in the army, in the burial-ground, till now only Teresa and her children filled his house, and only Teresa's habit of becoming idiotic through terror ever thwarted him. Though Don Saturno could never be his, the indifference which made a sacristan and a respectable householder nothing to Don Saturno made Don Saturno's village think a great deal more of Don Gil. For prating of philanthropy and progress, Don Saturno paid no real attention to the people, did not censure or chastise; and thus left open a career for a lesser authority. Though Don

Francisco affected to be a free-thinker, his pique at being ignored by a free-thinking patron blew him into a different course; disappointed in the castle, he had relieved his feelings by patronising the church, or rather, the sacristan; and a little well-adjusted toadying had made his toady indispensable to him. The village had suffered from droughts and bad harvests, he had loaned money to most people. Even over the inn and the mill, both solvent, his writ ran; for though the rest of that family were demons incarnate, Bernardo Hernandez and his eldest son Angel were extremely devout; and though Dionio Gutierrez lived in the inviolability of an obsession, his daughter led him by the nose, and between that daughter and Don Gil there had been certain transactions which laid her under an obligation to him. It was eighteen months now since she had brought him a sum of money—her father's savings, she said; and asked him to put it out for her at interest. What a good thing, said Don Gil, to see a daughter acting so prudently on a father's behalf—the more so, when the father was a little careless about money. Her green eyes enlarging under his stare she had replied that in truth her father had no head for such matters.

As the fig-tree spreads out its roots to the water Don Gil extended himself through Tenorio Viejo, forever striking new bargains between other men's weaknesses and his own power. And so he led a very happy life. But since the night of Doña Ana's vigil the sacristan's appetite had been disordered. His former moderate diet contented him no longer. It was no pleasure now to harass Don Tomas with statements that the candles were being stolen and the devil stalking through Spain. It was no pleasure to bully Teresa, to rub salt into Don Francisco's wounded feelings, to pay neighbourly visits to indebted households. He loved the sense of power; and his being was still disorganised by that love-night he had spent sitting outside the church-door with the lady inside and the key across his knees. No cage-bird with its eyes put out had ever sung so delicious a strain as her silence had sung to him. She was young, she was rich, she was noble, she was beautiful, she was proud; she was in an agony of mind; and all night she had been his.

If on the morrow she had got into her coach and driven away, it would have been easier for him. For he knew himself a practical man, not given to yearning after the unattainable. But she was still within reach. Daily he saw her. Daily she brought and conveyed away again the treasure which for a night had been opened to him and laid in his keeping. Hearing of Don Ottavio's accident he had thought, She will show signs of this. But she had shown no signs of it. Hearing the rumours about Don Ottavio and the chaplain he had scanned her demeanour for the appearance of a wife neglected and a woman insulted. She was perfectly serene. Then it struck him that perhaps she knew nothing about it. If she was their dupe? . . . In that case, a word, one of the casual words flying about the village, might at any moment undeceive her. Bruised with the shock, the rare scent of her agony might flow again, once more she would be as she had been that night.

At the thought that she might hear the news from other lips than his he became almost frantic.

Should he go now, himself, and tell her of the scandal, make sure that no other hand but his should break the alabaster box and loose the spices? He longed to go, he almost did go. But the habit of being circuitous was too strong for him. He stayed at home, thinking how he could encompass her. And began to encompass Leporello.

Once more Leporello was invited to tell his story of the death of Don Juan. But he had told it too often. The evening at the inn had spoilt his nerve, and now it seemed to him that all these invitations had but one intention, to catch him out and discredit him. The death of Don Juan was becoming too much his personal affair, it was taking on the semblance of being his responsibility; and now he preferred to stress his gratification at being in a respectable household. A religious household, no doubt? Very religious. And the chaplain? A little timid and retiring, perhaps, but a saint. One could not call him otherwise. One would not expect so well-made a man, said Don Gil, to be timid. He is not timid at table, Leporello replied. And for a moment he came out of his decorum, describing the astonishment of the castle servants at Don Isidro's appetite, and the inroads he made upon the sweets and conserves. The remainder of their conversation was perfectly fruitless and exemplary.

Yet in both minds the impression remained that they had something to get out of each other, and on their next meeting they were as affable as though they had exchanged a thousand confidences. The sacristan, with scarcely a gloss on the wickedness of gossip, went lightly from the state of Don Ottavio's leg to the state of Don Ottavio's affections; and Leporello as candidly replied that there was no truth in the story at all.

'Would there were! Life up there is so boring, one would welcome a little intrigue. But they are all as chaste as a packet of pins. And a poor servant is the poorer for it.'

So there was no hope of her that way. The sacristan leaned back, sighing profoundly. Who would have supposed the old fogy to be so sympathetic, thought Leporello. He must have taken a fancy to me.

'But whether one serves a beaver or a goat, it's the same story. The one does not require your talents, the other does not requite them. The money owed me by Don Juan . . .'

Out of his despondency Don Gil raised his head, his goggling lacklustre carp's gaze. Money was interesting too.

'A great deal?'

'Much more than I care to go without. But now I ask myself, shall I get it out of Don Saturno?'

It would be much better, thought the sacristan, that any money should go to Leporello. If Leporello were paid the irrigation might be forestalled. A landowner does not put his hand into an emptied pocket. A waterless Tenorio Viejo would suit him better, he had no mind to see his captives go sliding away from him along their ditches. And now he dredged up another consideration. The miller's daughter owed him some dues of fear and uneasiness, another hook in that plump cold-blooded victim would not come amiss. He considered awhile.

'What you need is money,' he pronounced.

'Ah?'

'In order to get more. Money calls in money. Has it never occurred to you, my good sir, to look round for a little dowry?'

Celestina. They had talked about her at the washing-place; and listening, he had decided that the other one, the Hernandez, sounded better fun. Then he had seen the mother. Then, hearing on all sides of the dangerous temper of the village, he decided that it would be wiser not to fish in such troubled waters at all, and the thought of marriage had been put away. But now Don Gil, who seemed so shrewd and had taken such a fancy to him (Ah! what a pity that Don Gil had no girl among his grandchildren!), urged Celestina upon him; so Celestina let it be. Certainly, the girl had commendations. A saving disposition, that is a commendation; and a dying father is an even greater commendation.

By now everyone knew that the miller was dying, and

the spirit in which he was meeting his end caused considerable disapproval. 'I paid him a visit,' recounted the widow Sobrino, 'as it were to say a godspeed to purgatory. And what did he speak of? He said his silkworms were dying. How does that strike you, eh? A man at the point of death!—and instead of attending to his salvation he does nothing but grieve over the death of some silkworms.' Her listeners agreed that the miller's avarice was inordinate, even for a miller.

Such a father would make a very advantageous father-in-law, especially if he were a dead one. And walking to the mill Leporello rehearsed the compliments he would pay before the lattice. The night, the sweetness of the air, the bright stars under the young woman's brows. Then one began to fondle the hand a little. It was all quite familiar, as familiar as the order of the mass. A turn to the right, a turn to the left, three paces forward, and the voice flowing in a certain modulation. The hand on the heart, the hand outstretched, a start backward, and the whining sighs of the lover. He had listened to it often enough, he was not likely to have much trouble with the daughter of the miller of Tenorio Viejo.

And yet as he walked on he was traversed by strange feelings of uneasiness and apprehension. It was as though that other wooer, cloaked and scented, were walking beside him, a critical and censorious ghost. He crossed himself once or twice, to be on the safe side. For with such a one as Don Juan there was no telling. He might be yonder, or he might be here.

There was the mill, and there, just as she should be, was the girl. How large her face looked, like the moon in water. The calmness of the night, the sweetness of the air. A melancholy stink rose up from the river mud.

'My poor heart is ground like a grain of wheat between the two stones of your beauty and your hard heart,' he began.

'We grind only rye at our poor mill.'

It was to be one of these repartee courtships, was it?

'But now I bring you wheat.'

The moon-in-water face turned this way and the other.

'I don't see the sack,' she said.

The hand on the heart, the hand outstretched. He thumped his chest.

'Here!'

'Only the donkey.'

It seemed to him that the cloaked and perfumed ghost gave a malicious laugh. Ah, devil take it, this was what it was to be born of low degree! No petticoat, be she countess or kitchen-slut, had ever called Don Juan by the name of donkey. And the pity of it is, he thought, scratching out philosophy from the back of his head, that I have looked on so often at high-born doings that when it comes to my own affairs I am all at a loss. I couldn't get a lady, and I can't get a miller's daughter.

He began again, saying that on such a donkey a girl could ride away from Tenorio Viejo, exchange bare feet for heeled slippers and country mire for the pavements of a city. His rancour gave him eloquence, and as he abused the backwardness of the country the stink of mud seemed to grow stronger, the tattered roof to sag more hopelessly, Dionio's snores to ring out louder and more woebegone.

There he straddled, pacing to and fro like a cock. Well, he would be a husband—if marry she must. But she did not want to marry, in her bedroom she had already all the husband she wanted, tied in a handkerchief and hidden under the boards. To live quietly and gather money: that was the life she wanted, and the life she had in mind. Slow and cold and inarticulate, like some sluggish water her ambition percolated towards the convent. Some day, when she had dowry enough to make her desirable, she would betake herself and her money to that asylum. And there would be the large clean rooms and the smell of beeswax and the sun defeated behind shuttered windows; and there no robbers would come, and no suitors, and no beggars; and there would be no scrubbing and no trudging, for lay-sisters would see to that; but an easy life, and the esteem of the world and the approval of heaven, and money forever amassing and never to lose. But yesterday Don Gil had come, telling her that she must now marry; and here at the window straddled the man.

'Your hand, your little hand.'

The hand drooped from the window. He began to caress it. It was large and cold and impassive. God, what a lumpish young woman! However, she was not difficult, the first threat of shrewishness had quite died down; and Don Gil's recommendations had been emphatic, and though the father's snores sounded most viable everyone concurred in the assurance that he would soon be dead. Meanwhile, here was the hand, smelling like a freshwater fish. Now would such a girl prove intolerably fertile? That too was a question.

If only she had never trusted herself to Don Gil! He had laid out the stolen money well, and paid the interest regularly, and gave her the leather-covered account-book. He seemed a sure friend. But now he threatened her with exposure, saying that he would tell not only her father but all the village how she had helped herself to the money entrusted to her keeping. She did not much dread Dionio's reproaches: him she could soon weep down. But all through Tenorio Viejo there would be talk and mockery, her secrecy would be torn away by those voices; and without secrecy what would become of her joy, and the sweet slow spell that brought penny to penny and pence to crown-pieces? Perhaps, after all, it would be better to marry, if indeed he would take her away as he promised.

'Will you not give me one kind word?'

'Another night, who knows?'

Another night, another night! In such a tone of voice, stockish and inattentive, the words meant nothing. The girl was cold as a fish and probably as slippery. And so she supposed that he was ready to come night after night, to hang about making soft speeches and caressing a hand that smelled like a carp. No, thank you! He had spent too many nights already hanging about under windows, and whether one wooed or watched another's wooing the pain in the calves of one's legs was the same pain. And now the cloaked and perfumed ghost laughed louder and with greater malice, as though to say, *Wait here for the present, Leporello.* Blood of God, the nights he had spent in shrubberies or in draughty doorways, bitten by mosquitoes or shuffling for cold, while some ten feet higher his high-born master was enjoying himself! Suddenly his peevishness caught fire, and with a resolute hallucination that this time the master should wait below while he, the valet, went on to conquer, he began to kiss the hand that smelled of carp, to nibble the fingers and breathe on the palm.

'Oh no, you cannot be so hard-hearted, you cannot speak of another night. It is to-night that I love you and that you are beautiful.'

The hand began to twist and tug.

'Yes, pull with your little hand. I will not let go, you shall pull me up to your window, through the bars and into your bedroom. And there, ah, what a treasure I shall find!'

He knew, then! Don Gil had told him of the knotted handkerchief under the boards. He had come to steal.

'Thieves, robbery! Help, come quickly!'

Her cries roused up the water-birds, their hooting screams joined with hers and one could scarcely tell the one note from the other.

'For God's sake, don't make such a screeching. Are you gone out of your mind?'

'Thie-ieves!'

'*Whee-ee! Whee-ee!*' echoed the birds.

'Let go my hand, you little fool!'

But she clung to it with the grip of hysteria, do as he would he could not wrench it clear of those imbedded nails. And now a door was unbarred and a man came rushing round the side of the house, seized him by the shoulders, shook him and kicked him.

'You leave my girl alone!'

Who would have believed there could be so much strength in a dying father? With a thundering kick Dionio landed him in the river-bed. He picked himself out and ran.

Dionio said no word. Celestina said no word. And by the morrow all knew exactly how Leporello had gone wooing and how the miller had leaped from his death-bed and sent him flying. The news rejoiced the castle kitchen, and rising in the world came to Doña Pilar just as she finished the one hundred and thirty-second pansy, shaded in silver and black. Her upper lip with its silver and black bristles lengthened as she sucked in a smile.

To hear of anyone's misfortunes made a welcome break in this interminable visit, better still that the misfortune should have befallen Leporello. She had disliked him at first sight, she had disliked him more when he entered Don Ottavio's service, now her loathing had reached such a pitch that she refused to consider him one of the Ottavio-Ana household, and thought of him as one of 'that Tenorio lot': thus contriving to hate the castle the more for owning Leporello and Leporello the more for belonging to the castle.

She leaned back, pensively stinging her cheek with little stabs of the needle, thinking at once of Leporello in the mud and of the expanse of satin which lay across her knee. Sixty-seven pansies since the night of the vigil and the morning of Don Ottavio's accident. Sixty-seven grey pansies, and each one of them accomplished in a more hideous state of boredom than the last. Boredom—at any rate, tedium—was her lot, was the colour of the state of life in which it had pleased heaven to deposit her. Even in those early days, slashed with the Commander's fits of temper, the chief of her time was spent in listening, in embroidery, in discretion; and she was quite prepared, after the brief coranto-measure of Doña Ana's love affairs, to settle down to a further spell of discretion, listening, embroidery, and baby-clothes. But implicit in her acceptance of her lot had been the understanding that the boredom should be amid surroundings of which she approved. And she did not approve of Tenorio Viejo. From eating great hunks of goat to listening to Don Saturno: from being supplanted as a physician by the village schoolmaster to finding a wild-cat in the privy, she hated everything about the place, and most of all that there seemed to be no prospect of getting away from it.

As for why they were there, she for one had no illusions. They ate strange meats and listened to blasphemies and were plagued with flies and wild-cats because Doña Ana's infatuation for Don Juan still endured. Because of that infatuation, they had come; and because of that infatuation, as far as she could see, they would remain. The pretext might be Don Ottavio's sprained knee, but the truth was Ana's obsession. And had it not been that throughout the night in the church she had kept obstinately and furiously awake, she would have been ready to believe that Doña Ana, levitated by her passion, had flown through the church window a little before dawn, had entered the castle, got her husband out of bed and tumbled him downstairs, in order to have a reason for staying on. *It is the will of heaven*, Doña Ana had said. It was the will of Doña Ana.

In the village too many grinned about Leporello, with the more pleasure in his mishap since he was known to be a pet of Don Gil's. As for Dionio, it appeared that kicking a suitor must be a cure for the wasting sickness. No one could maintain that Dionio was a dying man who saw his round flat countenance shining with contentment and every now and then puckered with suppressed laughter as the surface of a pond is puckered with flaws of wind. For a whole day he went about whistling, and without a mention of the silkworms. The widow Sobrino's cat was astonished at the vigour with which he shooed it from his bed, and towards sundown his sense of well-being became creative and expressed itself in a plan.

For why, said he, should they waste any more time in debating whether or no Don Juan was dead? Let them take the bull by the horns, let a deputation visit Don Saturno and ask him, civilly but plainly, whether he would carry out his long-standing promise of irrigation. People were so delighted with the kicking bestowed on Leporello that they overlooked the obligation to mistrust a miller; even those who had been most violent against him at the inn now weighed his plan and approved of it. The deputation was chosen—Pedrillo, Esteban, Andres, Diego, Ramon.

'You also, Dionio,' said Diego.

The miller shook his head.

'No, why should he come?' remarked Esteban. 'It is not his affair, he has water already.'

'He has mud, at any rate,' Ramon put in.

Amid the laughter Dionio said gravely,

'If it comes to that, water would benefit me too. You would grow better harvests, more would come to my mill. But I think for the present I will spend my evenings at home.'

The deputation consisted of five. But everyone was deeply interested, and the five were accompanied to the castle by another thirty, giving parting words of good advice or proffering last-moment reminders of points to make and principles to stand firm on. Thus it was that Doña Pilar, her boredom and malevolence a whole day riper, perceived a disorderly crowd approaching; and pointed it out to her companion, Don Isidro.

He was not her companion by choice. She thought him a very dull dog, one of the Commander's more deplorable protégés; and latterly he had been too much her companion. Of all those whom Ana's resolve and Ottavio's indisposition pinned in Tenorio Viejo, Don Isidro suffered the most. He was not only bored, uncomfortable, pained by Don Saturno's conversation; he was embarrassed and in considerable fear. The rumours of an unworthy connection between him and Don Ottavio had reached him, not only by the veiled condolences of Doña Pilar but by the abuse of the outside world. Boys had laughed at him, women had derided him, and on another occasion an old cabbage stump had been thrown. Trembling throughout his great bulk, he moped withindoors, convinced that at any moment an ignorant though moral peasantry might lay hands on him and beat him within an inch of his life. He clung, whenever possible, to Ana; and when Ana discarded him he clung to Doña Pilar; for if there was safety anywhere, it must be in the neighbourhood of a petticoat.

The air was still, the parting words of good advice and good wishes made up a noticeable tumult.

'What fly has stung them?' said Doña Pilar.

She moved towards the balcony.

'I shouldn't show yourself, Doña Pilar. Really I shouldn't, if I were you.'

'They seem very turbulent. And they are certainly coming this way. Holy Virgin, my dear Don Isidro, what horrible countenances they have! They might be wolves and tigers by the look of them.'

'Pray step back a little! Pray do not show yourself! It might provoke them. One never knows.'

'And the women'—continued the lady—'are worse than the men. I have never seen such viragoes. There are a great many women.'

'Misguided animals!' said the chaplain.

'I suppose all peasants are savages—I have never seen any before we came here—but I must say it seems to me that the Tenorio peasants are peculiarly debased. Do you remember that pack we encountered on the road here?'

Don Isidro assented with a hurried sigh.

'Doña Ana remarked then, that (now they seem to be choosing out leaders. One old fellow looks fairly harmless, but the other four!)—remarked that they were more like demons than men. *Profligate boldness* was her phrase, I think. They certainly look bold enough. But I believe they are not profligates. On the contrary, they uphold a very harsh and rigid morality, so I have heard.'

There was a timid crunching behind her. Don Isidro was fortifying himself with a comfit.

'There! The five leaders have actually been let into the house. What on earth are they here for? I must say

I find it a very unpleasant thought that we are under the same roof as those wretches. The other wretches are still waiting outside.'

She slid round a glance of her flat parrot eye on the wretch waiting inside. It was a very pale and damp and melancholy wretch, and its cheeks twitched with a convulsive motion as it urged its barley-sugar from jaw to jaw.

'Fortunately Doña Ana has the courage of an eagle. For I can't believe that our host would be much protection to us, if anything unpleasant should come of this.'

Meanwhile the five were standing before Don Saturno, their set speeches melting from them, discomposed by the conversibility of their foe. Not one of the five but disapproved of him, often to the pitch of hatred. But when it came to talking with him, it was impossible not to feel at one's ease; and the interview of the five and the one, which was to have been a combat, had turned into a conversation amongst six Spanish gentlemen. Diego, the most passionately embattled of them all, was now the most inveigled; for his rage sprang from a peculiar sensibility, he could never have felt such rancour against Don Saturno if he had not an appreciation of all that Don Saturno had and, having, withheld from him: the grace and agility of culture, the vitality of a mind freed from ordinary prejudices. Quivering like a pleased cat he stood listening to the well-modulated voice, the masterly choice of language.

At the mention of irrigation, Don Saturno's face lit up

with perfectly genuine pleasure. Remembering his former enthusiasm for such a project, it seemed to him that now, at last, his tenants had learned to share the same enthusiasm. With a bound he was with them, was leading them on: pointing out advantages they had overlooked, and offering them arguments which they had not thought of.

He fetched out a map he had made, and explained his long-projected scheme. Here the dam, and there the aqueduct; and the crosses that meant wind-pumps and the circles that represented cisterns. It would mean a vast deal of labour; but the advantages. . . . It would be very expensive; but how much better to spend money on irrigation than to throw it away on objects of superstition or fritter it in nondescript expenses.

'At this moment a ridiculous convention obliges me to spend a small fortune in entertaining my town-bred visitors. They arrive with a horde of lackeys and great fat mules—a friary of mules is devouring my stables. They must have this, they must have that—pillows, ice-water, the Lord knows what. If they stay much longer, I shall be eaten bare. You would not believe how they devour me.'

If they found pleasure in him, he no less was enjoying their company. Their sunburned faces bent over the chart, the severe comeliness of their wiry limbs, their melancholy magpie clothes, delighted him like beholding a work of art after walking through a gallery of simpering wax-works. The tang of their speech comforted his ears after so much polite conversation, and it seemed to him that there was more Castilian in one sentence from Pedrillo than in a sackful of Anas and Ottavios. The Spain that he loved, pungent and austere, the Spain he studied in his library among histories, documents, charts, pedigrees, portraits and music-books: it was here in these five men talking about water; it would remain, long after his insipid and expensive puppets had gone back to their town-house.

'We too had visitors from the city, once,' said Esteban. 'My wife's niece and her man. He had been a little unfortunate—they dropped on us without warning—a chalice that he had been re-gilding, and it happened to be mislaid. They brought a little dog with them. A terrible little dog. All these town people are the same. They don't come near us unless the Law has come near to them. But you are fortunate to be spared a dog.'

At the sound of distant laughter Don Isidro said,

'Listen! I hear laughter. It can't be so bad if they are laughing.'

'It depends what they are laughing at,' replied the lady.

She continued to look out of the window.

'Those down there don't laugh. Heavens, how sullen they look! And they stare and stare at the castle windows, as though they were dogs waiting for a bone to be thrown them. Ah, what a lesson against reforming novelties this place can give! These schools, these telescopes, this reading and writing. . . . What's the result? Religion perishes. I don't suppose those creatures down there have any more respect for the sacred calling than I have for a flea.'

'To rob the poor of their religion is to rob them of their only consolation,' sighed Don Isidro.

'How very true! And I would venture to add to that. I would say that to rob the poor of their religion robs them of the only restraint that can keep them from rushing headlong into crime.'

'Do—do you really think so, Doña Pilar?'

'I am convinced of it. This natural morality that Don Saturno and his like are relying on is nothing but a danger to society. Some little act offends them, some trifling incident misleads them. And instead of waiting for Holy Church to deal with it their fine natural morality inflames them and they take the law into their own hands. Hands like those hands down there.'

It was as though she had finished one of her pansies.

She continued to look out of the window, at intervals shaking her head, or making foreboding clicks with her tongue against the roof of her mouth. At every click Don Isidro, gazing at her profile, stiffened himself as though expecting her to say something more; and finding that she did not, relaxed again, like an enormous dark bun taken out of the oven. The murmur of voices below the window rose and fell. A child's voice enquired, 'What are we waiting for?'

'O Mother of God, what's that? What's that behind you, Don Isidro?'

He did not look round to discover what was behind

him. Toppling on all fours he hastened with agility under the table.

'There, there! Oh, how he glares at me! What do you want? Whom are you seeking?'

The table-cover quivered.

'Where have you come from? What do you want? Heaven protect us, it would be better to say what you want than to stand there glaring. Bloody, too. Ah! He's coming nearer. He's looking for something, his eyes roll. Heavens, how he scowls and bites his lips! Oh! Oh! The Virgin save us! . . .'

'He's gone,' added Doña Pilar in a voice dramatically flat and dumbfoundered. And she sank back on a chair and breathed hard.

After a while the table-cover stirred, and a cautious face, draped in yellow velvet, looked out. Instantly Doña Pilar passed into a fit of hysterics, and the face withdrew.

The hysterics continued until several maid-servants had come hurrying; until Don Ottavio, leaning on Doña Ana, had appeared; until Luis had fetched Don Saturno. By this time the chaplain, though still on his knees, was disencumbered of most of the table-cloth, and only seemed to be praying in an attitude of unusual reticence.

Doña Pilar, thrusting away a handful of burning feathers, choked one or twice, and recovered the power of speech.

'An apparition,' she said. 'I have seen a ghost. Don Isidro saw it too.'

There was a general stir, a flutter of hands signing

themselves with the cross. Don Ottavio turned pale, Don Saturno asked what kind of a ghost it had been, in a tone suggesting that ghosts of all kinds might be expected; at which Don Ottavio turned paler. Doña Pilar shuddered, and gestured towards Don Isidro.

'I can scarcely speak of it—Don Isidro—ask him.'

'A terrible ghost! Indescribable! A fleshless spectre. . . .'

'It entered by the door, but yet the door did not open. . . .'

'It seemed to glide through the door,' explained Don Isidro.

'It stood there, frowning and rolling its eyes. . . .'

'Yes, how they rolled! Supernaturally.'

'It wrung its hands and ground its teeth. . . .'

'It would be truer to say tusks,' corrected Don Isidro.

'Very white teeth. Not one missing. I saw them clearly.'

'Deadly white.'

'Its features were contorted, it seemed to be in a frenzy of anxiety. . . .'

'Blood dripping from its hands. . . .'

'It glared round the room as though in search of something. It came towards us as though to threaten us. . . .'

'Dressed all in white and dragging a chain,' cried the chaplain.

'Don Isidro, upheld by the courage of faith, confronted it and made the sign of the cross. And in the flash of an eye it vanished.'

'With a yell,' added Don Isidro.

Don Saturno, raising his voice above the comments and exclamations, enquired what the ghost was like, its sex, age and appearance. Doña Pilar, corroborated by Don Isidro, described the ghost in detail. She gave a remarkably accurate description of Don Juan.

The delegation was still examining the map when Don Saturno re-entered. He had no doubt that they were already perfectly conversant with what had occurred. But just as good manners would forbid them to show they knew, good manners must forbid him from showing that he knew they knew. The conversation was resumed where Luis's summons had interrupted it, and continued as though it had not been suspended for half an hour.

He was very glad to be amongst them again, their company shielded him from the unpleasant necessity of coming to grips with the ghost, or rather, since he did not believe in ghosts, with the ghost's consequences. Any previous ghosts—there had been half a dozen or so—had been dealt with by Doña Isabel as part of the household administration. There were exorcisms, or fumigations, or some such measures; and while the process was going on he went out for a ride if it were fine; and if it were wet, sat in his library. But now, he supposed, the laying of ghosts would become his responsibility, unless he could shoulder it off on Luis.

He did not believe in ghosts. But his theory of the universe had sometimes dallied a little with the notion that those alive, and most of all, those in the act of dying, might project an appearance of themselves. He wished most heartily that he had never allowed his theory of the universe so much latitude. But what was done was done, he could not now call back that straying fancy, having contemplated the possibility of such apparitions in general he must contemplate it in particular. And though Doña Pilar's story did not seem to him an assurance that Juan was dead, nevertheless it made him seem less living. But that is a common delusion of the mind, he said to himself, continuing the mental argument while Pedrillo described a fall of red snow that had taken place forty winters earlier: if one sees a man escape death, even though he comes out of the peril unharmed, for some hours at least one's mind refuses to accept him as being ordinarily alive; he may seem more alive for it or less; but his existence is qualified by what has passed.

'And what proved that the red in the snow was blood,' concluded Pedrillo, 'was the way the vines flourished the next summer. For everyone knows that blood makes a fine manure.'

'Suppose the vines had done badly?' said Andres.

'Well—there would have been some reason for it,' said the old man.

'Nothing happens without reason,' added Esteban.

What a history one could compile out of the memories of old men like Pedrillo! There, in the village, stored in smoky hovels, or at the inn, at the well, among the vineyards and the olive-yards, are the real archives of Tenorio. Here, in my chronicle-chest, I have only the faded old clothes of my ancestors; down there, in the memory of the people, their flesh and blood is preserved; the way they looked, the very manner of their speech, their whims and passions; my great-grandfather's limp, and the mole on the neck of my great-great-grandmother. Suddenly the realisation of what it would be to die without an heir swept over him. He began to tremble, his lower lip drooped, and he raised his hand to hide it.

At this moment Diego happened to look up. He had been examining a Venice glass, which he had taken off the table to admire more closely. It slid from his hold and smashed on the floor.. Without attention to this he exclaimed,

'We have no right to stay so long, fatiguing our host. In the pleasure of conversation we forget that Don Saturno has many cares; and he is too hospitable to remind us.'

Slightly bewildered, the rest began to say their thanks and take leave. Now that their hands were removed from it the map briskly rolled itself up.

'I beg you to stay,' said Don Saturno. It was the conventional politeness, but it sounded like an appeal. 'And if I have seemed inattentive, pray forgive me. My mind has been a little distracted, I must admit. Some silly people say they have seen a ghost'

—Andres gave a sympathetically judicial snort—

'the ghost of my son. All nonsense, of course. But for the moment these things distract one from oneself. There have been rumours, too—doubtless you have heard them?'

'We have heard of them,' said Ramon.

His eyes searched their faces.

'Who knows?' he said. 'But I have been a long while without news of him. Perhaps—perhaps he is dead.'

'We can feel for you,' said Pedrillo, coming forward as spokesman. 'We too—each man of us here—have lost child or children. For a child to die before the father is not natural. Yet it is the way of the world, though turned topsy-turvy.'

'If he is dead,' Andres added, 'we shall consider the water as his monument.'

In a sense the remark was timely. As Andres afterwards explained, the last blow fastens the nail, and without some such reminder the old whirligig would have been left thinking they had gone there merely to condole with him. Perhaps it might have been better expressed; but no one cared to argue with the speaker. They went out, and met those awaiting them; and like all delegations felt they had done pretty well until the comments of those they had represented made them feel they had done pretty badly. The news of the ghost, however, was well received.

'For a damned soul more or less up at the castle,' said Maria Hernandez to Maria Perez, 'won't make much odds. And if he's damned, he's dead. That's all we need care about.'

'I would rather see the water,' said Maria Perez.

On the next day the dawn-wind, snuffling in the mountain, did not subside with the rising of the sun. It grew stronger, it drove into the valley, a parching wind thick with dust. When the men set out for work the wind blew grit between their teeth. By mid-day half the olive crop had fallen.

In the village the doors and windows were barricaded against the dust. The goats had to be fetched in, the air rang with their angry bleating, they drummed with their forefeet and butted and fought each other. Every now and then some woman would recollect something left out of doors—a faggot of beans left drying or a bunch of maize—and would tear out, her head muffled in a cloth. Tiles blew off, the vine on the tanner's house was ripped away and trailed on the ground. The wind howled like a pig-killing, the clouds of dust rode over the landscape. As time went on there was nothing to do but sit still and listen to the wind.

No children went to school. Don Francisco sat alone in the Moor's House, staring through an arrow-slit window in the two-foot stone wall: a panelled view that showed him the hind-quarters of the church, a huddle of roofs, and beyond them the shifting fish-belly white of the blown olive-trees, and the profile of the mountain. This would be the end of the olives; and there was talk of a mildew on the vines. On the other hand, Don Saturno had promised water—for what his promise was worth. He sat weighing the possibilities of that riot Don Gil was so sure of, and whether misery, or the habit of misery, would prevail. Which would he prefer? Riot might endanger him, but it would break the endless boredom of his days. And if there were a riot, it would be put down, and that would make the people civiler. On the whole he hoped for a riot.

He had not gone to the castle again. He had not been invited. Now they had the ghost of Don Juan there, so he heard. They were welcome to it.

At the presbytery Don Tomas lay gasping for breath, and in the kitchen Doña Adriana limewashed the walls, singing an interminable ballad with a howling octave-leap at the end of each verse.

In the oak-woods the swineherds had driven the little pigs into the pound, which was called the Hermitage of the Angels. The old animals, frantic with the wind, tore squealing through the woods, the falling acorns pelting against their hides like stones from a sling. The gnarled boughs grew so low that they were like rafters, they creaked and swayed, looking pale in the dusky air. The dust sifted down through the leafage, troops of withered leaves volleyed past as though bent on the assault of some invisible castle. Sheltering against the masonry the men sat talking in low voices, their hoods pulled forward over their heads. They were arguing about robbers, whether robbers would do better in prosperous times, when travellers were richer, or in the lean times when travellers were less well-armed. And Jesus told the story of the Chapel of the Good Thief, a fine and large building, and fitted up more magnificently than any cathedral in Spain; but so well hidden in the Guadarrama mountains that no one knew of it but the robbers themselves. A priest served it, and when he died another was kidnapped and brought there blindfold. But they are so well fed, said Jesus, and so much delighted with the magnificence of their church, that they make no attempt to get away. And to this chapel come robbers from all over Spain when they feel the hour of their death nearing them; those who can ride, ride, and those past riding are brought on litters; so that they can receive absolution and get a good burial in the parish of the Good Thief. But only robbers are buried there. The dead priests are carried off and their bodies thrown down a precipice, for a priest can get to heaven anyhow, one need feel no responsibility for him.

The boy Enrique looked up in his face and said,

'I did not think you felt so well disposed towards priests.'

'I have no objection to a robbers' priest,' said Jesus. 'He does his duty and robs no one. His heart is full of goodwill.'

'Aye, but is it so?' said another of the swineherds. 'For he is carried off willy-nilly to his parish in the

Guadarramas, and his heart may be heavy with hatred against the robbers and against his duty.'

'He will come to love it and them,' answered Jesus. 'To keep good company is to learn good manners. And the beauty of the church is a wedding-gown to him.'

'That is true,' murmured the questioner. 'Beauty persuades one to peace—if it is not fastened on a woman.'

'But if the robbers only come there to die, there must be times when he is left all alone? And left alone it might come to his mind to escape.'

'They cast lots'—Jesus smiled—'every month, as to who shall remain with him and sing in the choir.'

'Suppose the King's officers should find this Chapel,' said Enrique. 'What then?'

'Another would be built. Be sure of that.'

A man who had been listening now joined in.

'For all that, unless one is of the nobility of thieves, a robber's life is painful enough. To be out in all weathers, night after night to watch with an empty stomach on the mountain, to have the chief part of the world against one—there is not much difference, that I can see, between being a poor robber and being a poor man.'

'I can hear a horse on the road,' said Enrique.

'One of them, maybe. Well, if he comes, he will get a poor reception from us.'

They listened.

'I can hear nothing.'

'Nothing. Only the wind and the trees and the swine. From talking of robbers he goes on to hearing them.'

The boy shook his head, unconvinced.

'I heard a horse on the road.'

He ran off, they saw him stand at the opening of the wood, peering out. He came back blinking, his eyes reddened with staring against the wind.

'What did you see?'

'Only the dust and the wind.'

Teresa Mauleon sat down to spin. 'Because you can't work out of doors is no reason to idle withindoors,' said Don Gil. 'Your children cost a fortune to feed, I must pay for their education too, since schooling is so much the fashion. They will learn nothing but evil, but I suppose you do not wish them to be behindhand in wickedness. It is a pity you are not with the other baggage-wagon wives. My house would be the cleaner and my purse the fuller. But since my poor boy dumped you here—I do not wonder at it—the least you can do is to bestir yourself a little. Perhaps at this moment he lies dying on some battlefield, wishing he had made a better match, I dare say. You had best accustom yourself to the thought of being a widow with a pack of children to support. If you are not a widow, you will probably be the next thing to it. A soldier in the King's service wants something brisker than a mother-of-sorrows with a backache. And I shall not be able to keep you much longer, make up your mind to that.'

Though the shutters were closed and cloths hung across the windows the dust blew in and clung to the thread. It broke continually. Tears ran from her eyes, partly because she had been scolded again, partly because her eyes were weak, and the grit had inflamed them. She thumped the treadle with an aching foot, and the wheel went round unsteadily, and in her mind was the thought of an eternity of torment. For Don Juan's ghost had come, the strange woman's chaplain had seen it. It had wrung its hands and yelled when the sign of the cross had dismissed it from a minute of respite back to the pains of hell once more. What had Don Tomas said that morning when he came out from behind the artichokes?

'Suppose he has been in hell and come back again? *To tell us?*'

The wheel went round. The thread snapped, but was reknit again. In hell the limbs of sinners are broken and mended, broken and mended. Men and women lie pell-mell together, naked as in the marriage-bed. There is promise of water, but no water. There is no light and yet they see the new torments approaching, and the stony looks of the devils standing by. The tears dried on her cheeks as she sat spinning, and thinking of hell. In hell, too, as in heaven, the tears are dried. For all the anguish, for all the despair, no tears can break out over the burning eyeballs. Now Don Juan had come back from damnation to tell of it. She could not put out of her mind the look Don Tomas had as he bent over her in the garden, like some terrible Jesus come out of the sepulchre. He too feared hell; but feared it as one fears the bull that has got one down and drives against one, feared it as a woman fears the first thrust of the labour-pains, feared it as one fears the thing which one has no power to turn aside. And if indeed Don Tomas had no power against hell, what hope for those who depended on him?

The dust was blown into the castle. But Doña Pilar scarcely troubled to brush it away, thinking how soon she would shake off dust and castle together. Her trick had done it; and now they were all seething together as in an alembic, and by to-morrow the elixir would be brewed. For now there was no fear that Don Isidro would go back on her. She had him doubly sure. By talking so much about the ghost he had talked himself into a terror of it; and seeing that every word hastened a departure from a place where the peasantry was so savage, so moral, and so misunderstanding, he talked of nothing else. Meanwhile Don Ottavio dared not be parted from Don Isidro, in case the ghost should appear again, and no one be there to exorcise it. What with rosaries and ghost-stories the two chattered incessantly, and with every word inflamed each other more. There was no crevice in their conversation wherein Doña Ana might slide in a spiritual or a practical dissuasion. She had tried both, saying that for her part trust in God seemed to her all the comfort one needed against ghosts; and again, on a new tack, seeing a very threatening appearance about Don Ottavio's knee. But she could neither blackmail her chaplain into courage nor her husband into a fright. This morning, with the coming of the storm, she had assailed Don Ottavio from another quarter. Worn out with watching, stifled with dust, she had a heart-attack, and fainted. But Don

Ottavio, full of solicitude, declared even more emphatically his intention of leaving the very instant the wind slackened, he loved her too much to expose her any longer to the dangers of Tenorio Viejo. Suppose she should be taken ill there, in a house full of ghosts and without a physician? No, no! Let the mules be got ready, the trunks packed. Her safety was more to him than life itself, even at the risk of inflaming his injured knee they must set out as soon as possible. And actually the knee was much better. See, he could get out of bed unaided, and walk about.

Even Don Saturno had fallen into Doña Pilar's alembic, and was plainly doing all he could to get rid of them. The ghost, reverberating through the castle, had caused a violent outburst of feeling between the servants of the household and the servants of the visitors. Doña Ana's waiting-women, Don Ottavio's valet, their coachmen and footmen, received the ghost as the crowning outrage of a period of outraged sensibilities. Their resentment was only equalled by their terror, and if plague had broken out in the castle they could not have been more anxious to get away. Their fears and their airs provoked the castle people into a braggadocio of insensibility to spectres. To prove how little a ghost meant to them they belaboured the visiting retinue with stories of innumerable ghosts, each more frightful than the last, but nothing to them, since these ghosts had haunted the castle from time immemorial, a blazon of the antiquity of the family, and were looked on more in the light of family friends by the family's retainers. What, were there no ghosts in the family of San Bolso, in the family of Quebrada de Roxas, not a headless man nor a nun of gigantic size among them? How paltry! How deplorable! There could be little credit or satisfaction in serving such ungarnished families. Well, well! Where the herb grows there is an ass to eat it.

These pedigree aspersions had the most satisfactory results in enraging the visitors. But loyal imaginations, recalling all the ghosts of tradition and inventing others, rebounded on themselves; and after a few hours of this contest the castle household had talked itself into seeing and believing, so that the shrieks of Luisa Pintada were answered by the shrieks of Luisa Perez, and the uproar of injurious genealogies in the kitchen broken by a crash and a petrified silence when the cook saw a white lady hovering in the buttery.

If Doña Isabel, so capable with apparitions, had been alive—but she was dead, she might at any moment become an apparition herself. And the only hope, thought Don Saturno, is to get rid of them as soon as possible. Accordingly he congratulated Don Ottavio's knee with inhospitable fervour, saying briskly,

'Well, now I fear I shall scarcely keep you after tomorrow. But my loss is your gain. And I am sincerely delighted to see you moving about once more, even though I know it means you will soon be moving on.'

The sound of a household run mad penetrated even into his library, where he shut himself up to think about the irrigation, and how it should be paid for. On a happier day the pleasure of adding new touches to the project would have been enough to occupy him; to-day, with everything going so unpleasantly, the thought of the cost kept edging its way into his mind. Would it be sufficient to sell more pigs? Or must he raise another loan?

The property was encumbered with mortgages, old and recent borrowings. To pay for the building of the church his great-great-grandfather had pledged his wife's dowry—a valuable stretch of salt-land near Cadiz. This was one of the few pieces of family property that had brought in a steady income. Once or twice it had been near redemption, some accident had always estranged it again, but the interest on the loan was kept up. Another mortgage commemorated his great-grandfather's career in the embassy to Paris, and a third—comparatively a small one—the passion of a great-uncle for collecting tulips and monkeys. During his own minority his mother—disgusted perhaps by this monotony of mortgages—had paid for his education by selling some of the olive-yards of Tenorio outright to a nunnery in Avila. In a fury he had bought the land back; but at a price so far above the sale that the only way to recoup was to let out the land piecemeal. His tenants paid pretty well; and he had the pleasure of thinking that he was rearing a sturdy peasantry, each with his own holding; but it was irksome to look out on those stretches of hillside and think how much better the yield could be if they were properly worked by up-to-date methods. His wife had brought a fine estate of corn-land in La Mancha and some river-dues on the

Ebro. But the river-dues had gone with the expenses of her death from an inherited skin-disease, and part of the corn-land in La Mancha was involved in that same transaction which presented him with Don Francisco—a bad bargain, as things turned out; but it was too late to change. Meanwhile he had been improving his pigs; partly as a national gesture: pigs were, he said, the most useful Catholics in Spain, a guarantee of orthodoxy and the support of letters, since the poorest scholar can afford a sausage; partly because his pigs and his oak-woods were about the only part of the property still entirely his own. They roamed through the oak-woods and over the plateau, where they picked up a few vipers to improve their flavour; they increased up to the fullest expectation of swine; and if he could have cured them on the estate they would have been even more of a profit. But there ignorant fashion stepped in, and it paid better to sell live pigs half-yearly to a dealer in Extremadura, where they were given a final fattening, killed, cured, and sold as Montanchez pork.

A further contract for pigs . . . in a way it would be a pity; at present the equilibrium between the size of the herd and the resources of their feeding-ground was so well adjusted. As other landowners like to think that their woods are full of dryads Don Saturno liked to think that his woods were full of pigs, and it would be a sad day when the chorus of grunts and screams sank to a semichorus. But nature is bountiful, and the depletion would in time be made up; whereas acres of corn-land do not breed more acres. The territory in La Mancha gave him no pleasure. The money came from it, true, but with the money came incessant complaints, and the regular threats of the bailiff saying that it would soon be impossible to collect the revenue, that one cannot wring blood from a stone, that only by his exceptional devotion and industry, etc. Don Saturno had long been convinced that everything was going wrong, that the bailiff swindled him; and decided often enough to go there to see for himself and to set things right; but the thought of the bailiff as often deterred him, there is something peculiarly repugnant to a magnanimous character in the prospect of confronting a person who has been steadily defrauding him. Moreover, the land having got into such a bad state, who would buy it, except a religious community? Only religious communities have enough capital to improve bad land; and he would not sell to a religious community. A mortgage? The same objections applied, and the estate was overburdened with mortgages.

His heart altered its rate, a sickness swept over him. He remembered again, and acutely, that he was an heirless man, that there was no one to come after him except a wretched second cousin in the female line, a dreary corpulent fellow whose only interest lay in the taking of clysters. Whether he sold or mortgaged, it was all one.

A second realisation followed, as bitter as the first. Though Juan were alive, mortgages or sales, pigs or water would alike mean nothing to him. He was as much immured in profligacy as in a cloister, a vocation as irrevocable as the vocation of a St. John of the Cross fastened him to the card-table and the alcove. Father and son, for years they had had nothing in common. Only for a few months had their relationship any validity, a twelvemonths perhaps during which the boy had been inseparable from him, looking through a telescope, arguing about freewill, reading Lucian, learning to reason, to question, to discriminate. But for all that came of it, this twelvemonth of intellectual enfranchisement might as well have been spent in the Religious Exercises of Loyola; for out of the brilliant adolescent crystallised the man enslaved to a vocation, climbing patiently from one conquest to another, treading the narrow path to the position of General of the Company of Libertines.

A careerist—and worse, a willy-nilly careerist. And bound as inevitably for the cloud-cuckoo-land of hell as the Saint for the cloud-cuckoo-land of heaven; and, like the Saint, appearing after his death. Ah, there was a condemning summary! If I could tell Juan that immediately after his death he had appeared to a priest and an old lady, that might bring home to him the fruits of an excessive devotion. But it would not, he answered himself. Death is not more deaf to argument than vocation.

Ah, what an odious day! He would be glad when it was ended. By to-morrow the thought of Juan's death would be less physical, less like something going wrong with his own process of vitality. By to-morrow, too, the wind would have fallen, and he would be nearer getting these visitors out of the house. Then he would be able to give his mind to the irrigation, to finding a better schoolmaster, even to the La Mancha estate. He would get rid of that bailiff and introduce some modern methods. With no one to save for he could spend the rest of his money and the rest of his days in accordance with the ideas he had ripened through a lifetime.

And by to-morrow, he thought, taking his place at the card-table, you may all be gone. And instead of sitting here, striving against boredom and sleepiness I shall either be usefully busy with the water-map or perhaps lying in bed with a book and some chocolate; and a smile came to his lips as he remembered the last time he had ordered his chocolate to be brought to him in bed and how, sans chocolate, his dressing-gown about him, he had stood at the stair-head directing the succour of Don Ottavio. But to-night the card-table was set in the library instead of by Don Ottavio's bedside; for Don Ottavio's knee was mending with such rapidity that he was able to walk up and downstairs with ease.

And you will take Leporello with you, he thought, listening to the noise of the wind. The wind was certainly falling. Though at that moment he recollected Leporello's account-book, still lying on his table, the recollection went by without disquieting him, an appurtenance only of Leporello's departure. He had been very unobtrusive since that misadventure with Dionio's daughter. Earlier in the visit that pompous idiot, Don Ottavio, had explained to him the reason for taking Leporello into service. Leporello was the last person to behold Doña Ana's father. The last person tobehold my son, too, he thought; but he felt no inclination to challenge Doña Ana's claims to him.

And though you are not, I suppose, by long odds the last woman to have been in my son's arms, his thoughts continued, while the game of hombre pursued its stately carnage of this card trumped and that, yet you were probably among the last half-dozen; but even if you had been the last, I should not want to keep you here. He looked at her across the table. To-night for some reason she seemed rather subdued. Undoubtedly she was a very beautiful woman; and the cloud on her spirits this evening was no cloud on her loveliness, indeed it was even an embellishment, it made her more credible, less like a triumphant and exemplary demonstration. But for all your beauty, and that spiritual arrogance that moves under your good manners, your adventure, I take it, is over. You are married to a stupendously foolish husband, a man whose tediousness is such a bread and water diet that it would dispirit any woman into virtue, a man whose stupidity, even if you cuckolded him, would rob the act of any reality, for one cannot balance a pair of horns upon a perfectly empty head; and so you will be faithful to him, though really it is my son you will be faithful to. Time will woo you from that faithfulness, on your thirtieth birthday, perhaps, eating a sweetmeat or dipping your fingers in the holy water, you will ultimately horn poor Juan; and on your fortieth birthday you will be looking like Doña Pilar, that stiff and shapeless pillar of society.

She hesitated, frowning over her cards, her face doubtful and deeply absorbed. The card she played was so incompetent that it seemed she must have put it down by mistake. Don Ottavio trumped it, uttering a chivalrous word of condolence. I will not be a loser to Don Ottavio and Doña Pilar, he thought; and presently, taking Doña Pilar's card, there was a stir of discourteous malice in his voice.

'Matador.'

He glanced at her. Her mouth hung open, her eyes were bolting out of her head. In a voice stifled and whistling, as though her windpipe had been cut, she squeaked out,

'He's there!'

For she sat facing the door; and so she had been the first person to see the door open, and Don Juan walk in.

Don Ottavio looked over his shoulder. After one glance he turned pale, shut his eyes resolutely, and began crossing himself with a trembling hand. The behaviour of Don Isidro was even more emphatic. He had seen the newcomer at the moment that Doña Pilar did, and like her, had exclaimed. But his exclamation was a howl, and his first movement was to glance round for a hiding-place. No hiding-place presented itself, and so on a new impulse he shook his fist in Doña Pilar's face, and cried out,

'It's all your fault! It's your doing entirely, I will take no responsibility, I tell you. Blaspheming hag, what have you done now?'

He fell on his knees between the two women, his face peering over the card-table, his fist swaying under Doña Pilar's nose. Only Doña Ana, after one swift glance towards the door, sat calm and motionless, her cards in a steady hand, her gaze fixed on them as though she would read her fortune there.

Don Juan surveyed them from the door. He seemed a schoolmaster, entering on a noisy classroom, he beheld them with a look of weariness, malevolence and distaste.

'I think you know our guests,' said his father.

'Oh, yes?' The tone implied a contemptuous uncertainty.

'If they seem surprised to see you, it is quite natural. They were under the impression that you were dead.'

Don Juan remarked that it was very kind of them.

Doña Ana got up. She stood with her back to Don Ottavio's chair, as though to defend him, as though to conceal him. They exchanged a formal bow and curtsey. Ottavio sat on. But he had ceased to cross himself, and now his pallor changed to a furious sullen scarlet. When at last he rose it was to bow hastily and clumsily and to sit down again.

'My knee's getting stiff again, Doña Ana,' he said. 'But I shall be able to travel to-morrow for all that.'

'Are you all leaving to-morrow?' enquired Don Juan. 'I should be sorry to think I had scared you away.'

He advanced towards the group, began looking at the cards on the table.

'Hombre. A favourite game of my father's, my grandfather's, my great-great-grandfather's. Doña Pilar, if you will allow me to say so, you have kept your heart too long. It is no good to you now.'

He began to look through the cards, to criticise the play. The candlelight showed him travel-stained, his eyes reddened with dust, a flush of fatigue on his face. And Don Isidro, thinking that a traveller from hell might look just so, crossed himself warily.

When he had set their play to rights, and remarked that the candles needed snuffing, and that the snuffers needed cleaning, he leaned back, silent, balefully attentive, a schoolmaster.

Don Saturno began to fidget his way to the door.

'Where are you going?'

'To find old Luis.'

'Is he so old you must go in search of him?'

'It is better,' replied the father, 'I want to tell him that you are here; and that he is to tell the household that . . .'

'That I am not dead. Exactly. Well, tell them to express their rapture quietly. I don't want to be swarmed over by a rejoicing population.'

'I expect they will take it quite quietly.' He was not ashamed at speaking bitterly; but a sense of hospitality made him add,

'And I will tell him to take good care of your horse.'

'He must go up the mountain, then. The jade was frightened by some pigs, bolting across the road. It lost its footing, and came down. So I left it there, and walked the rest of the way. An agreeable ramble, half choked with dust and through this pleasing Arcadia of yours.'

'I have an heir again,' thought Don Saturno, and went slowly from the room to announce the fact. Don Juan turned to the rest of the class.

'There are more encouraging places than Tenorio Viejo in which to rise from the dead. And that makes me the more obliged to you all for making up this unexpected little party to receive me. Have you been here long?'

'We came in May,' said Don Ottavio. 'We leave tomorrow.'

Don Juan looked at him, and looked at his sword, and smiled.

'Or the next day,' said Doña Ana. 'My husband has injured his knee, I am really not sure if he should travel so soon. At any rate, let us leave any decisions till tomorrow.'

The words, and still more the tone in which she said *My husband*, reinforced Don Ottavio's self-esteem. She does not want me to fight, he thought. She loves me. How gracefully she manages things. And certainly I cannot fight until my knee is well. There will be plenty of opportunities later, and meanwhile let poor Ana be spared any such prospect. And with stern civility he acknowledged Don Juan's good wishes for the knee.

'I cannot help taking a certain posthumous interest in myself,' said Don Juan. 'Do tell me how you heard I was dead.'

There was a pause. 'We heard it from Leporello,' said Doña Pilar. And added, remembering that remark about her heart, 'He told us you had been carried off by devils.'

'Ah, Leporello! And I suppose I have him to thank for the ghost I heard them chattering about downstairs? Who has seen my ghost? Have you, Doña Ana?'

'No,' she said, smiling a little.

'Have you, Don Ottavio? Have you, Doña Pilar? No? Your face belies you. I can see that you saw my ghost. What did I look like?'

'Grimy,' she said, looking at him steadfastly, 'and in rags.'

'How discourteous of my ghost to appear to a lady in undress!'

Doña Pilar bounced in anger, and again Doña Ana smiled.

Don Saturno had come in again. He stood listening, a prey to hospitality. Now he said,

'Doña Pilar has told you about your ghost. Now will you not, in return, tell us something about the living Juan?'

The schoolmaster manner returned as Don Juan said,

'Trifling apart, surely one death in the family is enough. Tell me about Aunt Isabel.'

He thought to himself, It is something serious. He needs me, he needs my advice. How unfortunate that he

should find these people here, and all this nonsense about ghosts. But when they have gone to bed, Juan will speak. Underneath ran the thought: It's money he wants.

But when Don Ottavio offered Doña Ana his hand to lead her to bed, Juan got up also, yawned, and declared himself dying for sleep. And no sooner were they gone than Luis appeared with a long story about how the wind had confused the castle's economy, in especial upsetting the coop in which the cook had penned up two cockerels to fatten. The coop had broken open, the cockerels had flown, and now there would be nothing for the soup. The roof of the stables, too, was damaged, and rats had got into the visitor's coach and eaten a nest in the cushions. It was an hour before Don Saturno could escape.

'You look heartily tired,' said Carlos. 'Shall I make you some chocolate?'

'No, no! The chocolate is for to-morrow night, when I can drink it in peace.'

But in his bedroom it seemed to him that the chocolate would have been very welcome; for he felt chilly, discouraged, in need of comfort, and with a hot drink inside him it would have been easier to stand knocking at his son's door. There was no answer. At last he went in. Juan was asleep.

He lay sleeping as though he had riveted himself in a casket of slumber, as though his last waking thought had been to defy any power on earth to rouse him. His fists were clenched, his teeth were set, he drew his breath slowly and contemptuously, as though he scorned the trouble of breathing. He looked profoundly old, and profoundly evil.

There was something so insulting in this slumber that the old man, sitting down by the bedside, did not look again. Though the sleeper turned about and moaned, he remained staring at the floor; and even when Juan woke, and cursed at the light, and asked what he wanted there, he delayed a little before looking at him.

'Yah-ow! Eee—yah-ow! Well, now I suppose you want to talk. Well, I want to talk too. Why in the devil's name have you got these people here?'

'They came to tell me you were damned. I was surprised, but concluded they meant it as a civility. Then Doña Ana prayed all night and Don Ottavio fell downstairs and hurt his knee. And they have been here ever since. It is difficult to dislodge a young lady with a one-legged husband.'

'And how did Leporello get here?'

'He came with them. They have taken him into their household.'

'What? Do you mean to say he has gone over to them?' He sat up in bed with a look that boded ill for Leporello. Don Saturno went on as rapidly as he might.

'It seems that Doña Ana wished it. According to Leporello's story, which she believed, Leporello was the last person to see her father. How she will feel about it now, though, is another matter. She is a remarkable young woman. But rather too visionary for my liking.'

'Visionary? As visionary as a money-lender!'

For the first time that evening his voice was genuine, the voice not of a schoolmaster but of a man smarting under a grievance.

'Malicious, cold-blooded, cunning! The woman's a monster! Listen, and then tell me if she's a visionary. Do you know what she did? She made me a laughing-stock. Me!'

He sat leaning on his elbow, his eyes burning, the words jolted from him like life-blood.

'I ask myself why I ever went after the shrew. Other men had more sense, no one would look at her, for all her face and her fortune, only that nincompoop Don Ottavio, and he only because the old man had bought him. *She was betrothed to Don Ottavio.* God, the times she told me that, mincing out the words like a lemon-ice. *Don Ottavio, one of His Majesty's officers. . . .* As much as to say, *Such epaulettes strike terror.* If I should look at her she would be at my side with her prate of Don Ottavio. What was I to do? Submit to this teasing, or take up the challenge? So I set about her, rolled my eyes, panted for breath, paid for serenades. *O you dreadful man, do you not know I am betrothed to Don Ottavio?* I'll send you to Don Ottavio with a dowry, I thought. And one fine evening, when she had told me she would be in the garden thinking of Don Ottavio, I presented myself. She was very happy shrieking in my arms, but unfortunately she shrieked too loud, and out stalked the Commander. My father, I beg you will never draw your sword in defence of my virtue. No doubt you were an admirable swordsman in your day, but things move faster now. That's what the Commander found out while he was brandishing his *bottes de Jésuite*. The old fool!

'But I was the worse fool,' he added. 'I killed the father and raised up a fury. There she stood vowing revenge. Revenge! The truth was she could not forgive me for attending to her father instead of settling her business.'

Don Saturno took snuff. The last words embarrassed him. But at the same time he was enthralled by a narrative so different in manner and matter from the conversation he had been enduring from his guests, and by the unprecedented flattery of his son's confidence.

'If I had had a grain of sense, I should have left Seville there and then. But how could I? And have it said that I had run away from Ottavio? Instead, I remained to be persecuted.

'Persecuted!' he repeated, raising his voice. 'Pestered, harried, goaded, teased, pricked and jabbed like a bull that won't fight, tormented and plotted against and held up to ridicule. And all by that woman. God, what malice, what brazen unwomanly effrontery! There is nothing so shameless as a virtuous woman. She was so modest, wasn't she? She could scarcely speak in public without lisping and looking round for her duena. She was so chaste, such an icicle! She would find something to blush at in the hymns to the Virgin, if she saw a bedpost she would hang her head and fidget. What did she do, this Calista? Off she went, fast as a she-cat, and hunted out an old whore of mine. And Doña Ana and Doña Elvira and Don Ottavio hung themselves with black and put on masks, and wherever I went, wherever I turned, this junta dogged my steps, squeaking out threats and reproaches. It made my life a hell. It was so notorious that every beggar and old woman in Seville knew of it, and the comedians joked about it in the theatres.

'I heard the people in the streets laughing at me!' he exclaimed. 'Well, since they made it impossible for me to go into good society, I thought I would distract myself with a little low life. For I was going out of my mind with mortification, I could not sleep, my nerves were in fiddlestrings, I needed a woman as I had never needed a woman before. I found a silly little chit with her head on one side and one pair of cotton stockings. And by the grace of God, she did not laugh at me. Ah! For a moment I could have loved her for that. I thought I was safe, I thought I'd got her, she was mine, when they ran me down, my three black tormentors. Doña Ana preached the sermon, the other two sang the responses. And after that Zerlina was added to the junta.'

'My poor boy,' said the father.

'And then *you* began to take a hand in tormenting me!' said the son.

'I?'

'You! You who chose out for me a mother with the scrofula. My hands, my face, my feet began to burn, and were covered with swellings and blotches. Nothing would cure it, not medicines and not ointments. Sometimes it would vanish and then it came back. The pain was intolerable, it was all I could do not to tear the flesh off my bones. The pain was intolerable, and the shame was worse. I had been made a laughing-stock, now I was to be a leper. I, Don Juan. You can think how I blessed you.

'So I ran away,' he went on. 'I could not face them with a face covered with blotches, and I could not call in a doctor to cure me, for he would blab, and there would be something else for Seville to laugh at, and Doña Ana to preach about. I bought a mask to wear over my hideous face. I ordered my last dinner in Seville and hired musicians to play to me—but they played in the next room. I could not let them see me. Leporello was there, I had meant to take him with me. But in the mirror I saw him laugh at me. I gave him the best thrashing he has ever had, told him to invent some story if they should ask where I had gone, hired a new servant, and departed.'

'Why did you not come here?' asked the father.

'I suppose because I was feeling too exhausted for parricide. Bah! That's exaggeration. I did not think of you. I thought only of curing myself.'

It seemed this would be his last confidence. With the last words the schoolmaster had returned, and he lay peevish and torpid among the pillows. But why has he come here now? thought Don Saturno. It must be money. Doctors cost as much as pleasure, I suppose. Well, I may know in the morning. He sat for a while.

It seemed that Juan was asleep. He got up softly. The black eyes opened, a hand was stretched out.

'It is not cured yet. Look! On my wrist——'

There was something immediate and childish about the words and the gesture of the hand that went to the father's heart.

'It's nettlerash.'

Choosing his words as discreetly as he could he explained that the disease was not serious.

'It comes with agitation, with nervous strain. I have sometimes had it myself,' he added.

The schoolmaster looked at him with a smile, patronisingly incredulous, faintly amused.

He went, not to his bed, but to the library. He unlocked the chest of walnut wood, bound in an elaborate lace of iron, and took out a bundle of family documents and the de Tenorio pedigree. There they were, on a tree sprouting from the stomach of a recumbent founder—their names, their qualities. Three Admirals, a Beatified, thirteen Bishops, five royal favourites, eleven soldiers, one man of letters: just like any other family in Spain. One Admiral had been a man of valour, one of the royal favourites had been a man of integrity. How many of them had been like his son?—a shallow spiteful cur, yelping because fate had landed a kick on him.

In this hour of nocturnal clairvoyance he had renounced

every illusion but one. Juan was not a good character, not intelligent, not courageous, not magnanimous; not bold even, nor cunning. All this he could admit; but could not bring himself to admit that Juan was uniquely a discredit. He could not bear the unparalleled reproach, it must be distributed through centuries, other fathers than he must have begotten such disappointing sons.

Turning over the shrivelled documents, he searched for Juans of the past. Here was Don Ermengildo, one of the Admirals, an intolerable braggart and bore. Here was his namesake, a Bishop of Segovia, a man moved in all his doings by malignant triviality. Here was the Beatified, a monomaniac, incessantly whoring with hairshirts, spiked girdles, whips and cactuses. Yes, there was corroboration enough. The only thing he could not find was corroborating vulgarity. But vulgarity, he said to himself, is a fleeting perfume, and a few decades can dull our nostrils to it.

He put back the papers and shut the chest. He had found enough in it to comfort him. He had found matter for philosophy; and philosophy—he had practised it for so long—was as comforting as an old dressing-gown.

There had been other Juans. And they had begotten some very respectable members of the family. It is all a matter of chance, or perhaps it forms part of a design too intricate to be seen as such. In any case, it is the way of the world.

'After all,' he said to himself, 'I might have begotten a Don Ottavio instead of a Don Juan. He is probably quite an upright fellow, and now that he has married a wife with money will pay his bills very punctually. But for all that, I should find him a most mortifying son.'

On his way out he paused once more by the sword which had belonged to the seventh Don Juan, and drew it from its scabbard. It was a beautiful blade, a masterpiece of the craftsmen of Toledo. His Don Juan, too, spent his money with distinction, had good taste.

Luisa Pintada, half-dressed, was shaking Doña Pilar. The old woman's eyes opened, and rolled like a hen's, but she was still a long way from waking.

'Doña Pilar! Doña Pilar! A message from my lady.'

The shaking redoubled, thc bedstead creaked. You old hag, thought the young woman, I'd like to wake you with my nails. But you'd make me pay too dearly for it.

'Doña Pilar! My lady sends to ask you how nearly you have finished the petticoat.'

'Eh?'

'The petticoat.'

The word, sent screaming down her ear, flew into Doña Pilar's dream and converted itself into a threat of rape. She sat bolt upright, gathered the sheet about her, and looked round snorting.

'Girl, you are not decent.'

'My lady has sent me to ask you if her petticoat is finished. The embroidered one with the pansies.'

'Eleven pansies more.'

The ravisher whisked back through the ivory gate, the world began again. To-day they left the castle. Drat the girl, here she was again!

'My lady asks for the petticoat. She wishes to wear it.'

'You fool, did I not tell you there were eleven pansies yet to finish? When will you learn to carry a plain message? Are you so depraved by living in this madhouse of immorality and impiety that you can't understand plain Spanish?'

'My lady says it does not matter about the eleven pansies. She wishes to wear the petticoat.'

'Then why could you not say so before? Talk, talk, talk! Your tongue will wear out before your feet and your fingers do. There it hangs, take it. Stop! Bring it here. No, take it, I don't want it. Take it, I say! Why do you stand dawdling? Is this rebellion, or just idiocy?'

For she had remembered that the needle was left in it. Never mind, let the needle stay. It might be better for Doña Ana if there were a hundred needles. What a moment, and what an occasion, to forsake her mourning! Her father's murderer has slept under the same roof, and she runs headlong into an unfinished grey and silver petticoat.

She jumped out of bed crossing herself, wiped her face with a cloth, licked her finger and rubbed it around her eyes. She pulled on her stockings and called the girl to come and lace her. While the girl pulled at the laces she snatched her rosary and whisked it between her fingers. Hail-Mary-full-of-grace, I think I can match you, my mistress, and I certainly mean to: fruit-of-thy-womb-Jesus. You will take a little time, hail-Mary-full-of-grace, putting on your new petticoat and seeing how it sits. I may be an old woman, but I can dress as fast as you at a pinch, Hail-Mary, or faster. You think you can get your own way, the-Lord-is-with-thee, 'Girl! You're all thumbs!' Your husband, Hail-Mary-full-of-grace, was born I think with wool over his eyes. But if he can't see through you, I can. Ow! What torment to be laced the moment one's out of bed, thy-will-be-done-on-earth-as-it-is-in-heaven, but I'll bear it and be even with you Amen! Hail-Mary. . . .

Doña Ana walked in.

'I thought you would like to see the petticoat,' she said. The rosary paused, swinging madly from the speed of its journey. In spite of her principles, Doña Pilar was swept away on a flood of pride and admiration. Never had the child looked more beautiful. She went on her knees and began tweaking the folds so that they should hang handsomely.

'Please finish your dressing quickly,' added Doña Ana. 'We must not be late for our mass. Don Ottavio is coming with us, his knee is perfectly well this morning, and I am so happy.'

Blameless as a flower her beauty opened on the parched and dreary morning. As they drove back from mass she looked out of the chariot window, her glance resting with delight on the dust, the havoc, and the weary anxious faces of the people standing in the street.

'Look, Ottavio! Look, Father! What a hole in that roof! And those poor creatures, I suppose, are wondering what they'll do about it.'

Her sympathy was as serene as a child's. Don Ottavio said it was a frightful mess, Don Isidro remarked on the hand of heaven.

'But I suppose it's nothing to the storms they have in the Americas,' said Ana.

'Oh no, nothing. Nothing at all.'

A knot of people was standing at the foot of the castle steps, and the Hernandez twins were sliding down the balustrade. Three little boys hissed their admiration as Doña Ana went by. She turned round with a smile, whereupon they became abashed and pretended it was the twins they were admiring.

After all, thought Doña Pilar, why should one oppose love? It is the most powerful wine in existence, the scriptures assure us that many waters cannot drown it, and even those who are not drunk themselves receive a slight agreeable intoxication from the breath of those who drink it. In a house where love is, there is always something going on; the servants, the friends, the dependents, the poor relations, though it is no affair of theirs, share in the banquet, have their secrets to tell, their surprises, their rich meditations, so generous is the table of love. Though cuffs and sharp words may circulate, money circulates also. There are letters to carry, doors to watch, one's wits are kept burnished. Even the husband has something to gain. His house becomes fashionable, animated with guests, and his servants take pains not to displease him. Meanwhile, his wife becomes immensely improved. Her beauty increases tenfold, the family jewels are displayed to the best advantage, in a very large number of cases she becomes much more amiable, and even fits of bad temper are less scathing and sooner abandoned. So why should I intervene? Now in my old age perhaps I am going to see some fun. Don Juan is detestable, a libertine, an atheist, and not in good taste; but it is not I he will embrace.

Ana's beauty had opened like a flower, candid and absolute as the vivid blue monstrance of the morning glory, that evening crumples and throws away. At mid-day it remained as absolute, but its candour had changed to a more resolute quality, it was not so much candour as defiance. For Don Juan was still in bed, sleeping off the journey of the previous day. The trunks were packed, the mules harnessed, everything was ready for departure. She had said, 'We cannot leave the house without saying good-bye to Don Juan. It would be uncivil,' and sat on imperturbable. It was hot, the conversation sagged and stuck fast, in their many silences they could hear the murmur of voices outside.

The knot of people had swelled to a crowd. They loitered about, talking among themselves, some left, and others came. They did not seem to have come on purpose, it was more as if some eddy in the course of the day collected them there; for the men carried the implements of their labour, the women balanced pitchers or carried bundles of clothes for washing. They loitered about, talking among themselves, and the children played.

'They have gathered to wish you a good journey,' said Don Saturno, for the fifth time.

Suddenly there was a yell like a spurt of flame.

'See! There he goes!'

Silence followed; and after a moment the party in the library began to converse.

It was Leporello they had seen, traversing the court between the house and the stables. Doña Adriana had joined the crowd. Her face wore a stern expression, and catching sight of Ramon she went up to him and began arguing. What was the use of standing around like this? What were they waiting for? He shrugged his shoulders.

'You at least should have more sense. Or has the wind blown away your wits?'

'You are here too,' he replied.

'Yes. And the more fool I. But I at least have finished a good morning's work, I have not been here since daybreak.'

'And what work should my husband do, Doña Adriana?' Maria Perez bristled up. 'Take a broom and sweep up the little olives? They would do well, wouldn't they, to feed us through the winter?'

Doña Adriana sighed. Her large dark face looked doubly grim for looking compassionate.

'Well, I suppose we are all here for a diversion,' she

said. 'But believe me, he is not worth waiting for, whether he comes from hell or from Seville. Listen to that child!' she added, her grave countenance cracking into a smile. 'Is it Fernanda or Engracia? I cannot tell one monkey from the other monkey.'

It was Engracia. She had decided that what this gathering needed was a centre-piece. So now she stood on the steps of the castle and sang. Her voice was as raucously sweet and powerful as a new wine. It flowed miraculous and unimpeded out of the narrow body that she jolted to and fro on the beat of the tune, wrenching herself from side to side, stamping with her bare feet. Over the right shoulder and then over the left her small pale face watched her audience with an intent and unswerving regard.

In the library Don Saturno began to beat the air lightly with his toe, and Doña Pilar's head wagged from side to side. The younger members of the party acknowledged the music only to the extent of beginning to talk about the opera, regretting that good music received so little encouragement in Spain. Recalling himself to good manners Don Saturno spoke of Farinelli. Don Isidro said that the most beautiful music in the world was that of the Choir of the Sistine Chapel. 'They sing a Miserere there which cannot be written down. It goes rather like this. Mi-hi-hi-se. . . .'

'Is no one going to play the flageolet?' enquired the voice of Don Juan. 'Tweedly-tweedly-weedle. . . .' And he looked with a flat snake's eye at Don Ottavio.

'My husband will, I am sure. He plays very well, you

should hear him. Don Ottavio, will you oblige me by fetching your flageolet? I saw it last in the dining-room.'

Now I wish Ana had not said that, thought Don Ottavio. It is very chivalrous of her, but really she need not always fly to my defence so rapidly. And I don't feel inclined for the flageolet just now.

'How foolish I am,' exclaimed Ana a moment later. 'I have just remembered, the flageolet is not in the dining-room. It is on the garden-terrace. Don Isidro, would you be so kind as to tell Don Ottavio that the flageolet is on the garden terrace, not in the dining-room?'

'It seems to be a very forgetful morning,' said Don Juan. 'I find that I have forgotten my watch, my scapular and my snuff-box. It will take me some little time, I fear, to repair these omissions. But I hope to be back in time for the music.'

The insult was so deliberate that Don Saturno and Doña Pilar both jumped up on a confused impulse of partisanship. They saw Doña Ana rise also, and walk very calmly after Don Juan.

They sat down again, and looked at each other. It was impossible to keep up the pretence, and Doña Pilar said,

'Times are changed since we were young.'

'How very odd it is to reflect,' said Don Saturno, 'that if I had had the happiness of knowing you when you were Doña Ana's age, we might have fallen in love with each other; that is to say, we should have become locked in the same mortal combat of the male and the female.'

'Speak for yourself, Don Saturno,' said the lady. 'I, at any rate, have always known how to behave myself.'

'What a pity!'

'They will be coming back in a minute,' she said, 'with the flageolet.'

'Or without it.'

'What shall we say?'

He rose and offered her his arm.

'Throughout this visit I have promised myself the pleasure of showing you some of my sister's embroidery. It is not too late, I hope? We go out by the other door.'

He was standing by the long mirror, waiting for her with a sneer on his face. Like a sleep-walker she came up to him, and laid her hand on his sleeve.

'I did not believe that story,' she said, 'I could not believe it. Something told me we were destined to meet again.'

'So you filled up the time by getting to know my family,' he answered, 'and marrying Ottavio, of course. You were always a prudent virgin. Pray, are you a virgin still?'

She shook her head, smiling.

'Well, I too have lost my virginity since we last met. It is a delightful experience, is it not?'

The hand that had rested on his sleeve lifted itself, moved slowly backward like an interrogation.

'I knew we should meet again,' she repeated.

'But that is no reason to be idle in the meantime, is it? She was a most exquisite creature, slender as a nymph, delicate as snow. And, would you believe it, she was quite ill-bred . . . the daughter of a quack who treated me for a certain malady which I can scarcely mention to a delicate lady like you. I wooed her and I had her. So she was not obliged to run after me, mewing and spitting and caterwauling.'

The hand went back towards her bosom.

'You devil,' she said. 'You filthy devil!'

'No more a devil than you,' he replied. 'No more filthy. It's how we are made, you know, people like you and me.'

'Like you and me,' she repeated. 'So you admit we are alike, Juan? You feel we are akin?'

'Brother and sister. But do not look so excited, Doña Ana, for I have lost my passing fancy for incest.'

Out on the steps Engracia turned two somersaults and began a fresh song,

> Is it a lady or is it a nightingale
> That cries so sweetly, that cries so sadly?
> Lady, though you sang to a harp of angels,
> You would not fetch Don Juan from hell,
> No, would not fetch him.'

'Shall we go back to the flageolet?' he said. 'Or do you prefer our native howlings? You wish to stay? Perhaps you will allow me to go alone?'

'Stop!' she cried, and ran after him, and pulled him round to face her anger. For a while she could not speak for fury, and when the words came it was a phrase invented long before, and stale now as a speech from a last year's tragedy.

'Don Juan, I have called on man and on heaven to destroy you. Both have failed me. Must I kill you with my own hands?'

'If you want to know it's well done, do it yourself. It's the libertine's motto.'

She pulled out the knife from her bosom and struck at him. He took hold of her wrist and disarmed her easily enough, and handed back the knife with a bow.

'Bravo for the performance.'

He slapped her face with a resounding blow. Mechanically, without a word, she put up her hand to rearrange her hair.

Doña Ana's chief coachman looked through the iron door of the stable court.

'How am I going to get the mules round with all that rabble there? My beasts won't stand that sort of thing.'

The crowd had grown larger. Those who had left it earlier had come back again, almost all Tenorio Viejo was there. Even Don Francisco and Don Gil had come strolling arm in arm, and now stood at a little distance, watching. Engracia continued her ballad, voices from the crowd joined in.

It was the song they had sung at the inn. Everyone who had been present remembered this, and Diego, catching Ramon's eye, aimed a wry grin, as much as to say, 'You've won this round.'

Every time that hell was mentioned in his daughter's song, Bernardo Hernandez, listening with pride, crossed himself.

'The other sings just as well, you know,' he whispered to Serafina.

'They're Cherubim and Seraphin, everyone knows that,' she answered sourly. 'How much longer are we to be kept waiting?'

The words were on other lips also. Faces were growing sullen, and at the end of the ballad no one remembered to shout an encouraging word to the singer. Abashed, she looked round, began to come down the steps, paused, and stood on one leg scratching the shin with the heel of the other. Behind her the door opened and Luis came out on to the top step.

'Good-day, ladies and gentlemen. Our visitors are just about to leave. The carriages must be brought round. Would you have the goodness to step back a trifle?'

Nobody budged. A voice from the back of the crowd called out,

'Where's Don Juan?'

A score of voices took up the cry,

'Don Juan! Where's Don Juan?'

'He arrived last night,' said the old major-domo.

'Aye, we know that. We want to see him. Where's Don Juan? We want to see him. It's our right.'

Don Gil turned to Don Francisco, pursing up his lips, and nodded. Now all the voices cried out,

'It's our right.'

No one moved till Luis had gone in again. Then as though with one unanimous movement they pressed round the foot of the steps. There was a clatter of hoofs, and a whip-crack, and the first chariot came out through the stable court.

'Make way there!'

No one stirred. The mules tossed their heads and fidgeted, and boys began to flip stones at them. The coachman began to curse, and then fell silent. Out of the crowd came the noise of breathing.

Once more the major-domo came to the door, spread out his hands, and retreated. A child began to whimper, and the mother hushed it desperately.

At last a shutter was pushed back, and Don Juan appeared at the window. He threw out a handful of small money, and said,

'If you wish to see me, here I am. Juan de Tenorio, at your service.'

No one said a word, and no movement was made to pick up the money.

They looked up at him and he looked down on them, and saw on every face the same sullen despairing recognition. A moment after, the doors were thrown open, and Doña Ana appeared on the top step. Looking out on the crowd she said in a ringing voice,

'He lies! Do not believe him, good people. He lies!'

He leaned from the window, grinning. But nobody looked at him, the whole crowd shifted its massive attention to the woman on the steps.

'He lies,' she repeated. 'Before God and the most Holy Virgin I swear to you he lies. He is not Don Juan. I, who speak to you, have known Don Juan well. I have loved him and lain in his arms. A woman who loves is not mistaken in the man of her love. I tell you, this man here is not Don Juan. He is some impostor. He may deceive everyone else, but he cannot deceive me. He is only an impostor.'

She stood looking out over their heads as people look out over the sea. It was as though some indifferent angel had come to deliver a message. She stood looking at the crouching pale-faced houses, the church with its lop-sided cupola, the speckled hill-slopes, the profile of the mountain. Behind her in the shadow of the doorway stood Don Saturno, and her husband and her household.

At last the old duena stepped forward and touched her arm.

She turned at the touch, and gave a little nod.

'It is time for us to go, is it not?—Good people, we have to go. Will you please make way for our coach?'

The crowd fell back from the steps. The chariot came round and they got in. The servants arranged themselves in the other two coaches, the reins were gathered up, the first coach was already off. Don Juan, still at his window, called out,

'Leporello!'

The face of Leporello appeared at a coach-window. 'In God's name, drive on!' he said.

Pale with fury, Don Juan slammed to the shutter.

The dust rose up behind them.

About a mile beyond the mill they encountered a band of men coming down the road. Ottavio, brooding in a cloud of bewilderment, happened to look out, and recognised the swineherds who had halted them on their journey to Tenorio Viejo. On an impulse he ordered the coachman to stop, let down the window, and said,

'Where are you going?'

They answered him with another question.

'Are you from the castle?'

'We are leaving it.'

'Tell us, is it true that Don Juan is there?'

'Yes, he is there.'

'In the flesh, and alive?'

'Alive,' said Ottavio.

They looked at each other grimly, and marched on.

The coach went on, swaying and creaking. No one spoke. Ana sat fingering her cheek, where a bruise already showed itself. Sometimes her lips moved rapidly, but no word escaped from them. Doña Pilar sat gazing at Ana, slow tears streamed down her face. Don Isidro read a book of devotions.

For women and priests, thought Ottavio, life is very easy. They have nothing to do but give way to their emotions. For a man, life is a sterner contest. For a man of honour, the course is always plain.

Nothing could be plainer than the course for him. He should kill his wife, and challenge Don Juan. Meanwhile, he was driving with the one away from the other.

He looked round on his companions. There sat Ana— and he felt the words of reproach and anger rising to his lips. But if he spoke to her, she would not attend, would not understand. She sat there, stroking her cheek, absorbed in her misery, inaccessible as a mermaid in the sea. And there sat Doña Pilar, the grey-haired go-between. She, if he spoke to her, would attend all right; but then she would answer him, and he guessed how, and he had no mind to bandy words with a virago. And there sat Don Isidro, reading his book of devotions. Nobody felt for him, nobody thought of him. He was utterly alone.

And yet, by rights, he should be the centre of their attention, they should all be on their knees, trembling, propitiating, begging him to moderate his fury, the fury of an injured husband.

He looked out. Already the valley was out of sight, and they laboured up through gloomy oak-woods. Ah, hateful ill-omened journey, why had they ever come on it? And he remembered himself sitting by Doña Ana, not even married to her then, trying to dissuade her from an undertaking that he knew by instinct to be a mistake. It would have been better, after all, if he had given way about those masses. But he had been weak for lack of sleep, and further weakened by anxiety for Ana's health; and while the journey or the masses had been in debate it had darted into his head that the journey might be made conditional upon the marriage; and he was tired of wooing Ana, and of her repeated postponements, and the long engagement was becoming a great strain, both on his nerves and on his pocket.

Once more he looked round on his travelling companions. And they were just as inattentive as before.

Yet surely he deserved a little sympathy? In a quarter of an hour he had lost his illusions, his peace of mind, his honour. Carrying the flageolet, he had returned to the library. It was empty. Racked with anxiety, he had waited, sometimes playing a few notes, a Ranz des Vaches, as it were; at other times giving himself up to the blackest misgivings. Then, at the one door, had entered Ana and Don Juan, and at the other, as though with the connivance of a ballet, Don Saturno and Doña Pilar. Ana had turned to him alternately a cheek crimsoned with shame, and a cheek pale with terror; and he had not known what to make of it, but had tried to think the best, relying on her virtue, and on the short interval of absence from the room. The parting refreshments had been eaten, the parting good-byes said, Don Juan had gone to show himself at the window, the rest of them were gathered on the steps.

And then, in front of all, in front of that rabble even, Doña Ana had declared her adultery and his shame.

He took out his watch. If, in an hour's time, no one had spoken to him, no one had bothered to notice his existence, he would leave them. They could fend for themselves, and he would return to Tenorio Viejo to challenge Don Juan.

Sometimes he looked at the watch, sometimes he looked at the view. The time and the journey crept on, and the coach left the oak-woods and came out on the windy plateau. Fifty-three minutes had elapsed when Don Isidro, rearranging his legs, chanced to kick Don Ottavio's shin, apologised for incommoding him, and began to comment on the dreariness of the scenery.

After the coaches had driven away a few people detached themselves from the crowd outside the castle, shuffling off in silence, or murmuring pretexts that no one listened to. Since the fun seemed over the children went off to play elsewhere, and some of the women remembered their work and went back to it, saying that they were not man-kind, able to stand about all day if they chose. Those who remained closed their ranks and argued over what they had seen.

Who knew what to believe? It was many years since Don Juan had been in Tenorio Viejo, and though the man at the window resembled him, yet resemblance is not everything. The woman had said plainly that he was not Don Juan. Why not believe her? Believe the word of a woman who admitted herself a strumpet? Why, man, that made her more credible yet. A woman bold enough to speak the truth about herself is not likely to hide any other truth.

Doña Adriana, elbowing her way among them, added her word.

'Neighbours, I tell you this much. The woman was mad.'

'Mad? No such thing! Did she slaver, did she tear her clothes? Why, she spoke as calmly as though she were giving the death-sentence.'

'I have seen many mad, men and women, cattle and dogs.' It was Esteban who spoke. 'Never a one of them was like her.'

'No, indeed. We know madness when we see it, she was no madwoman. A shameless woman, certainly. But not mad.'

'Mad!' cried Doña Adriana. 'Crazed for love.'

'But the mad rave, there is no coherence in what they say. This woman spoke to the point.'

'Mad for all that.'

Her persistence was beginning to have effect. The old woman had a knack of being right. Serafina hobbled up and began her say.

'It's true enough, women do run mad for love. Look at our own Conchita Hernandez, clean out of her senses when the tax-gatherer would not have her. But it's for lack of a lover, I think, that women run mad. And Doña Ana has not suffered from *that* sickness, we had her own word for it.'

She glanced round to collect their suffrages. But her reputation was among the women of the village only, the men who had listened to Doña Adriana though but to disagree with her did not listen to Serafina. The Daughter of the Church observed this, a scornful smile twitched her lips. Serafina's wheedling tones changed to a hoot of fury.

'And if Doña Ana is mad, then I say she is mad after the fashion of Catalonia, where those in their senses are called mad and only the mad are thought wise.'

'God in heaven!' shouted Esteban. 'We shall all be mad if these women come among us with their chatter. Why are they here at all? It is no place for them. This is not a lying-in.'

More voices took up the same cry. Women, making their way out of the crowd, began to say how undecorously other women had behaved, putting themselves forward to shout and dispute. Most of them found it a relief to be dismissed. Only a very strong communal excitement could have pulled them so far from the customs of Tenorio Viejo as to mix without embarrassment in a crowd of men. Such a cancellation of sex-consciousness was alarming, it was as though some transcendent catastrophe, a fire or an earthquake, had compelled this change of manners; and now with a sense of escape they moved off and gathered into a separate group some twenty yards away.

As though a room had been swept and a seat dusted for him, Don Gil observed the retreat of Doña Adriana, and came forward.

'Kill the dog, and take on its fleas. Get rid of the women, and up comes the sacristan.'

It was Andres who spoke. Don Gil heard him but feigned not to hear. Portly and musing, he circulated among the crowd. Everywhere backs were turned and a path opened for him. He listened and loitered, snuffing up the smell of anger.

'It's him, right enough, let her say what she will. I would know that ill-omened set of features anywhere.'

'But you believed the valet's story fast enough.'

'More fool I! I should have known it was too good to be true. He go to hell, forsooth! No, he'll stay on earth to plague us.'

'Trust him to turn up just now.'

'Yes, we can whistle for our ditches, if he's about.'

'It's as though he had come on purpose, that's what I think.'

'Mother of God, if I thought that! . . . Yet it's likely, too.'

'How could he know?' asked Andres.

Don Gil paused beside them. Diego was fast convincing himself that Don Juan had come on purpose to frustrate the irrigation, and Andres continued to ask how he could have heard of it.

'Of course he could have heard of it.'

'But how? Who could have got word to him, how

could he have heard it in time? Messages don't fly over the mountain.'

'On Sunday, the day before yesterday, Don Saturno promised us the water——' Ramon spoke, and was interrupted by a clamour of voices.

'Promised? Promised? Why did you not get more than a promise? He'll promise anything. Oh, you managed it badly! If you'd listened to us . . . If you'd done as I said . . .'

Don Gil said smoothly,

'It appears to me, just as an onlooker, that there are two people who might have sent a message to Don Juan. One is his own father'—he paused—'the other is the miller.'

'If we've been tricked by the miller!' exclaimed Diego. At the same moment Ramon said bitingly,

'I can think of a third. The sacristan.'

Things might have gone badly for him, but now the swineherds joined the crowd. To the angry hum of discussion was added the sharper narrative accents of those telling their story of Don Juan at the window and Doña Ana on the steps, and the third counterpoint of questions and ejaculations from the new arrivals. These were in a more genial mood than the rest of the crowd. Their employment made them less concerned about the irrigation, it was the news of Don Juan's return and of the village anger which had brought them down from the mountain; they had come for the story's sake, and in order not to be out of any row that might be happening. People who arrive in a band, too, are always pleased with themselves. Their pleasure at being a reinforcement, and their pleasure at finding the story so much enriched by the incident of Doña Ana, made them seem almost rollicking by contrast with the careworn anger of those who had been there all the morning. Combating this, the narrators threw a more violent passion into their story. They picked up the money that had been thrown to them, brandished it in hands shaking with rage, spat on it, and trampled it underfoot. To point out the window at which he had appeared they threw stones at it. Dionio Gutierrez, shaken out of his usual puzzled melancholy, cried out, 'There's treachery in it!' with such vehemence that even those who suspected him of being, somehow, the traitor, forgot their suspicion and shouted with him. Now everyone was declaiming at once, the new arrivals were as furious as the rest, and with a fresher fury. Like a connoisseur listening to a stormy music Don Gil moused from group to group, nodding his head in time to their outcries, and exclaiming, too, such words as, Deplorable and, Scandalous; though no one lent him an ear or even troubled to cold-shoulder him.

On the outskirts of the crowd he found himself face to face with Don Francisco, pale with excitement, gaping with the luxurious attention of the fire-raiser. Here was a wayside plum to be picked. In an undertone, he remarked,

'They say someone sent the news of the water to Don Juan. That would be someone who could write a letter.

I'm sure I hope they won't take it into their heads it was you.'

The words fell flat. Looking more attentively at the schoolmaster, Don Gil realised that the man was in an ecstasy. With his dull eyes bolting out of his head he stared, not at the crowd, but at the castle, as though he expected, at any moment, to see it shivered by lightning. Between his thick lips the tip of his tongue quivered, bruised with tooth-marks, and he rocked to and fro on his heels.

Making a mental note that Don Francisco hated the castle even more than he had supposed, Don Gil moused on. He was interested, he was hopeful; but he was not happy. It tantalised him to see all this fury and turmoil, and to have so little control over it. He had not raised it, he could not direct it, it was not even directed against him; and he felt in a way slighted that the village should feel a wrath against Don Juan such as they had never felt against Don Gil. Suffering and misery would certainly come of it; but it was not so sweet a drink to look forward to, a misery which he had not brewed and spiced to his own taste. It was galling, too, that all this wrath should be aimed at Don Juan, with whom he had no particular quarrel, for whom, indeed, he felt a certain forwarding approval; for such a man must have humiliated many hearts, and tormented dozens of women as silly as Teresa. Why could they not rage against Don Saturno, that invulnerable old monkey?

And he could swing them to it, one word would do

the trick. Once get that notion into their heads, and the thing was done. They were a pack of dolts not to think of it for themselves; but they had not thought of it, and might not; as usual, all the fine thinking for Tenorio Viejo was left to him. Once get that into their heads . . . but how was he to get it there? Though he should burst himself he could not make himself heard; moreover, he was so well hated that his wise word, coming from the silliest mouth among them, would be better received than coming from him. He moused and listened. There was the spokesman right enough, that bellowing Jesus; but this same Jesus was the unlikeliest man there to tolerate a word from him. The word must go round-about. He thought of the schoolmaster, wondered if he could be taught to carry it. No! No hope of it. Lost in his silly undiscriminating joy, the schoolmaster stood there gaping and rubbing his hands like an idiot before a house on fire.

Just in front of him stood Esteban, and Esteban by virtue of having seen Don Juan at the window was getting the better of Miguel Sobrino, one of the swineherds, who inclined to belief in Doña Ana's statement.

'I tell you, it was the man himself. Did I not see him?'

'You saw a man. But one man can resemble another. And with these lords, there is nothing to tell them apart by, their faces are so smooth.'

'It was he, I swear it.'

'Very well, very well, it was he. And yet she swore to it, it was not he. It seems to me it was six of one and half a dozen of the other. The worst of it is, we have been fobbed off again. Fobbed off by Don Juan, fobbed off by an impostor, what's the odds?'

Pleased with the phrase, he turned to Pedrillo, saying,

'What's the odds, eh? One way or another, we're fobbed off.'

—'Eh?' said Pedrillo. At the same moment Don Gil said to Miguel,

'I wish you'd been here. You would soon have seen which one of them was telling the truth.'

All the answer he got was a grunt. But he persevered, calling up all his arts as he spoke of Doña Ana, how she had appeared of a sudden, to confess herself a sinner and denounce the false Don Juan.

'Pale as death, trembling before us all. . . .' He had to stop and suck the moisture off his lips, so profound was the emotion with which he recalled the moment which had given her back to him once more, agonised and appetising as on the night of the vigil. But it had done the trick, Miguel was listening.

'No man of experience could doubt she was telling the truth. That is why I wish you had been here.'

The humble middle-aged Miguel Sobrino, a man of very moderate experience and outrageously bullied by his widowed mother, pursed up his mouth.

'A wronged woman will revenge herself. In the dark, I suppose, she did not know this one from the other one.'

'You should have seen, too, how chopfallen Don Saturno looked,' pursued the sacristan.

'Don Saturno?'

'Hearing his cheat exposed before us all, his stratagem to pass off this impostor in the place of Don Juan. It makes one tremble,' said Don Gil, raising his voice a little, for others might be listening too, 'to think of such scheming, such hypocrisy. His son in the grave, himself on the brink of the grave. . . .'

'He's not so old as I am,' interrupted Pedrillo, 'for I can remember the day he was born. His mother wasn't too bad a woman, God rest her soul, she gave me a real once, when I pulled her little dog out of the water. She bore eleven children, but only three of them lived. Our Saturno, and Doña Isabel, and another daughter who married a gentleman from the province of Lerida, I don't recollect his name, but it was in the year before the red snow fell.'

Don Gil gnashed his teeth. A hand caught his shoulder, and he was swung round face to face with Ramon.

'I see what you're at, old poison-mouth! And I tell you, you may keep your slanders for yourself, for Don Tomas and Serafina. Here, we can do without them.'

'Why, what was I saying?' gasped the sacristan.

'That rather than pay for the irrigation, and to have an excuse not to pay for it, Don Saturno is tricking us with a false Don Juan. That's what you're saying. And if you say it again, I'll stuff the words down your throat. We have enough wrongs to move us, we need no lies.'

There was no need to say it again. The words ran through the crowd, in a moment he heard the accusation on all sides, and Jesus shouting,

'He thinks to cheat us, does he? He'll give us another Don Juan instead of the water? We'll see to that!'

A roar of anger went up.

In the dusk they were still there. But no longer as a crowd. A little before sundown, after a storm of stone-throwing, they had tried to break the door in. The tough iron and the walnut-wood held, and Don Juan, aiming through the chink of the shutters, had wounded two of them, Andres and the boy Enrique. Clasping the wound in his leg Andres had railed against such an ignorant strategy, analysing in his strident voice all the defects of a straightforward attack.

'That's it. March up to be shot. Knock on the door and ask them to do you the kindness of a ball through the head. That's courage, that is. That's the old Spanish valour.'

Inordinate with pain, his voice could be heard quite clearly inside the castle.

'I wish you had not shot Andres. I have a great respect for the man. Besides, it's so foolhardy. Every time you make a hole in them, you let in more sense. Now, mark my words, they'll invest us.'

Don Saturno was not afraid. With a considerable part of his being he was even enjoying himself. The Art of War was an art which he had studied as appreciatively as astronomy, economics, agriculture, music, chemistry, heraldry, and the drama; and in his young days he had had some practical experience of it under de Lede. His house was very defensible, in spite of the visitors it was still well victualled; and a few hours earlier he had gone over its weak places, such as the poultry-yard and the bakehouse, contriving various fortifying arrangements. But two things qualified his enjoyment: one, that he was being besieged by people whom he thought of as his own, and as friends; the other, that his son was included in the garrison.

'All we need do,' he had said, 'is to endure each other's company for two or three days till they come to their senses again. Do you remember Ulysses, when he was attacked by the Thracian dogs? "Ulysses, being a wily man, threw away his staff and sat down." Well, we must model ourselves on Ulysses. Do nothing to annoy them, and sit here till they go away.'

'The only word of sense you have uttered, so it seems to me,' replied his son, 'is the word *dogs*. However, I am glad to hear you will do nothing to annoy them. I thought you might intend to make them another speech.'

Don Saturno winced. With the first bout of stone-throwing he had gone out on a balcony, prepared with a few words of rational rebuke and an invitation to a rational parley. Seeing him, they had yelled out, *Cheat!* and *Old Cozener!* He was furious. Stones, yes, but not insults. Abuse, yes, but not abuse in these terms. Quivering with indignation, he had retired, to nurse his wounded pride and his wounded feelings. He might not be a model landowner—who is? His projects for their betterment might be misunderstood, or turn out half-baked because there was never money enough to fuel them. He might have been neglectful sometimes, or have turned a deaf ear to their incessant misfortunes. But he had always dealt openly with them, they had no reason to call him cheat. Worst of all, they had called him cheat in his son's hearing.

His pique, taking a magnanimous twist, now compelled him to praise their characters to Don Juan, and even, as far as possible, to praise their behaviour; and it was in the tone of an advocate that he reported,

'They're doing just as I foretold. They're investing us. They've placed themselves all round the house, a group here and a group there. They're commanding every possible sally-port. They've really done it remarkably well. Their women are bringing up provisions, and no doubt they mean to beleaguer us all night.'

'What a pity they have no artillery,' said his son.

'Artillery and starvation are not the only means of reducing a garrison. Several treatises of the Middle Ages recommend the introduction of bees and hornets, I have seen a wood-cut of the assailants, mounted on scaling-ladders, tossing bee-skeps into a machicolated tower. Fire, however, is a more practical threat. By wounding two of them you have taught them the principles of investment. I must implore you not to quicken their invention any further or we shall be smoked out—which would do a lot of damage and terrify the maid-servants.'

After a while Don Juan said,

'I wish I'd never come.'

'Why did you come?'

'You'd believe it, wouldn't you, if I told you I came here for a little kindness?'

His nettlerash had come on again, he was scratching himself furtively, like a schoolboy. Too much like a schoolboy, thought Don Saturno, embarrassed by the whining voice.

'It appears to me, Juan, that after a certain age is reached the kindness of parents can do very little. It is like giving an old-fashioned toy, at no time is it appropriate, and at the best it is only amusing for a minute or two. You are in the prime of life, indeed, you are already rather past it. I am an old man. Kindness from me to you would be a species of doting.

'Advice, yes—if you will take it,' he went on. He paused, there was no answer. 'Well, perhaps you do not want advice. Or a little philosophy, if only the reflection. Here is somebody old enough to be my father, and still finding the world tolerable enough to remain in it.'

He paused again, longer this time, looking sadly and shrewdly at the man.

'Sympathy, if you could take it. Information, stories of times past. Or practical counsels. Or perhaps money,' he added.

'Yes, I shall want some money. And that reminds me. What is all this talk about irrigation? Just one of your usual projects, I suppose?'

Don Saturno began to speak of the value of irrigation, irrigation in general. He quoted figures to prove how with a steady water-supply the land would give a greater yield, in some cases two harvests instead of one. He described experiments in land-development which had been made in other countries, the antiquity of terracing, the reclamation of English bogs. He sketched the arguments for supposing the aqueduct of Segovia to be of Roman construction, and those for supposing it to be the product of an earlier civilisation. He talked for some time, and did not once refer to the irrigation of Tenorio Viejo; for he did not wish to inaugurate the siege by inaugurating a quarrel. It seemed to him, branching off by Father Flores to a discussion of Spanish antiquarianism in general, that he had led the talk into a region of safety, and that Juan was looking reassuringly uninterested, when Juan said,

'Well, why don't you irrigate Tenorio Viejo?'

A trap. It was degrading to have a son who laid traps for one, it was also degrading to have to avoid the trap. But in the interests of peace he skirted the question, and spoke of the local antiquities, various fragments of masonry lost in the oak-woods, the possibility that they represented some forgotten hillside city.

'I can't be interested in the past,' said Juan. 'I want to know why you don't irrigate this place. Surely it would be very profitable?'

'Who knows? The land is very bad. It might not be worth it.'

'I suppose the difficulty would be to get enough water.'

'Oh, no. There is plenty of water.'

He spoke of the winterbourne brooks, the wasteful floods that followed the melting of the snow and poured themselves away to nothing, the springs hidden in the rocks. There would be plenty of water.

'You seem to have it all at your fingers' ends. Why don't you draw up a plan?'

'I have a few sketches,' said Don Saturno carelessly.

The water-chart was fetched, and together they studied it. How I must have misjudged him, thought the father. It seems he is really interested. Perhaps now he is growing older he will begin to take a liking for this sort of thing, to develop tastes like mine. Juan sat calculating the cost of the scheme, the value of the increased harvests. Even for a confirmed gamester his mental arithmetic was brilliant.

'It seems to me that in five years' time there would be a twenty per cent. profit.'

'One must allow for accidents.'

'Even allowing for accidents.'

He had to remind Juan that since nearly all the land to be irrigated was leased out it would be the tenants who would profit.

'I suppose you still get a certain amount of obligatory labour out of them?'

'Well, yes, a little. But it doesn't do, you know. To get anything done one must employ overseers, and all overseers cheat. It's a bad system.'

'I was thinking that as the irrigation will be so much to their benefit they might be told to do some of the stone-hauling, and digging, and so forth in return.'

'Yes, that would be possible. They certainly want water. The day before you came some of them were here, talking about it. In fact,' he added, 'I believe it is their anxiety about the water which is at the bottom of this trouble now. They have a notion you might be an obstacle.'

'Not at all,' said Don Juan. 'But don't run out and tell them so now. Remember Ulysses, let us sit down till our dogs have gone away. They would think us unduly silly if we were to march out saying, Now you have given us a stoning we will give you water.'

He continued to study the chart. Presently he asked to see the other estate maps, the division of the land among the various tenants. Don Saturno repeated the story of that unfortunate sale to the nunnery in Avila, the extortionate terms of the nuns.

'I was young, and too impetuous. If I had not seemed so anxious to repossess myself of the land they might have come down, and then there would have been no need to let. They were very good olive-yards then. Of course, with water they would become good again.'

Don Juan nodded inattentively. After a while he asked what was the term of the leases.

'Yearly. For at first they were so suspicious that they would not take a longer lease. They thought I had some device against them when I offered them land. And now, though they all talk of *My land*, *My inheritance*, they are too conservative to change to a longer term.'

'I know some of them,' said Juan. 'Esteban Flores, a tall red-headed fellow.'

'No, you are thinking of Jesus Morel. He is a swineherd, and works for me.'

There, I should not have said that, he told himself. Just when Juan is taking so much interest in the estate, how tactless!

'Andres Ribera. Who's he?'

'The man you shot in the leg.'

'Ah yes. The strategist.'

She stretched herself, yawned, scratched a little, and settled back to her former position. Since she had last drowsed off, dusk had taken the place of afternoon. It was the hour when the smell of water came into the house; but now there was only a trickle of water left, the mill-wheel stood still, and instead of the smell of water was the smell of mud. Stealthy and adept, the widow Sobrino's cat bounded from the cask to the penthouse roof, strolled along the ledge and disappeared through the little three-cornered window.

What a long day it had been!—long and agreeable, and not yet over. Since the early morning she had not done a stroke of work, drowsing on the window-sill, listening to the noise of the people gathered round the castle. It was a day in which to look on, to listen, to sit still. A little after mid-day the cavalcade of the departing visitors had gone down the road, the coachmen beating their mules and shouting; and then she had bestirred herself enough to go to the other window, in order to watch the coaches out of sight, praying to the Virgin that Leporello might be in one of them; but as the coach windows were screened against the heat it was impossible to know. Then she had gone back to the east window. Later her father had come in, excited, talking a great deal and giving her a great many directions about barring doors and shutting up the ass. Then he had gone out again. Silent and empty, the house became very agreeable. If it had been rather cleaner she might have imagined herself in a convent, and the noise up at the castle the noise of the world forsaken and shut away. They were as busy as bees swarming. But it was no affair of hers. Her lot was to sit in the window-sill, sometimes to pass a comb through her hair, sometimes to say a few Hail-Marys, sometimes to sleep.

Now I believe I am rather hungry, thought Celestina. But she was still too comfortable and too languid to go in search of food. She went on looking out of the window instead. Everything was quieter now. The road, pale and faintly patterned with ribs of dust like the surface of simmering milk, ran straight towards the village. Now on the road appeared a man.

It's my father coming back, she thought with annoyance. What a nuisance!—for now she must move herself, put food on the table, see to the ass, sweep out the dust of the house into the dust of the road.

But the man on the road walked too slowly to be the miller, and was a much heavier man. She rubbed the sleep from her eyes, and recognised Don Gil.

Swift and smooth as a cat she ran out of the room. In her narrow mind, clouded with the fumes of sleep, was a single determination: to escape from Don Gil. For either he was coming to bid her marry Leporello or else, if Leporello were gone, then Don Gil would marry her himself. He had often pawed her, saying that with her dowry and her cool flesh she would make a pleasant wife. One good fright will undo a stupid mind, and ever since Leporello's wooing Celestina had been idiotic with fear; only her sluggishness lay like a film over her terror; and now, with the sight of Don Gil and with that cat's flounce from the window-sill, her sluggishness had yielded, she knew her terror and her opportunity, and knew nothing else. She pulled up the loose board and took out the knotted handkerchief. Then, going to her father's room, she opened the chest where he kept his money, and took that too. There was no time to count it, there was just time to remember that overnight her father had brought back some money paid him by the tanner, a handful of coins which he had left in the niche that held the holy-water jar. She knotted all in the handkerchief, flicked herself with the holy water, and ran from the house.

On the road, he would see her. But keeping to the river-bed the bushes hid her. Even when she heard him tapping on the door she did not know any particular fear. It seemed the most natural and easy act of her life, to be running away to a convent with her father's money tied up in a handkerchief. Even the thought of crossing the mountain called up no uneasiness. The road went on, she had only to keep to the road. All the swineherds were in the village, no one would see her, no one would ever know where she had gone. The night was still and serene, there would be a moon presently; and beyond the mountain she would find the world and a refuge from the world.

The news came that the boy Enrique was dying. It had not seemed a serious wound, little blood came out of it. But now he was dying.

Ramon was one of the detachment set to keep a watch on the north side of the castle, where a door opened on to a stone terrace whence a flight of steps went down into the formal plantation of box and ilex. He sat on the ground, his back against a tree, his gun beside him (for now to the best of their ability they were armed), looking at the house, pale in the ashy northern light, and at the fantastic tufts and bulges of the half-clipped alleys. But what seemed fantastic to him was not the contours of the escaping branches but the sheared lower portions of the hedges and clumps. It seemed madness to shape a bush into the form of a wall. It seemed madness to end a life of twelve years between six in the evening and midnight.

'And here are two pieces of bread,' said Maria Perez. 'Take both, for you will need them, and eat this garlic a little before dawn, it will keep off the bad airs—and do not trouble about us, we shall bar the door and do well. And do not fret too much, husband, for the loaf comes out as the oven wills, care killed the cat.'

The life of man has its shape, as a tree has its shape. One grows up, one learns a livelihood, one marries a woman and begets children. As one grows older one grows tired and in the end one dies. That is the pattern of the life of man. He looked at the pale house and the mis-shapen trees, and thought of the dying boy. He thought of his business in this garden, and how foolish it was. He thought of his companions, and knew himself at odds with them.

He could hear their voices, though they were talking softly. He could have listened to their words, but his own thoughts were louder.

He was a man of certain steadfast ideas—not uncommon in that, and the ideas were nothing out of the ordinary. What made him peculiar was the steadfastness by which he lived according to his creed. The world is no pleasure-ground, there is an inherent hardness in the life of man, and probably it would have been better to remain unborn; but being born into the world man could better it, and amend what he could not abolish. Though one cannot turn aside a drought, one could combat it with water-storage. Though plague and lightning go where they will, the tribe of lesser evils can be foreseen and guarded against. Though some madnesses cannot be withstood, not every bite is the bite of a mad dog. Though the seed of death lies in every quarrel, many quarrels need not happen. The world is not so bad as we make it. As we have hands given us to work with so we have wits given us to think with. There should be justice to the poor; for though Death is welcomed to the house of the oppressed and driven away from the door of the rich man, yet in the end he knocks on both doors. Neighbour should stand by neighbour.

These were his ideas, and all his life he had held by them. And he was even respected for them, or for his doggedness in keeping faith with them; and even those who disliked him admitted that he was a prudent man, a man with sense in his head, a man of his word. And yet these same ideas, which appeared so moderate, so reasonable, appeared also to be under a curse of miscarrying. The advice he gave led to confusion, his sense of justice roused one turmoil after another, and he had only to speak of reason for everybody to run out of their senses. *The loaf comes out as the oven wills*, Maria had said. If that were so, then surely he had a most ill-willing oven; for what could be worse than this last batch of his baking? The strangers had come to Tenorio Viejo with their story of Don Juan's death, and in the common excitement he had seen a chance for common action, for that policy of neighbour standing by neighbour which was part of his creed. But first it was reasonable to find out if the story were true; and it had been his suggestion that they should meet, and Leporello submit the story to them. It was so silly a story that even those who said they believed in it mocked at it; and yet by the end of the evening the story had divided those who had come together, and the only thing they seemed agreed upon was to hate the miller. You've botched it again, he told himself. And swore to meddle no further. Though he had gone with the deputation, he had kept in the background, said nothing. Don Juan's arrival had proved him right in disbelieving Leporello, but too wary to remind them of this he had kept his own counsel. They will come together of their own accord, he had thought, watching them gathered before the castle, watching their anger harden and take shape. If they will hold for an hour or two longer, we shall get the water; for though the old man is too scatter-brained to give it from compassion, and too proud to yield it from fear, yet his honour will shame him to it now; he must keep his word when he sees how desperately, how unitedly, we hold him to it. He had watched Don Gil, too, sly and mischief-making. I must root you out, he had thought, before you spoil this harvest; and patient and silent he had followed him till the moment came. A passion of disgust had shaken him to see this scabby and limping slander let loose to distract honest men, and he had spoken with the indignation of honour; and the denunciation was barely out of his mouth before Don Gil's lie was re-minted as Ramon's truth, and voice after voice cried out, Ramon says, Ramon has hit it, Ramon has found out the cheat.

And as a result the boy was dying, and they were sitting round the castle like mad wolves, and he was with them. For neighbour must stand by neighbour. But I might as well be sleeping at home, his thoughts lamented. I've set them all against me, they think I am a turncoat. Steadfast and hopeless, he had tried to turn them back to their senses, disowning the words that had been put in his mouth, asseverating that they were dancing to the tune of Don Gil, reasoning this way and that—and only blackening the disaster.

No hay remedio. There was nothing to be done. Meanwhile he sat watching the castle, patient and attentive, with his old gun across his knees.

Honour demanded it. There was nothing else he could do. The horse twitched its ears, the moon was rising, the air was filled with the dry whispers of night. Honour demanded it, he must kill Don Juan, or try to.

For at Fuentes, the straggling little town at the mountain-foot, Don Ottavio had hired a riding-horse at the post-stage and turned back alone. Perhaps he would not have done this if Fuentes had not happened to be full of soldiers. Some officers were drinking at the inn, and among them he recognised a former acquaintance who told him that they were returning from taking part in a ceremonial occasion where they had been reviewed by a Prince of the Blood and an image of Our Lady of Carmel.

He introduced the other officers. They complained of the heat, of the tightness of their uniforms, of the inadequacy of Fuentes where they were billeting that night; and congratulated him on his fortune in quitting the army for a good marriage and a quiet life. How little they guessed!

But the thought came that though they did not guess now, in time they would know for a certainty. The news of his dishonour would not remain bottled up beyond those mountains, sooner or later it would reach the world and the ears of his fellows. A wife who proclaims at the top of her voice that she has loved amiss leaves no alternative to a man of honour. He had been a soldier; and now he was a husband. There was nothing else he could do. So he paid for drinks and sat awhile listening to their healthy natural gossip of women and horses and promotion and bets and money-lenders, and felt happier than he had been for months. Such happiness undoubtedly came from a right decision. Addressing a farewell to Doña Ana (to which she was as inattentive as a stone) he was even more convinced that he had decided rightly. To look at her now aroused in him sensations not only of grief and disillusionment but also of painful embarrassment. Apart from her unchastity, that a woman whom he had made his wife should be able to love as vehemently as she had done was deeply shocking to him; and if the passion she had disclosed had been a passion for him it would have been almost as bad. With relief he bowed and went away.

He reined in his horse and sat looking down on Tenorio

Viejo. The moon was coming to her full, she cast a light that was brilliant and derisive. Looking down on the pattern of light and shade he realised the tatterdemalion squalor of the place which had heard him put to shame. He seemed to be looking at the tumbled bleached bones of an ossuary. There, where the poplar-trees growing along the river barred the earth with long black shadows, were the ribs of a skeleton; and the church, looking at him with its hollow socketed doorway, was the skull. A bad omen. Don Ottavio crossed himself.

He rode on, past the olives, and the vines casting their jagged shadows on the white earth. He rode past the black bars of the poplar-trees, past the mill and the first scattered houses. The dogs barked. No one was about, there was no sign of life.

There was the castle on its hillock, its fortress contours breaking down into the clustered out-buildings, and the iron gate of the stable court, and the flight of steps masoned into the rock. He rode into the square. Men arose from the shadow and halted him.

'Are you for the castle? You cannot pass to-night.'

Others came out from other shadows, too many for him. His horse was tired; though he drove in the spurs it would not rear. All it would do was to snort and sidle backwards.

His thoughts had been so entirely occupied with meeting Don Juan that he was unprepared for any other encounter. He could not think what to do or to say. He was not afraid, but he was baffled.

One of the men came nearer, and said,

'Are you not Don Ottavio?'

'Let me pass.'

The man turned round, conferring with the others. He sat haughtily, looking at the castle, trying not to hear what they said. For they were speaking of the events of the morning and of how Don Juan had wronged him. It was highly painful to sit here on a jaded horse, thwarted by a gang of peasants, and hearing his dishonour canvassed among them.

The spokesman returned.

'If we knew your reason for wanting to get into the castle, maybe we might let you through.'

Furious at their impertinence, bewildered by his own misfortunes, he asked himself what he should do now. He could not ride back. Honour demanded that he should stay, and anyhow the horse was too done to carry him. He could not spend the night out of doors, he had no mind to go to the inn. An expedient occurred to him, and in a snappish voice he asked where the priest of the village lived.

'Why, you've no quarrel with him, surely?'

'My quarrels are no concern of yours, I suppose.'

'That's a pity,' said the man, 'for if we had known your quarrel we might have helped you to it.'

From the group of men an aged voice, interested and helpful, cried out,

'Speak your mind, Don Ottavio, you've nothing to fear. If it's Don Juan you are looking for, why, he has wronged us as well as you. If he's your quarrel, we'll let you through soon enough. Though whether you'll get in is another matter.'

They made way for him. Nothing could have been more exasperating than to find himself befriended by these clod-hoppers. It was in his mind to turn and ride off. But now there was no escape from their good offices. This one would hold his horse, the other bang the knocker for him. He dismounted in silence and walked up the steps, feeling their attention resting on his back like a load of bricks. The friendly old yokel dogged him.

'Knock again, sir. Knock louder. Shout to them who you are.'

But the door did not open and he had to return to their sympathy and their advice.

The maps were still on the table, account-books and treatises on agriculture had been added to them, and Don Saturno was still talking about the duties of a landowner. Hearing the knocker hammering on the door, he had broken off to say how pleasant it was to feel such security from interruption.

'They will soon leave off knocking, and we can go on talking. As I was saying, the La Mancha estate has often given me a great deal of uneasiness. I have felt that if only I could go there and supervise a thorough remodelling—new methods, rotation of crops, you know, all that sort of thing—and get rid of that cheating bailiff, it could be improved out of all knowledge. Indeed, I blame myself that I have not gone. I should have gone. But I have always been attached to this place, perhaps I have concentrated too much on Tenorio Viejo. You too will find it a temptation. One tends to sink into one's native soil, one identifies oneself—it is very natural—with the traditional family acres. You will be wiser, I hope.'

'I certainly don't intend to sink into Tenorio Viejo,' said Don Juan.

He had not spoken for a long while. Perhaps that was why his voice sounded so peculiarly unsympathetic, so raw, as it were, and unassimilated, like beans that have grown too dry and resist the concoction that should have embodied them in the stew. I hope I have not talked too long, thought Don Saturno, but I expect I have. What a pity, when we were getting on so surprisingly well.

'No? Well, of course, it will be for you to decide. Maybe you will yet change your mind. Anyhow, I shall die the happier for thinking you have an interest in the old place, even if you do not settle here.'

'As you remark, it is for me to decide. And I think it will save a great deal of wasted chatter if I tell you my decision. First, I shall not change my mind. Secondly, I am not interested in the old place. As I told you, I hate the past, I hate the old. It is the new place I am interested in.'

'Quite right! One should look forward. As a people we are far too traditional. A new Tenorio will grow from Tenorio Viejo. One could not inaugurate it better than with the scheme for irrigation, I understand why that idea pleases you so well. We must . . .'

'I am coming to the irrigation. This plan here: how am I to know if it will work? I don't want bungles and delays, you must get a surveyor to examine it.'

'Certainly, certainly. As you say, we don't want bungles. As for delays——'

'Well, there's this to be said for your dawdling. If you had done it sooner, you might have mismanaged it.'

A trifle stiffly, Don Saturno said,

'There is this also to be said for my dawdling. One cannot impose a scheme on people until they are sure they want it themselves. First, you must convince them that they will be the gainers by it; then you must make them acquainted with the theory. . . .'

'And that is the third thing I must make plain. I have no intention of being a philanthropist. It is my own good that interests me. I don't see myself depending on the card-table for my supplies for the rest of my life.'

'You mean, you would raise the rents?' said Don Saturno.

'Not at all. I should abolish the rents. Once the thing is in order, I abolish the rents and take over the land again.'

'You cannot do that!'

'I can do it whenever I please. The leases are yearly. You told me so yourself.'

'And the men?'

'Can work my land for me. Or I can fetch others.'

They looked at each other: the old man shaking with indignation, the other placid and smiling.

'Then there shall be no irrigation while I live,' exclaimed Don Saturno passionately. 'I will be party to no such thing. You shall never dishonour me like this.'

'There will be irrigation the moment you die,' said Don Juan.

He remembered how they had called out *Cheat* and *Old Cozener.*

'I could kill you for this,' he said.

He took the map and tore it into shreds. He went to the window, threw open the shutters, leaned out, crying,

'*Oye*, you there! I have something to tell you. Shameful tidings, but you must know them. There can be no water. We have fallen into bad hands, you and I. There can be no water!'

His high-pitched voice, shaken with passion, trailed like a lamentation for the dead.

He must try another door, they had said to Don Ottavio. Let him not be discouraged. Revenge would be sweet, whichever door he came to it by. There was a place in the east wall where one could climb over by way of the old mulberry. Once in the grounds. . . . A man came running, cast himself into the midst of them.

'My girl's gone! Celestina!'

In his flat face his mouth opened like a wound.

'She's gone! I went home, as you know, to see that all was well, the doors locked, all safe and tight. The door was open, the house was empty. The moment I went in I knew it was empty. Oh, I could tell! She's gone!'

'She's gone to a neighbour, maybe.'

'No, she would not do that. She was never a gad-about. Besides, I have searched, I have asked, I have been everywhere. No one has seen her. She's gone!

'And I know where!' he cried furiously, shaking his fist. 'She's been stolen. By him. He's got her in there, damn him! And wasn't his pandar, that Leporello, down at the mill? That's how he heard about her, that's how it's been done. Let me get at him! He shall never go after women again.'

He staggered about, beside himself with rage. He beat himself with his fists, twisted himself, tore his hair, he was like a man in the extremities of colic, he was terrifying and ridiculous. The others thumped him on the back, shook him. Don Ottavio withdrew a little.

'Well, there's a pair of you. For here's Don Ottavio, come back to avenge himself. He's for a wife; you're for a daughter. He's bent on getting into the castle, and you had best go along with him.'

Don Ottavio put out his hand in protest. The miller grasped it, and wrung it.

'We'll go together,' he said.

It was all arranged. One of the detachment was told off to go with them and to precede them into the grounds.

For those on guard within must have Don Ottavio explained to them, the appearance of a gentleman might be taken amiss. It seemed a long way to where the mulberry sprawled its heavy limbs over the wall, whose coping was broken with their weight. Dionio went over like a cat, Don Ottavio, a heavier man and a taller, got halfway over and then became entangled in the branches. The tree creaked and swayed, Dionio caught hold of his legs and tugged, a stone was dislodged. Two men came running.

'Who's there? Dionio?'

Hauling on Don Ottavio's foot, Dionio began to explain why he was in the tree.

'If you'll let go of my leg, I can get down.'

One of the men unclasped Dionio's hand. From afar off a high-pitched voice wailed out something about water. It was answered with an outburst of furious shouting. Scratched and bruised, he leaped from the tree.

'Here, what's happened? What are they shouting about? Has he broken out? Are they after him?'

They had begun to swarm up the wall, to lean over and listen. Dionio turned to Don Ottavio, saying,

'Which of us is to have him, say? Shall we draw lots?'

Ottavio could find no answer. Closed in under the straggling trees, breathed on and jostled by strange men, he seemed to be in some frightful nightmare. Far off was furious shouting, and here, furious whispers. Hearing at last a voice at ordinary pitch he turned in relief towards the speaker.

'Friends, what has become of you, are you run mad? Let us go back to our place.'

'Aye, but listen to the shouting. Suppose he's escaping there?'

'Well, they are there to see to it. But let us go back to our watch. For all we know, it may be a trick, he may be escaping this way.'

'Ramon's right.'

'Yes, he's always right. It's his way.'

But they ran back, dodging through the trees. Ottavio walked slowly after, stopping to look round, to listen to the shouting, to ask himself if he was in his senses. The fellow who had lost his daughter turned back for him.

'We'll get in, we'll get in,' he said. 'For Ramon Perez is here, and his niece is one of the castle servants. It can be managed, he'll get us in. But which of us is to have the man?'

He ran, hauling Don Ottavio after him, and speaking in snatches.

Now he recognised where he was. He had walked in these overgrown alleys, with Don Saturno chattering, with Ana leaning on his arm. It was a relief to find that this Ramon who was to arrange things was the man who had spoken in an ordinary voice. He seemed more respectful, at any rate less frantic than the others. He led them, Don Ottavio and Dionio, by a little path into a courtyard where there was an old wheelbarrow, some rakes and spades, and a woodstack. The tumult beyond had broken out again, more furious than ever. Ramon climbed the woodstack and crawled along the roof of an outbuilding. A shutter moved a little, was thrown back, and a girl leaned out, brandishing a skillet.

'Don't you come nearer. Don't make so much noise. Tell me, what's happening?'

'You should know that better than I. Where's my niece? I want to talk to her.'

'Shouldn't I do as well?' asked the girl, waving the skillet like a fan.

'You'll do better. It's Antonita, isn't it?'

She put up the skillet, and hid her face, and giggled.

'How are you getting on in there?'

'It's awful,' she replied. 'We're terrified. Old Luis walks up and down with a sword, all the doors are barricaded, the men must sit up all night, and the cook is starving us. Why don't you go away? And what's it all about? If you're after the fat priest you've missed your chance, for he's gone. What a mouthful!'

'Where's Luis with his sword?'

'Eh, how should I know? He's waiting behind the great door.'

'Antonita, here's a gentleman. He wants to get in.'

'Let him knock, then.'

'He has knocked. Luis was deaf and did not hear.'

'What does he want?'

'He wants Don Juan.'

She spat.

'More than I do. He's an ugly sulky beast. In here, we all hate him.'

'Out here, we hate him too. Antonita, how can my man get in? It must be a gap wide enough for a man and a sword.'

She leaned out further, stared with bright round eyes, whispered,

'Who is he?'

'Don Ottavio.'

'Oh—h!'

Her face was pinched with excitement.

Never again will I trust a servant, thought Don Ottavio. What traitors they are! Who would have believed it possible? His features assumed a sterner expression as he remembered that anyhow all women betray.

She twirled the skillet to and fro. It lagged, it came to a standstill.

'Ramon Perez, I dare not, I'm afraid.'

'Antonita, my man is two men. The other one is our Dionio. He has come to find his daughter.'

'Celestina? But she is not here.'

'She is.'

'She is?'

'It seems, he carried her off.'

Her face grew hard.

'They must come this way. In through this window. All the men are on the ground floor. He is in the library. From here you can march straight in on him. It would be a good riddance.'

Already Dionio was climbing the woodstack. Ottavio's mind was a whirl of horror and forebodings. He climbed the woodstack too, and crawled along the roof. Ramon hoisted him up to the window. I ought to tip him, thought Ottavio. His cuff caught on a nail, and tore, a hot, hard little hand came out of the darkness and pulled him in. He was in a dark gallery, stiflingly hot. He heard whisperings, giggles, and the rustle of skirts. His head knocked against the sloping ceiling, there was a strong smell of dry-rot, when he caught hold of an upright beam he felt the wood come away in powder. She pulled him on, into another room, down a stairway into another gallery, up stairs again. Passing a window he looked out, and saw for a moment a view of the square and a throng of men surging to and fro.

Ahead of him a door opened. He saw Dionio silhouetted against a lighted room and recognised where he was. They had come in at the other end of the library, through the door opposite the main door.

He saw Dionio pull out a knife, and leap forward. He saw Don Juan jump to his feet. He ran after Dionio, and tripped him; and as the miller struggled to get his footing again Don Ottavio hit him with all his force on the back of the neck. Still clutching the knife he fell, and lay still.

'I am very much obliged to you,' said Don Juan.

Don Ottavio tried to reply, and could not. After so long a strain, after so much anxiety, disgust, and self-control, the excitement of striking down a man had been too much for him. He felt the blood rushing to his face. His eyes dazzled, his heart pounded. Far off, like the sea, the noise of the besiegers rose and fell. An emotion of nobility swept over him, like a drunk man he became aware of himself as a separate being, a figure to be at once admired and pitied.

Now he noticed Don Saturno, looking old and ill, who had got up out of his great chair and came forward, saying,

'I hope you will not think me inhospitable if I ask how you got in?'

How puny he looks, thought Don Ottavio. How old. What a despicable figure. The spectacle of Don Saturno restored to him the power of speech. Turning to Don Juan, laying his hand on the hilt of his sword, he made a formal bow.

'I returned here at the bidding of honour. But in an hour like this honour can remember no personal quarrel. We must stand together in the face of a common enemy.'

Don Juan also bowed.

'Don Ottavio, your deeds have gone before your words. I only regret that the rabble should delay me from offering you what satisfaction I can. But let us hope we shall soon see the end of them.'

Meanwhile, Don Saturno was examining the miller.

'Is he dead?' asked his son. 'No? I suppose you know who he is and all that. One of your enlightened tenants, I take it? By the way, Don Ottavio, are there any more of them about, do you know?'

'He was the only one that I saw get in. But there may be others. I must tell you at once, he was let in by one of your servants.'

'Indeed?'

'A girl called Antonita.'

'Antonita? Father, do you hear that? Your garrison is false to you. My father assures me that a siege is nothing, almost a matter of course. I must say, I find it annoying. And it's even more annoying,' he went on, his tone sharpening, 'to have semi-conscious assassins sprawling all over the floor. Unfortunately, this is not my house. I do not know whether he will be secured, or left here till he is strong enough to attack me again.'

With reproachful civility, Don Ottavio begged that the miller might be removed to a place of safe keeping.

'I don't think you realise how serious things are. Do you know that your grounds are full of these men? And that your servants seem to be in league with them?'

'My servants are not afraid of them, if that is what you mean,' replied the old man. Then, with a sigh, he rose from his knees, and walked slowly to the door and called out for Luis.

'Dionio!' exclaimed the major-domo. 'Who would have believed such a thing?'

'Now they will go off and fuss over him as though they were the holy women weeping over Jesus,' said Don Juan, with a laugh. 'Between ourselves, Don Ottavio, this shock has been too much for my father. He has let everything slide for years. Now it has turned serious, and he has gone to pieces.'

'How many men have you got here—men you can trust?'

He shrugged his shoulders.

'A handful of cook-boys and stable-boys. And some old grey-beards like Luis, who think my father is Alfonso the Wise. And all of them related to somebody in the village. Otherwise—our two selves. You came in by that door, I think. We had better lock it.'

Don Ottavio looked with disapproval at the flimsy lock. Outside, the uproar went on.

'It sounds as though the whole village were there.'

'It is,' replied Don Juan.

'This is exceedingly serious!' exclaimed Don Ottavio. 'We do not know how or where it will end. The country is in such a state. . . . Don Juan, let me beg you to have a detachment of troops to restore order.'

'Excellent, if we could get them. But short of sowing dragons' teeth in the flower-pots. . . .'

Don Ottavio spoke of the troops he had seen billeted in Fuentes.

'A word to their commander—I know him well—and they would be here within twenty-four hours from now. But we must send at once, or they will have gone on.'

Don Juan looked up.

'I think I have it. Did you say the girl was called Antonita? But I am afraid I must ask you to accept for a moment the painful imputation that we have fought, and that you have been the loser. That girl,' he went on, 'knows you got in, but knows no more. I have only to ask her to tell her friends in the grounds that a priest is needed. A priest can pass in without interference. He can carry out our message.'

Don Ottavio said warmly that it was an excellent idea.

'You are sure that you do not object to the imputation that I have got the better of you? Of course, it might be the miller——'

'Not at all, not in the least. I waive all that. But your father?'

'—Need not be consulted. Now for Antonita.'

Luis brought in wine. Don Saturno returned. Sighing, he let himself down into his chair, uttered a few words of hospitality, and seemed to fall asleep. Don Juan also returned and sat down near the window and beckoned to Don Ottavio.

'It will be worth watching,' he said.

It shocked Don Ottavio to see him settled there as though at a theatre. With very different feelings he saw the acolyte come in sight, ringing his bell, and the priest following him. The crowd opened before them. The shouting was hushed, they fell on their knees as the priest went by carrying the sacrament. Tinkling his bell the acolyte mounted the steps.

Don Saturno sat up with a start.

'Write out that letter,' said Don Juan. 'I'll see they're let in.'

The bolts jarred, the door creaked on its hinges, and for a moment there was a growl of anger. But the bell tinkled louder, and the door was bolted again, and Don Juan had ushered Don Tomas into the room.

'It appears that your miller has asked for the priest,' he said. 'Unless you would like to accompany Don

Tomas, perhaps you will leave it to Don Ottavio and myself.'

Wrinkling his face like an old monkey, Don Saturno seemed to be hunting for words. No words came. With a look of embarrassment he held out a key.

Outside the servants were on their knees. When Don Ottavio appeared there was a ripple of astonishment; but no word could be said and in silence they trooped after the priest. Luis came forward and took the key. With indignation Don Ottavio realised that Dionio had been laid in the room which had been Don Isidro's. He had begun to recover consciousness. When he saw Don Tomas his face took on a look of melancholy astonishment.

In his confession he began to speak of Celestina. With extraordinary energy the priest urged him to forget earthly things, to die in peace with all men. 'Your salvation depends on it,' he said, his eyes bolting out of his head as though he saw some terrifying object. That evening Don Gil had been with him, talking of the bloodshed that must certainly come, of the souls dismissed unabsolved and in a heat of anger, and of the possibility that the seeming Don Juan was in truth a fiend, straight from hell, sent to Tenorio Viejo to scourge it for past wickedness, to inflame it to more.

Ottavio had been rather perturbed to find that the last offices of the Church were being bestowed on a man who seemed to be making a very good recovery from a knockout blow. But he reflected that the miller might be worse than he looked, might even die during the night; and in that case how providential it would be that a stratagem necessary to preserve law and order should also have necessitated the formalities of a christian death-bed. But casuistry was soon swept away by devotion. Deeply moved, he knelt at the foot of the bed, joining in the responses in a voice rich with feeling as he recalled the events of a day including such injuries, such dangers, and such a climax. He had returned to fight Don Juan and instead he had saved Don Juan's life. He felt the drama and the chivalry of the act, he felt also its inevitability. A right-thinking man could not have acted otherwise. And as though the viaticum had been given to him he found himself in a state of christian charity towards Doña Ana, Don Juan, and the miller.

Under his eyelashes, which were both long and thick, he glanced towards the man who had been his foe and was now his ally. For an atheist, Don Juan was certainly behaving with great decorum. And nothing could have been more masterly than the skill with which he intercepted Don Tomas.

'This letter, Father, is of the gravest importance. Otherwise, I would not trouble you at a moment like this. But it must reach Fuentes by daybreak, and I cannot send it by a messenger from this house, in case these misguided villagers should set on him. Give us your advice. Who can go with it?'

Don Tomas muttered something about the sacristan.

'He is very discreet—a light sleeper.'

'Has he a mule?'

'Oh yes, a very good one. Yet I do not quite like to disturb him.'

He would never do it for me, he thought.

'He is a poor man,' he said.

'He shall have as much again when I learn that the letter has been delivered in good time. And doubtless you have other poor men in this village. If you would be my almoner——'

Don Tomas looked with something like horror on so much money, and it seemed to him that it scorched his hand.

Waking with a start Don Tomas saw that it was day. His first thought was of the letter, which perhaps at this moment Don Gil was delivering.

On being asked to dress himself, saddle the mule and ride immediately to the Inn of the Escutcheon in Fuentes the sacristan had proved unexpectedly amiable.

'To some fair lady, no doubt,' he had said. 'Ah well, your reverence, it is no business of mine whom they send letters to in the middle of the night; nor of your reverence's either, till he comes to the confessional.'

'It is addressed to an officer,' said the priest, surprised that the sacristan had not mastered the address already.

'Then there is the less sin in it, I hope. But whatever there is in it, I shall go a roundabout way through the village. For I take it this letter is a letter that must not be spied on.'

'Go with God,' said the priest. No doubt it was the money that had done it. Wrapped in his great hooded cloak the sacristan had seemed like some enormous bird of night perched on the mule. If presently he had risen in the air, flapping dark wings, it would not have been altogether surprising.

As usual on waking a choking-fit came over him. He got out of bed and opened the shutters and stood gasping up the morning airs. On the window-sill was the money that had been given him for the poor of the parish, the money that overnight had seemed to scorch his palm. But now it was the ordinary coin of the realm, a handsome alms from a rich man and for a poor man a six-months' livelihood. But should I have taken it? he asked himself. And a phrase from holy writ came into his mind about being a consenter to iniquity. He realised that all night he had been dreaming of Don Juan.

The dream persisted into the waking. He could not rid his mind's eye from the recollection of Don Juan's face: a well-fed, well-preserved countenance, ordinary enough, the face of a man who knows what he is about; the face he had watched with such trembling curiosity during the rite administered to the dying miller last night. At first, in his simplicity, he had supposed that before those holy words and gestures the man from hell—if so he was—would quail and shrivel away; the atheist—if atheist he were—would assume looks of mocking contempt. But nothing so dramatic or so simple had been shown him.

Indeed, what had he seen? Nothing supernatural, nothing to be afraid of. A man of the world; and man of the world enough to behave as other men did, to bow gravely and speak civilly, to kneel in the presence of the Sacrament and to give an alms to the poor of the parish. That was all. No man from hell, a man of the world merely; a man whose concern with worldly things expressed itself in certain passing looks of thoughtfulness, anxiety, contrivance.

But the face of Don Juan re-minted by his dreams persisted in his mind's eye. It looked at him from under the brows of the medlar-tree, it peered from behind the artichoke hedge, it rested its chin on the crest of the mountain and looked down on the valley. There was to be no escape. The imprint on the money for the poor became the face of Don Juan, the face of a man tormented with endless calculation, a face where triumph was followed by uneasiness, uneasiness by weary cunning, as though traversed and shadowed by wreaths of smoke.

'Since he is a man, I should pray for him,' gasped Don Tomas. 'O God the maker of hell, O Jesus who descended into hell, strengthen me against the thought of this man!'

He took the money gingerly, and dropped it into the holy-water stoup, and fell on his knees. It was as though he had lowered himself that much nearer to the mouth of hell. He breathed its smoke, he smelled the fusty odour of eternal woe. His cough became worse, it was destroying him. He lay grovelling on the floor, rubbing his breast-bone against the bare boards. He sneezed, and his eyes ran. It was always worse in the morning. Ah, how slowly time went, weary as he! How long it must be before the evening brought him its dated relief!

He listened for sounds of his housekeeper, but she still slept. The village, too, how quiet it was! Then he remembered that all the men were on guard round the castle, that there had been a scuffle in which the boy Enrique had received his death-wound, that the life of the village was at a standstill. It was something to do with this trouble about the water, though it was Don Juan they were waiting for.

Absorbed in his ill-health and his religion of melancholy and fear Don Tomas knew little of his parishioners. Don Gil told him of their misdoings and Doña Adriana of their needs. But he scarcely knew them by sight, and the voices in the confessional all told much the same story, it was as though the voice of the wind breathed its monotonous cadence through the lattice. Now, for some reason, he began to think of them, saying to himself that at mass he would give a more particular attention to his congregation, a congregation which would be the more spiritually minded since the village was in this state of tension.

But the congregation was much as usual, and the absence of the sacristan made the performance of the mass seem hazardous and agitating. He had to think of the church-bell, the candles, the supply of incense, the punctuality of the server and what would happen if he were not prompted in the responses. He was aware that he disliked Don Gil; but he had not realised till this morning how completely he relied on him.

'My cloak,' he said to his housekeeper. 'I am going out.'

She looked at him with surprise.

He thought he would go to the village. But instead he found himself going to the Moor's House. The schoolmaster was alone, still half-dressed, yawning, and without his wig. He received the priest with an ill grace. Don Tomas began to speak of the children's religious education: did they read the Lives of the Saints, did any one of them show an aptitude for religion? The schoolmaster looked at him coldly and enquired after his asthma. Conversation was languid and formal till all of a sudden Don Francisco broke into a tirade of passionate complaint and self-exculpation, pointing to the faded maps, showing the three battered horn-books and the broken pair of compasses, the dirty scribbled walls and his frayed shirt, asking how any man could teach who was so ill-provided with the means of teaching, so ill-supplied with the means of making himself respected. 'I was fetched here to rot,' he said. 'No one comes near me, if I am considered at all it is as a horse-doctor.' And he repeated the words, 'a horse-doctor,' with bitter emphasis. After a pause Don Tomas uttered a few words about the dangers of ambition, the security of a life far from the world and its disillusionments. The schoolmaster took up a coat and began to sew a patch on it, and after a little the priest took his leave.

He walked through the village. He had expected that it would register the strain of recent events, that he would hear lamentations and cries of alarm, and find himself called on for consolation. But everything was as usual: at least, he supposed so; really he did not know, since he went abroad so seldom. The women were fetching water, driving dust about with their brooms, combing children's heads, the usual occupations of women, and looked no more careworn than they usually did. If anything alarmed them, it was seeing him out among them. The tanner's wife, leading her goat from the shed, caught sight of him, crossed herself, and went hastily back again.

He took notice of everything, as though this were the first time, or the last, that he would walk through his village. He busied his eyes with a rent in a roof, a broken crock by a doorway, a rabbit-skin nailed up in the sun to dry, a fig-tree with its young leaves drooping in the heat, a child crossing the road on all-fours, a woman scraping dandelion roots into a basin, the cactus-shaped pattern where some water had been spilled in the dust. He busied his eyes so intently that he scarcely noticed that he was being greeted, that the child on all-fours was hauled up by its mother and aimed towards him for a blessing. He did not want to look at people's faces, the rabbit-skin and the broken crock were better subjects for scrutiny; for they could not remind him of Don Juan.

When he came to the open space before the castle he flinched, and almost turned back. The men were still there. They were sitting in a patch of shade. They had fetched out stools and benches, they had a wineskin, and were playing the tarot. So much he saw, and went on with lowered eyes, studying the dust patterned with innumerable footsteps, as though a flock of sheep had been penned there. He came up to them. A card from their game lay on the ground, and he looked at it—the Madman.

They rose at his approach, and instantly he stopped some paces away. Perhaps it was because they were in the shade and he was in the sun that he received an impression that they were people of a different race, ambassadors from a foreign country. A choking-fit took him, the sweat burst from his forehead, he gasped and mopped himself with a handkerchief and thought how humiliating it would be if he had to go away without having spoken a word. Presently someone offered him the wineskin, and someone else gave him a dubious buffet on the back.

'Since when have you been here?' he began.

The big swineherd was shoved forward as spokesman.

'Since yesterday, Father.'

'Would it not be better to go away, my sons?'

'Any man can go away who likes,' replied the swineherd. 'We compel no man.'

Behind him Pedrillo, inveterate conversationalist, was bobbing up and down.

'Making so bold, your reverence, was it the miller you

carried our Saviour to last night? For we thought it might be that other one, since he, as a gentleman, would have the first turn. But now, from what we hear——'

'It was Dionio Gutierrez,' said Don Tomas.

Pedrillo turned to the others. 'There!' he said regretfully. 'It was the miller all the time. Well, it seems Death had nicked his ear. Only a week or so ago and he was dying. Thin as a lath, no stomach at all. Next thing we know, he had beaten Leporello and was as strong as a giant. But Death had nicked him, for all that, and he's met his end round another corner. May-his-soul-rest-in-peace!'

There was a general commendation of the miller's soul. Andres followed it by saying,

'Aye, but is he dead?'

'Cht!' said various reproving voices. Such a query was felt to be uncivil, an aspersion on the honour of the last rites.

'Well!' said Jesus. 'Death has nicked this one too, or I'm much mistaken.'

'We'll know when he comes out,' said Andres, holding to his point. For Don Tomas had mounted the steps. And his coughs must have identified him to those within, for the door opened a crack to admit him.

He was shown in on Don Ottavio and Don Juan, who were playing backgammon. His arrival just then—though he did not know it—was rather awkward. For only a few minutes earlier the castle had been aroused by shouts and hammerings from the dying man. Dionio had lain through the night very obediently expecting to die, but meanwhile growing increasingly hungry. As time went on hunger became too much for him, he had to admit that this increasing languor and emptiness was no part of a good death but the appetite of ordinary living. Hard on the heels of this had come the thought that, since they had given him the last rites, he was to be left shut up till he died of starvation. He began to shout, to bang on the door.

'He seems stronger this morning,' said Don Ottavio.

'These peasants are as tough as leather,' added Don Juan.

Left alone once more they laughed a little and went on with their backgammon. They were getting on very well together. Though neither man felt the slightest kindness for the other, in the face of a common enemy (as Don Ottavio had put it) and while waiting for a common succour, they sank their differences. A further bond, too, was growing up between them in the shape of a more or less open agreement to put down Don Saturno. Released from Doña Ana's decorum Ottavio found a schoolboy delight in flouting the old man whose hospitality he had been compelled to endure for so long. Of the two allies in this pursuit he was much the livelier; for he was enjoying a novel experience and putting his whole heart into the enjoyment. Once, indeed, he thought he had gone too far: a jest at the unennobled antiquity of the de Tenorio family might have been as much resented by the heir as by the father. But a glance at Don Juan reassured him. Don Juan was smiling—rather as a schoolmaster smiles at some happy sally from a pupil, but smiling nevertheless.

I have done it. I have seen him again, thought the priest. He was filled with a proud, with a victorious tranquillity, as though he had acquitted himself of some life-or-death obligation. Faith had supported him, the efficacy of the chrism had held good. He had looked evil in the face and had felt no fear. With no special protection, not warded with the sacrament or secluded in a holy ritual, he had visited Don Juan and come away unharmed.

He was walking off, rapt and oblivious, when the men in front of the castle came running after him.

'How is Dionio, Father? Is he alive or dead?'

'He is still alive.'

'How does he look? Will he recover?'

'I did not see him. There is no need for me to see him again. He is in a state of grace, he is making an exemplary death. *He is penitent*,' he added, turning on them with a sudden twang of authority in his manner.

There was no need to study fig-trees and rabbit-skins and children on his way home. The sun could not smite him, though a thousand should fall at his right hand he would not be moved. He reached the presbytery, and putting aside Doña Adriana's questions about the state of the village and Enrique's funeral, he lay down to rest, and fell asleep like a child.

'Adding eight to eight, the sum is sixteen,' said Don Saturno. 'One and six make seven. The sum of three eights is twenty-four. Two and four make six. The sum of four eights is thirty-two. Three and two make five. The sum of five eights is forty. Four and a zero, that is four. The sum of six eights is forty-eight. Four and eight make twelve, and the digits one and two make three. You follow?'

'Aha,' said the miller, wrinkling his nose. It was wonderful how they came out, these figures, one following another sure as the stars in the rising Orion. What beauties there were in the numbers, to be sure. If it had not been for the thought of Celestina, what heavenly happiness he would now be feeling. Here I am, he thought, sitting in this grand room, my belly full of good food, my mind full of learning—and yet, in the happiest hour of my life I cannot give myself over to happiness. For what has become of my girl?—that is the question that bites me in the heart. I am here like a blessed soul that sits in heaven all but one foot, and that foot the angel has forgotten to take out of purgatory. But good manners forbade him to interrupt his entertainer by asking about Celestina.

'The sum of seven eights is fifty-six. Five and six make eleven, two ones, and that makes two. The sum of eight eights is sixty-four. Six and four make ten, which is to say, one and a zero, one. Eight, seven, six, five, four, three, two, one.'

He had noticed Dionio counting the remains of his

meal, the olive stones, the halved apricot stones which he had split to get at the kernels. This had suggested divination and auguries as a subject for conversation; but after a while he realised that Dionio was not interested so much in divination as in numbers, and he began recounting some of the curiosities of the multiplication tables.

'With the next step it becomes more interesting. The sum of nine eights is seventy-two, seven and two make nine. This appearance of a nine seems at first sight inconsistent and surprising; but with the sum of ten eights. . . .'

How attentively the man listened! Good manners alone could not account for such listening, it must be the first murmuring resonance of a mind attuned to mathematics. But had he analysed more closely Don Saturno would have found that it was the miller's good manners which meant most to him. The way in which he had been treated by his son and his guest had mortified him deeply. He had been set at nought in his own house, he had been snubbed and cold-shouldered and laughed at. Keeping the ring round these attacks on his self-esteem was the larger circle of his other enemies. Wincing under Don Juan's sneers and Don Ottavio's horse-play he almost forgot that his house was still besieged, and that as well as being called Quixote and Old Fool, he had been called Cheat and Old Cozener. But they were there, and hated him. He compared himself to the bull, absorbed in combating its tormentors; and yet, did it look a little further, it would see the combat encircled with a ring of implacable spectators.

Meanwhile he continued to write down the figures, and they had reached the sum of twenty-six eights.

'Look! We're back again where we were. An eight, and then a sixteen.'

The miller's voice expressed an authentic delight. One could not be insensible to such goodness and simplicity; and it seemed to Don Saturno that in his prisoner, with whom he also was imprisoned, he had found a friend for life. He stretched out his hand, thin and bleached and a little tremulous, towards Dionio's hand that rested so solidly on the sheet of scribbled paper. But Celestina?—thought the miller. We have reached twenty-six eights, everything begins over again. Is this not a moment in which to speak of Celestina? He did not notice the gesture. Don Saturno hesitated, and drew back his hand. And it seemed to him that his old blood had stumbled to his face, that he was crimson with shame.

The water. The eviction of the tenants when the irrigation was completed. Do as he would, they were to be betrayed. Do as he would, they would never believe that he was betrayed with them. As long as a child's child lived in Tenorio Viejo he would be called Saturno the Cheat.

He walked to the window and looked through the chinks of the shutters. There they were. He looked at the landscape he had known all his life, at the place he called his. There was the river-bed, the poplar-trees, the speckled olive-yards, the green bands of the maize, the road. He saw something compact that moved at a steady pace along the road. A cloud of dust moved with it, and out of the dust flashed sharp prickles of light.

'They march well. But it's too fast.' The sentence rose in his mind, deliberate as a bubble rising. It exploded into meaning. He remained for some time at the window, swallowing, and driving the nails into the palms of his hands. The truth was, he was afraid to go downstairs and face the two men there.

Shutting the backgammon table Don Juan suggested that they should throw a main or two. 'You might be more fortunate with games of chance,' he said acidly. He was a censorious opponent in games of skill, it was ill-bred, thought Ottavio, to take each move so seriously, to go over the game afterwards so exactly and so pettishly, pointing out wherever one had been wrong.

The dice rattled, the flies buzzed. At intervals Don Juan looked at his watch.

'They seem quiet enough now,' said Don Ottavio. 'They are beginning to lose heart I expect, they are coming to their senses.'

'Snakes lose heart, don't they, when they lie still?'

'We shall certainly see a detachment before sundown,' continued Ottavio. 'Meanwhile I feel no alarm.'

Don Juan gave him a glance that said plainly, Dolt.

'A show of authority will be quite enough.'

'The smell of authority is better,' replied Don Juan.

How shabby to be so afraid of a pack of peasants, thought Ottavio: wretched creatures, half-starved and worse than half-armed. He recalled himself, a splendid solitary figure, confronting the swineherds. The situation had for a moment looked very untoward, yet he had not been afraid. A boar, a spectre, a cannon, a skilful duellist: before such things one might justifiably feel a certain alarm; but not before the lower orders. Don Juan, however, was undoubtedly feeling alarm. Only alarm could account for his restlessness, his impatience, his fits of abstraction, his asperity, and the expression which accompanied the fits of abstraction: an expression, as it were, covetous and musing. Very odd. Not very creditable. Perhaps he had learned timidity through so inordinately frequenting the company of women.

The flies buzzed, the dice rattled. The door was thrown open and the old fool walked in.

'Juan! A band of soldiers is marching down on the village.'

'I am glad to hear it.'

'Did you know they were coming? Did you—have you been poltroon enough to send for them?'

'Ah—yes. We sent for them.'

'You took it on yourself to order troops into my village? You, my son? And you, my guest?'

'I have a certain interest in your village,' said the son.

'Your village! Your rubbish-heap, your starveling bear-garden. You are not the only member of this family to have projects of reform. I have my reforming projects too, as I explained to you last night.'

Some way off a child's voice, a thin angular cockcrow, began calling and hallooing. Don Saturno rang his silver bell violently. Don Ottavio said,

'I must take exception to the word you used just then. Prudent, yes. But not poltroon. Order must be maintained, as your guest, as a younger man, I feel a personal responsibility for your safety.'

'Ass!' said Don Saturno. Luis came in.

'Luis! Without my knowledge, soldiers have been sent for. I am going out to meet them, and to order them back. You will open the door and accompany me.'

'He won't,' said Don Juan. 'No old men leave this house. We value their hoary wisdom too much to endanger it. No old men run to the window, either. We had enough of that last night. Sit down in your easy-chair, father. You must take a little nap. First, I will tie your arms, so——'

The major-domo ran forward. Ottavio caught hold of him.

'That's right. You deal with him. Next, I will tie your legs. And now, my dear father, here is a book of philosophy'—he walked to the bookshelves—'*de Senectute*, that will do admirably, which I will open and place in your lap, so, in order that you may continue your studies for the next hour or two. I do not suppose it will be much longer than that.'

'Bad son! Wicked and shameless man!' cried the major-domo, whom Ottavio had tied up. 'Don Juan de Tenorio, cold-hearted rascal, creature with the thoughts of an ape, may you be forever cursed for this, may your name stink before God and man and the devil! Beast, libertine, traitor, blood-sucker, ignoramus, blot on an honourable house, shame of the whole of Spain, why did you ever come among us? You were ill to bear even in your absence, your stink blew over the mountain like a poison, never named without a curse, never remembered without a groan. . . . May you have your reward, may you have a son worse than yourself! Hear the truth from an honest mouth for once. What are you worth, worthless one? No more than this fellow, this cuckold here. . . .'

'Fellow?' exclaimed Ottavio in a fury.

'Cowards, both of you!' shouted the old servant.

Don Saturno sat as though deaf and dumb.

In the river bank a little beyond the mill there was a nest of wild bees, and the children went there to play, lobbing stones into the cranny and watching the bees come swarming out. They were making so much noise that they did not hear the tramp of marching till the first soldiers were almost level with the bee's nest. Then Fernanda looked up, and saw above the fringe of bushes the resolute unanimous outline of a detachment of infantry. Before she had spoken the others had caught her thought, looked up and saw the soldiers too. Most of them fell on their knees and began crossing themselves, for they had no experience of a procession that was not a religious procession. Fernanda scrambled up the bank, hauling Engracia after her. Engracia slipped, scraped her knee, cried and dragged back. For the first time in their lives the bond that tied them gave way. She left Engracia, and began to run down the road. After she had run ten yards she opened her mouth in a scream. She ran and she screamed. Every now and then she looked back over her shoulder at the men and made a furious grimace. She ran so fast she soon left them behind, they were only a cloud of dust, pricked with flashes of light, when she reached the village. But still she ran and screamed, knowing that they followed on.

'*Ay! Ay!* They're co-o-oming!'

She ran past the opening into the square before the castle. Her father, who was one of the men on guard there, recognised her voice. Under the shade of the acacia where he had been drowsing he sat up, stared anxiously at the small figure running in the brilliant sunlight. 'She's been at the wild bees,' he said. And he half rose to follow her, a man ardently in love with his children. But he restrained himself, and sat down again; for his position with the others was a little awkward, his great piety made him rather suspect among them; and afraid that if he left his watch to run after the child his companions, who were also his customers, would be even more inclined to doubt his good faith, he stayed where he was, smiling rather sheepishly, and murmuring,

'That pair of mine falls from one misfortune to another. I never had such children.'

Women hearing the noise came to their doors, calling out to the child to know what ailed her. She did not answer, she ran on screaming, sometimes looking back over her shoulder to see if the men were coming into sight. 'Those two monkeys,' said one woman to another. 'Which of them was it? She went by so fast I could not see. She runs as though the wolves were after her, poor child!' They moved into a group, staring and wondering. All the dogs began to bark. Maria Perez jumped up from her mending, Maria Hernandez came out of the inn's dark doorway, brushing aside the curtain of flies. Fernanda tumbled into her arms. She stopped screaming, and the noise of men marching made itself heard. Hearing it, she began to scream again.

'They're coming, they're coming! The men! A hundred men, and all the same man. And a man on a horse.'

'What does the child mean?' said Maria to Maria.

Maria Perez listened. Her face became pale and saturnine, she reared her head and listened, with the haughty attentive look of a lizard motionless in the sun.

'Soldiers,' she said. 'Nothing else walks that way.'

Women were thronging into the streets, wringing their hands, running this way and that, dragging children after them and screaming to other children. Suddenly, with one accord they began to run up the street. They went by, crying out,

'To the church! To the church!'

'But half the children are down by the river,' said Maria Perez. Maria Hernandez shrugged her shoulders.

'How many of yours in the house?'

'Three.'

'Take them then. I have only this one.'

'There is not time to look for the others?'

'No. Let us save what we can.'

They joined in the flight. From every house came women driving their children before them. Some carried food or household belongings, Teresa Mauleon dragged a sack of wool, another woman carried an hour-glass and a heap of bedding. Even when they did not know what they were flying from, they knew they must take refuge. Calling to their children, screaming and chattering and lamenting, they crowded into the church.

Don Tomas was there, kneeling on the altar steps. They too fell on their knees. The crying children were hushed, nothing was heard except a heavy fluttering as they panted for breath.

He seemed not to know that they were there. More than an hour before he had come to the church to make an act of thanksgiving for the morning's victory. He knelt in an ecstasy, a man re-established, ascribing glory to his maker and gilded with the reflection of that same glory. He need never be troubled again. Don Juan or Don Gil, the castle or the village, what were they compared to him, Don Tomas, a priest of God's church? Like an armour his office braced and secured him; and the thought of hell which had so long obsessed him now sank into its place in the scheme of the universe, and was a fact and a doctrine instead of a dreadful dream.

Rattling through his meditation came the noise of firing. It was followed by a sound close at his heels, a sound as though a sudden wind had blown through the forest, shaking down a myriad dead leaves. He rose from his knees, bowed to the altar, and turned to the body of the church, frowning at the interruption. They began to shuffle towards him, and with the first voice a score of voices joined in, relating, questioning, imploring. Their cries grew to a tumult. They advanced on him, thrusting their children before them, snatching at his skirts. To quell them he had to raise his voice to a scream, reminding them to respect the presence of God and to wait in patience for the hour of vespers.

Coming into the square before the castle the soldiers were called to a halt. From under the shade of the acacia, from the doorway of the barn whence they watched the gate of the stable-court opposite, the men of the village gathered into a group, defensive, and still a little incredulous. Only half of them had guns, the rest carried pikes or hayforks or cudgels. They held their weapons tightly and awkwardly.

'Stand firm,' said Andres. 'This is only to frighten us.'

The soldiers stood panting and sweating. Their officer, a middle-aged man with a cross ceremonious expression, pulled out the letter which had summoned him, and re-read it. This was the castle, and these the rioters. So far, so good. But something always goes wrong, even in a well-regulated battle, and on a wild-goose chase like this he might expect a hundred hitches and cross-purposes. Why was there no rioting, only this group of sullen peasants standing as though in a market-place waiting to be hired? And where was Don Ottavio, who had written this ridiculous letter? He glanced round on his men, examining their exhausted stockish faces for a sign of indiscipline. Something must be done with them or they would begin to think; and he gave the order to take up a formation of fire. The men in the middle of the square watched the manœuvre with curiosity, and he heard the man with the bandaged leg expounding it.

Holy Virgin, do they expect me to do everything for them? he thought. This carpet-knight Ottavio, I suppose he is indoors picking his teeth. What do they want me to do, anyhow? Shoot the men down, or go on looking at them? How am I to know if these are the rioters, or whether they are the household militia? And the thought came to him that all this while his men were exposed to a surprise attack from a body of genuine rioters coming upon them from behind. Was this a mare's nest or a wasp's nest he had been fetched into? Remembering the fat old man who had come with the letter and returned with the detachment he decided that there was nothing for it but to appeal to him.

Sidling through the ranks Don Gil came modestly forward. An acclamation of fury greeted him. One of the peasants, a big red-haired man, raised his gun, took aim, and pulled the trigger. It missed fire. With a curse he threw it down and came bounding towards Don Gil, snapping his fingers as though they gnashed to be at the sacristan's throat. Another man followed him. A shutter opened. Don Juan appeared on the balcony. Shots and a hail of stones greeted him, he dodged back to hide himself.

The officer heaved a sigh of relief. Everything was straightforward now. He gave the order to fire.

Into the dusty mouldering stillness of the garden cracked the noise of musketry. They leaped up, ran, poured themselves over the wall. The smell of gunpowder came to greet them. Diego was the first over. His face, ordinarily so haggard and passionate, seemed smooth as an angel's.

'Hush! Keep close in to the wall. They may shoot from the house.'

It was a narrow sandy track, the wall on one side of it, on the other a piece of waste land, hummocky with heaps of fallen masonry and rubble, all overgrown with brambles. There had been houses here once, it was here that the great pestilence had started. After that this part of the village had been left to fall into ruin, nothing remained except these heaps of stone and the Moor's House, standing beyond. Where the lane ran into the square, between the side of the castle and the barn, there was a stone archway. Through the archway a man came running, he was bent double, he clasped his stomach, a stench came from him, blood ran through his fingers. His legs twitched him a few paces further, then he fell. Those following Diego leaped aside to avoid trampling him.

Diego motioned them back, from behind the shelter of the arch he looked into the square. The soldiers blocked the passage into the street, those in the front ranks were defending themselves in a hand-to-hand fight with the peasants, clubbing them with the butt-ends of their muskets. Behind them the others stood firm, still firing at intervals. All the centre of the square was empty except for half a dozen figures on the ground.

'Mother of God, if we'd gone the other way round the castle, we'd have had them between our teeth!'

Was there time to go back through the garden, to come out beyond the stable-court, to attack the soldiers from the rear? But already it was too late, for those behind him, pressing forward, had shown themselves in the archway. The officer had seen them, he pointed, and shots followed the direction of his hand. Someone else had seen them too. Andreas, sitting hunched on the ground, coughing and spitting blood, turned his head towards them. His face lost its look of stern abstractedness, he signalled to them to go back. They could see his mouth shaping words, but no words came. He mouthed and signalled. At the end of the square the men were going down under the musket-blows. The soldiers began to move forward. A man who had been lying motionless suddenly leaped to his feet and ran zigzagging towards them. It was the innkeeper.

'We're lost. They're too many for us. And it was the sacristan, God damn him, who brought them, he's there with them now. I'm going to fire his house.'

He set off across the waste ground, plunging unsteadily through the brambles, waving his arms and shouting. While they looked after him more men came through the archway, Miguel Sobrino with his head cut open, and Esteban, cursing with mortification, his face streaming with blood and sweat.

'Save yourselves, they're after us!'

The fugitives swept off those who had not fought. From a window of the castle Don Ottavio opened fire, and the first soldiers came through the archway. Diego shouted,

'To the Moor's House!'

If I can't kill one of them my heart will break, he thought. And suddenly he realised the advantages of the waste ground, and dropping under the cover of one of the rubble-heaps he took aim at one of the soldiers, and wounded him. Ramon and Esteban took up the same tactics, a soldier was killed. Though they were still retreating, it was no longer a rout, there was time even to notice the innkeeper, lying among the brambles, his legs twitching, death on his face. 'They have made me die without God,' he whispered. All over the stretch of waste ground they were taking cover and sniping, those who had no guns picked up stones and threw them. The retreat was almost changed to a stand when the advantage of the ground failed them. They had traversed the region of briars and hummocks, now between them and the Moor's House was a stretch of fallow, there was nothing for it but to scatter and run.

The ground sloped uphill, and that too was against them. Yet even here they had the advantage of being nimbler and more light-footed than their pursuers. It was here that Miguel Sobrino fell, shot through the heart, his body leaping and twisting among the thistles and spleenwort. His brother, a man so taciturn that he was always called the Deaf-Mute, chose out a large jagged stone. Poising it in his hand he ran back towards the soldiers, and hurled it with all his force at the officer, who had come riding up over the waste ground. The officer clapped his hands to his face, and crumpled up in the saddle. When he was helped off he did not seem able to guide himself, and blood streamed over his face. He was blinded in one eye. The Deaf-Mute stood and watched, his hands dangling, his jaw drooping, absorbed in a surly exacting scrutiny. Then he walked off to his brother's body, looked at that too. Then he ran on towards the Moor's House.

The soldiers had gathered round their officer, and this

gave the runners time to gather up their two wounded: Joaquin Espiga, and Ramon.

'What a pity I am so heavy,' he said.

'Weight of wisdom,' answered the Deaf-Mute, suddenly loquacious.

The flight of stone steps leading to the upper story of the Moor's House was on the further side of the building. It was a curious sensation to be out of gun-shot, they felt as though some chemical had been suddenly withdrawn from their blood. The door was open. Diego and the Deaf-Mute, supporting Ramon, were the first to go in. With a shriek like a wild cat's the schoolmaster jumped out from behind the door. He was frantic, his nerves had snapped, whoever had entered he would have attacked them. He struck with a hanger, jabbing and slashing, as though he were drawing some fantastic diagram on his blackboard. Diego thrust the burden of Ramon on to the Deaf-Mute and closed with him. Grasping him round the body he tripped him and swung him violently against the wall, as a woman bangs the dust out of a rug. With the third swing Don Francisco's head tilted to one side. His neck was broken.

The other men crowded the doorway. Diego said,

'There! I've killed Don Saturno's schoolmaster.'

His voice was slightly rueful, astonished and fatalistic.

Ramon sighed and shook his head. A schoolmaster, even a bad schoolmaster, was something valuable.

'It had to be,' said Diego, answering the look; and he went on to arrange their defence, the allotment of the narrow windows among those who had guns. The door was barred, the schoolmaster's mattress wadded against it, the two wounded men laid where they were least likely to be in the way.

The soldiers, disabled by the injury to their officer, were hanging back. They pointed to the Moor's House, and seemed to be arguing among themselves, and searching about for an approach which would not expose them. Some ammunition was spent in trying to pick them off, but there was not a gun that could carry so far.

They should not waste shots, thought Ramon. But he said nothing, it seemed he must always be under this curse to cavil and disapprove, first regretting the waste of a schoolmaster and now the waste of ammunition, and always too tardily to be effective. He looked at his smashed foot and thought, I shall be a cripple. Then he noticed that blood was flowing out from under his body, and that flies were coming to it. There must be a second wound somewhere. All his good intentions and all their miscarryings seemed to be in another world, to be in the story of another man; and in another world too, in another story, a story which he would never know, was the future of his children and of Maria. All he could do was to give a diminishing and wavering attention to what was around him: the Deaf-Mute, sharpening his knife on the stone threshold, Don Francisco's wig lying apart from Don Francisco's head, the unconscious man beside him, Diego wandering about the room, uttering a soft thin whistle, Esteban suddenly remarking,

'Suppose they just leave us here? Pretty fools we shall look then.'

To Diego the act of whistling was an accompaniment the pause in the fighting, like an interminable holding-note in music between one strophe and the next. From the moment when he had jumped down from the wall he had entered into a new life, a life of unassailable happiness, a life in which every detail, every horror, every bungle, stood out brilliant and unequivocal, as in a landscape bathed in sunlight. The mistrust, the unsatisfied egoism which had tormented him all his life long had shrivelled and vanished. He felt secure in the love of his fellows, brotherly affection laced them all, living and dead, into a harmony where there was no compulsion, no bending of the individual from its true intonation. Secure in love, secure in hate. His hate was released and ran loose, beautiful in the sunlight, rejoicing like some wild animal loosed from a cage in which it would have grown unmuscular and scabby.

He went back to his window and looked out. It was the window commanding a view down the village street. He saw a puff of straw-smoke rise up, and another, yellow in the sunlight. They thickened into a tree of smoke, Just so. The soldiers were setting fire to the houses.

Another tree of smoke rose up. Man after man jostled to the window, took his turn to ascertain with his own eyes, to stare and curse. Though the soldiers still hung back at the edge of the waste ground, their fury could not wait, shot after shot was fired and the fallow bubbled with fountains of sand. Now from the window commanding the village they saw other soldiers appear, those who had come up the street from the castle square. They were grimed with smoke and bulgy with pillage. And walking a little apart from them, fastidious and secluded, was Don Juan. Presently he mounted the steps to the church, and stood on the platform before the west door, holding up an optic glass and looking towards the Moor's House. It was not enough to take aim through the single slotted window. They threw open the door and swarmed out on the steps, shooting from there. He took cover in the porch.

They heard a shout. The soldiers who had been waiting on the edge of the waste ground were advancing.

'Wait till you can be sure of getting them,' said Ramon anxiously.

'That's true,' said Esteban. 'We haven't much left.'

Three shots were fired, the third brought down a man. It was a good shot. It was the last. There was no more ammunition.

'We've got knives, haven't we?' said the Deaf-Mute.

Cautiously, the soldiers were advancing on the house, still doubtful of another volley. The garrison watched them, commenting with scorn on their timidity. Diego, pacing to and fro, looking first from one window and then another, his face twitching with excitement, fingering this and that like some house-proud hostess awaiting the arrival of her guests, caught sight of Ramon. He knelt down beside him and whispered,

'You can't fight, they will take you prisoner. I can't leave you to them, Ramon. Shall I kill you? I would do it well.'

'I'll see it out.'

Kneeling beside him he brushed away a fly and smoothed the tumbled lock of hair off the brow.

'What are you looking at, Ramon? What do you see?'

'So large a country,' said the dying man. 'And there in the middle of it, like a heart, is Madrid. But our Tenorio Viejo is not marked. I have often looked for it. It is not there, though. It is too small, I suppose. We have lived in a very small place, Diego.'

'We have lived in Spain,' said the other.

'Aye.'

His gaze left the map and turned to the face bent over him. They looked at each other long and intently, as though they were pledged to meet again and would ensure a recognition.